FORTUNE'S FOOL

A Dark War Novel

ANGELA ADDAMS

ABOUT FORTUNE'S FOOL

Mercenary. Vampire Hunter. All around supernatural herder. That's me. You find yourself on my capture list and it's as good as done.

Consider that a personal guarantee from Jet Black.

The current job is to find the witch who was supposed to save the world and end The Dark War. Unfortunately, she's on Vampire Island, a notorious prison for supernaturals...one I've helped fill.

Once there, I'm forced to team up with some other inmates...in particular a certain lynx shifter, Jason, to whom I owe my life. Can't seem to keep my hands off him either.

So here's the problem...I've got a spell to get me and the witch off the island—a one way ticket for two. It's a death sentence for Jason if I leave him behind. But it's a death sentence for all of us it I don't. I have to choose between my heart and the fate of everyone. All because some sketchy little witch couldn't do the one thing she was born to do.

Saving the world can't be that hard, can it?

I guess that's for me to decide.

A NOTE TO READERS

You can start here and have no trouble following along. Even if you haven't read *The Dark War*, *Fortune's Fool* stands alone.

But really, why haven't you read *The Dark War*?

Dedicated to Michelle von Enckevort

I bet you were expecting Kali.
Queen witch.
Prophesy foretold, savior of the world.
Except no one's seen her for a decade, and I don't mean no one's seen her because she's invisible.
No one's seen her because she's gone. Hidden or hiding.
Captured or self-imposed isolation. Nobody knows.
But not dead. Of that I am certain.
And what's hidden can always be found.
Especially a fucking witch who everyone thinks owes the world something.
End the war or don't; it's all the same paycheck to me.
And I'm just the girl to drag a witch's sorry ass where it needs to be.
Of that I am also certain.
Kali Richards, I'm coming for you.

— Jet Black
Mercenary, Dhampir, All Around Badass.

I WOKE TO A LURCHING MOTION THAT MADE ME WANT TO vomit, and to the smell of those who had. Moans and whimpers echoed around me. For a moment I was confused, disoriented as I lay on the cold steel floor.

There were bodies crowded next to me. A quick assessment told me they were all women. Vulnerable ones. Their terror pinged against my skin and banged around in my already-throbbing skull. Their moans made me wince. I knew that I should be frightened too, but I wasn't.

Rage burned through my veins, giving me a jolt of adrenaline.

I'd been knocked out somehow. Loaded into this cell unaware. Betrayed.

I pushed myself up, my hair somewhat shielding my sensitive eyes from the harsh fluorescent light above. We were housed in a steel cage, behind bars too thick for me to bend with brute strength alone. There were a dozen or more women of all ages, but no younger than early twenties, by the looks of things. That was good. It would be worse if there were children. Nobody deserved cruelty like this, but especially not children.

My head hurt like a motherfucker. I reached up to touch the sorest spot and found a lump the size of a walnut, and by the sticky feel, blood too. What the hell had happened? Obviously dealing with some shady smugglers wasn't without its dangers, but I'd always prided myself on being able to sniff trouble before it could take me out. I was supposed to be on this boat, that was true, but not in a cell. I ran my hand along my waist, already knowing that my blades were gone. I definitely wasn't supposed to be unarmed.

There would be hell to pay when I got back home. *If* I got back home.

Oh, I'm getting back home. Jet Black does not go out like this.

The light suddenly died, plunging us all into darkness. A wave of screams echoed against my sensitive ears. I pushed myself up to my knees, ignoring the agony of my pounding head. There was a grating screech of metal-on-metal, a waft of fresher air that lasted for only a few moments. The screams intensified, a ripple of alarm washed over the confined space. I could smell blood. Not mine.

I licked my lips.

My eyes adjusted. There were new shapes moving through the cell, stalking, assaulting, taking what wasn't theirs. They wore night-vision goggles, they obviously had targets, and an advantage —none of the women could see them coming. Well, none of the women except me.

A hand snaked out of the darkness to my side, gliding along my waist, an almost tender touch and most unwelcome. With a sudden jerk, he hauled me to my feet, holding me by the hair.

"This one is mine," a gruff voice grunted. Foul breath invaded my nose, his face suddenly too close to mine. "You're a dirty girl, aren't you? I've been watching you, you hot thing. You've been lying there in your skin-tight clothes, taunting me. I'm gonna peel you apart. I bet you like it rough, don't ya?" He had me pressed against his body in what he probably thought was an impenetrable hold.

"Remove your hands." My voice was a low growl of warning. If I'd had my blades I wouldn't have bothered speaking. Steel on flesh was usually warning enough.

"You're marked for death, pretty lady. I'll be makin' the most of you now so it doesn't go to waste." He chuckled and slid his hand over my breast, his lips brushing against my cheek as he cupped my crotch, squeezing hard, digging his fingers in.

"You will not *touch* me." My body coiled, every muscle vibrating.

I twisted around and, in the process, yanked back two of his fingers. They snapped as I elbowed him in the throat and dropped him to the floor. I stomped on his chest, felt my boot sink in. The crunching of bones made me smile.

His screams brought others.

Humans were so fragile.

Lightning fast, I darted, ducked, jammed my fist into a throat, gouged my thumb into an eye, swept my leg around, taking one large man out. I crouched low, the sound of something metal whistling by my head. Blood splattered on me, the strong metallic smell making my mouth water. Even though I was not a vampire, I still savored the bouquet. It was in my DNA to want it, even without the long fangs.

I fought, kicking, punching, using my body as it was meant to be used. A weapon honed for battle.

My assailants lay in a crumpled heap around me, five in total.

Is that all you've got?

There was a click and a whirling sound. Something latched itself to my arm, embedding through my nylon suit, biting into my flesh. Before I could move an inch, I was jolted, frozen in a spasm of pain. An electric shock rolled through me and something oozed into my veins, burning on contact.

I crumpled down on top of my assailants. Paralyzed.
Effectively taken out again.

Fuck.

That was not part of my plan.

PAIN. EVERY MUSCLE IN MY BODY HURT. LIKE MY BLOOD WAS infused with fire and it was scorching through my veins. I lay on wet, cold concrete, the ground no longer swaying beneath me.

"Is she awake?" a voice filtered through the pain. Female. Scared. I continued to play dead, assessing, listening. A hand nudged my hip. "It'll be dark soon; she needs to wake up before then."

"If she's not awake in ten minutes then we leave her here. Plain as that," a second voice barked. Hard, gruff, very male.

"She saved my life. She stopped the guards from..." Her voice cracked, a strangled sob echoed in my ears. "I'm not leaving her behind."

"Suit yourself, you can both die here then. The monsters come out at night. Starved, crazed monsters." The gruff voice was hushed, menacing. Not lying. "You stay here with her and they'll drain you both dry. I'm not doing this for my own good."

Another foot nudged my leg, a hand on my shoulder—a gentle shake, then stronger. Her touch was like a hot poker against my skin.

I grabbed her hand, pulling it away from my flesh. "That

fucking hurts," I snarled as I opened my eyes and got my first look at the woman who was fighting for my life.

Shoulder-length mousy hair, skinny beyond acceptable, bruised and obviously battered, dirt and blood caking her face, she fit the typical victim profile. Her soft brown eyes opened wide with surprise. "You're awake!"

I grunted as I let her hand go and pushed myself up to sit, shifting my head to the side to see the other speaker. Tall, very tall, clad in dirty jeans and a simple use-to-be-white T-shirt. Muscles suggesting hard labor, dark hair that looked like it needed a cut, shaggy-looking beard that probably had once been well groomed, green eyes glaring, mouth set in a scowl. Shifter of some sort, if I were to guess. He swung a crudely made bow over his shoulder and adjusted the quiver on his back.

"You coming or what? Gonna be dark soon. Left it too late as it is." His voice held a ghost of an accent. Philly? New York? He nodded in the direction of the mousy girl. "She wouldn't leave without you."

Admirable, but unnecessary.

I flexed my muscles, forcing myself to do it despite the lingering pain. I grimaced as I twisted my back, my spine cracking.

"You hurt?" the shifter asked, his tone suggesting that I'd better not be.

I shook my head and stood, my legs wobbling slightly before I locked them up tight. "Nothing I can't handle," I said as I met his unwavering stare. This guy was all about the intensity. "You can go. I'm good."

He narrowed his eyes. "We waited for you."

"Would have been better to leave me be. I work alone." I turned toward the door where a steady stream of sunlight bathed the concrete. It was only then that I realized we were in a warehouse, my nose picking up the distinct scent of seawater as we moved outside. I shielded my eyes from the glare, my heightened sensitivity making them burn. The heat had me breaking out in sweat instantly, my discomfort amplified by whatever those assholes had zapped me with on the boat. The humans were always coming up with new ways to take out the supernaturals. They'd probably dosed me with some kind of vampire repellant, not realizing it wouldn't kill me.

As my eyes adjusted, I saw the huge loading dock that jutted from the warehouse. They'd unloaded their live cargo here, dumping us as prey.

"You're an idiot if you think you can survive on your own." He trailed me to the door, pointing toward the dense line of trees that marked the edge of a forest surrounding the empty harbor. "We have a camp not far from here. We try to rescue the supernaturals when we can. You don't want to go into the city."

I glanced to where he was pointing; a crude-looking road that had seen better days lay on the other side of the parking lot. The pavement was beaten, vegetation and forest threatening to reclaim it. It was hardly fit for a vehicle anymore other than perhaps a hardcore military one.

"I made him wait. They took the others back to camp already —another witch, and a lycanthrope, I think," the mousy girl said timidly as she came to my side. "You saved me from getting raped on the ship... Those men... I just, I mean... I think you should come with us. They have a safe place."

"Not interested." I shielded my eyes to scan the area once again. There were no obvious pathways leading into the forest, just trees on top of trees on top of trees. "You better go before the nasties come out to play." There had been a cargo of women on the boat. I didn't see a trace of them now. "You use the humans as bait."

The sun was moving toward the horizon. Time was definitely running out.

"If they survive the night we hunt them down, try to help. Usually." The shifter shrugged one shoulder. "Survival of the fittest. It's not like we have unlimited resources here. Life expectancy is typically no longer than six months anyway."

It was cold. Calculated. I could appreciate that. If it came down to me or someone else, I wouldn't be making a sacrifice. And I wouldn't be staying here longer than it took to complete my mission.

"Like I said, I can take care of myself." I nodded to the girl. "Best you get moving."

She looked like she was going to argue. Instead, she wrapped me in a ninja hug, sprang it on me like we were long lost friends. "I'm Amber, and I owe you my life. I'd give you a boon, if you wanted one."

I stayed stiff, stepping back so she would unlatch herself. "A boon from a witch who probably won't survive the night? What's the point?"

She flinched hard at my harsh words. I was not in the mood to cultivate friendships and my head was still pounding from the shit the humans had dosed me with.

"Never mind," she muttered as she fell back a step. "Let's go, Jason. Sorry I wasted your time."

The shifter was appraising me; I could see it in his cool stare. Judging what my odds were given my lack of weapons. "The monsters need to get fed at some point or they'll come looking for us to quench their thirst. Not my concern if you want to be dinner." He glanced over my head, squinting into the dying light. "We don't have a lot of time. Some of the bastards can tolerate dusk. Let's go."

A shiver licked down my spine, as if his words had conjured the vampires. They were coming. The first tingles of awareness jolted through my senses, making me vibrate with anticipation. I lifted a hand, felt the spot on my arm where the humans had latched the prong that had delivered the dose of whatever had knocked me out, and pulled my fingers away to find crusted blood flakes there. Between that and my head wound, there wasn't much red stuff, but it would do.

"We're pretty safe in the forest. They usually stick to the city," Jason said as they moved down the stairs and headed to the trees. "Stay off the roads if you do decide to go that way."

The last of the poison burned through me, finally dissipating. I closed my eyes as another wave of electric excitement washed over me. The vampire vibes were coming from the forest. They were walking right into a trap.

I watched them disappear, the forest swallowing them, foliage so thick that I couldn't even see a shadow moving. But I didn't need to see. I could feel the danger. A horde. Had to be at least half a dozen. Witch and shifter against a starved fang horde? They didn't stand a chance.

But I was no hero.

I jumped down from the concrete and pulled the amulet out of my bodysuit. Whoever had stripped me of weapons hadn't found where it was hidden. Probably helped that it was bewitched. The amulet sparkled in the light, looking like just a normal gem nestled in a silver setting. I held it in my palm. It pulsed to life, warming against my flesh.

She was here. That witch, Kali Richards, was on this island.

I winced, scanning the tree line. Somewhere in there, it seemed. The damn thing could tell me she was near; it could give me an idea of which direction to go in, but it couldn't tell me how to find her.

I looked back at the road. There was a city that I couldn't see, which would be an easier route, but the amulet definitely burned hotter when I held it toward the forest. That forest was thick—that meant hard trekking. And it looked buggy. I fucking hated bugs. It could take me weeks to find her.

The sounds of crunching leaves and thrashing branches touched my ears. I could go with Amber and Jason, save their sorry asses; get something more than just a boon. Would make hunting Kali easier. Quicker no doubt. That shifter seemed to know his way around. And they were heading in the right direction. As I'd recently discovered, sometimes the lore of a place turned out to hold some truth, and who better to know the secrets of this island than its current inhabitants?

Decision made, I slipped the amulet back into its secret spot in my suit where it would fade into my skin like a chameleon, then moved quickly after the pair, their clumping and heavy footsteps hardly stealth. Despite the fact that so far my mission had not gone as planned, I was at least in the right place. The witch who'd been on every possible wanted list—dead but preferably alive—was within reach. I was nothing if not adaptable.

I caught up to the pair in a few minutes, startling Amber as I moved in behind her.

"You might need my help." I bypassed her and moved in front of Jason, keeping him from taking another step. "I think you'll die otherwise." They were so close, the nasty vile blood suckers. "Can you hear them?" I closed my eyes, swayed a little as the hum of the horde sang to me.

"Who are you?" Jason's voice was full of suspicion.

When I opened my eyes, I knew how I must have looked to him. My pupils dilated, cheeks flushed, like an addict getting a fix. I licked my lips, shivered, took in a deep breath, exhaled and smiled. "Or rather, *what* am I?"

His eyes went wide, disbelief flashing across his face.

"Dhampir?"

I gave a tight nod, flashed a wicked grin, touching my little fangs with my tongue.

"You've got to be fucking kidding me. I knew I should have killed you."

"What?" Amber's voice was barely a squeak, her hand almost covering her mouth. "Why would you say that?"

"She's a Dhampir," Jason growled. "A vampire hunter on an island of vampires. You're bleeding aren't you?" He looked past

Amber. "That's why there's a horde on the way, right? Fuck! They're drawn to you. I can't believe this!"

When it comes to vampires, there were two kinds—Strix and Dhampir, the latter of which were a bit more complicated in physiology. Naturally, I was the latter and, for all intents and purposes, the better.

"You're a vampire hunter?" Amber gasped.

"More like a mercenary." I winked. "I'm an equal opportunity kind of girl. I don't only do vampires. Not anymore. But I *am* very good at killing."

"An assassin," Jason spat.

"Not always. Depends on the highest bidder. Sometimes I take them alive." I shrugged. "The way I see it, I'm your best defense." I took a quick inventory of the trees around me. It wasn't great but it would have to do. I reached over and snapped a good-sized branch from the tree next to me, breaking it on an angle to create a crude stake. I did that three more times. "You good with that bow or are you going to wolf out or whatever?"

"I'm not a werewolf," he scoffed before tossing the bow and then the quiver to Amber. "Here. Use this if you can."

Amber let the bow and quiver fall to the side then sank down to the ground, tracing her fingers in the dirt as she mumbled.

"Don't aim any of your spells my way," I warned. Witches were sneaky fuckers and their aptitude with magic was untrustworthy. This one didn't seem overly confident to begin with. I wasn't too interested in taking a hit from friendly fire.

But I didn't have too much time to think on it.

The Strix vampires burst through the tree line, a crowd. I counted seven to start, all in a frenzy of bloodlust so crazed that they appeared raving mad, fangs distended, foaming red-tinted mucous, their bloodshot eyes locked on me like I was beacon.

I turned toward them, two stakes in each hand. "Come and get me, boys."

3

A VAMPIRE IN A BLOOD FRENZY WAS A STUPID VAMPIRE. THAT was a fact. A stupid vampire was a dead vampire. That was also a fact. Two homed in on me right away. Red eyes locked on the only lethal target in the vicinity. Couldn't totally blame them though; my blood called to them, even the tiny, dried up little bit of it on my flesh. Dhampir blood was their nectar and they were starved for it.

I let them come, watching as they moved clumsily, tripping over the vegetation on the ground as well as their own feet. They were behaving more like zombies than bloodsuckers. Moaning, drooling, one even fell. Not the stealth, fast-moving predators that I was accustomed to. I made short work of the first one, dropping into a crouch and throwing him off his target. He stumbled with confusion. I sprang up with my crude stake, using my momentum to impale him with one fluid strike. I spun toward the other, stabbing him in the heart over my left shoulder. A shallow wound but he went down anyway, too starved to survive even that.

The others had headed toward the easiest target—Amber, on her knees still, was locked in a spell casting that was gonna get her killed. She was in the process of levitating, swept up in some magic. A vampire was right there, ready to fall on her and feed. A hair's breath away.

I flipped a stake in the air, catching on the pointy end so I could launch it at the bloodsucker. "Amber, heads up!"

Before I could throw, a giant blur of fur took the vampire out. I pivoted, using the distraction to nail two others with my stakes, dropping them just in front of Amber.

Her eyes snapped open. She flicked her hand out, sending two more vampires flying through the air. She slammed them into a tree so hard it broke, huge splinters of wood impaling them. It was impressive and unexpected. I guess she wasn't a slouch after all.

Jason, the cat apparently, launched himself at the last vampire, taking the grotesque thing in his jaw and snapping down, severing the head completely before knocking it away with a giant furry paw.

He looked at me, fangs dripping with gore, and settled back on his haunches with the smug expression that all cats wore.

He was a Lynx. Bigger than the average cat shifter, with giant furry paws and claws that could tear a man in half, no doubt. Beautiful dark markings outlined his eyes, trailing the sides of his gray face. There was dark fur poking up from his ears, making him look like some kind of mischievous creature, and a smirk that said he liked to play with his prey just as much as he liked to kill it. An unusual breed of shifter that didn't discriminate based on gender, unlike most of the werewolves and bear shifters I'd come to know. All cats in a lynx clan were treated as equals. A novel concept for someone like me who came from a decidedly patriarchal culture. Dhampirs were not known for their fair distribution of power.

I'd heard that there were more females than males in the Lynx community, a result of some kind of genetic snafu. So Jason the

Lynx was rare indeed, and suddenly much more interesting. Never been with a cat before, definitely not a Lynx.

"Good kitty." I smiled when he narrowed his eyes. "That was some intense witchcraft, Amber. You an elemental?" Would explain the directed wind gust.

Amber opened her eyes, grimaced at the bloody scene, then tried to stand, breaking the spell that was keeping her aloft. She braced herself against the tree behind her as her feet touched the ground. I didn't intervene. She needed to rebound quickly or she'd be dead. This wasn't a playground.

"Kind of," she said as she sucked in deep breath. "My mom was. I can harness it when I concentrate." She pushed herself off the tree. "It takes a lot out of me though."

"What do you need for a pick me up?" I knew a thing or two about witches. Most of them, the powerful ones anyway, needed something specific to replenish their magic. It could range from sunlight to sugar and anything in between; it really depended on the witch.

"Food, preferably red meat." She was moving sluggishly from one tree to the other.

"Hear that, kitty? You might need to hunt down a bunny—"

But Jason wasn't where I'd left him. Instead, he was standing right next to me and I'd been too distracted to notice. *Interesting.*

"Watch yourself, Dhampir," he all but hissed the words.

Made me snicker. "You watch yourself, pussy—"

He crowded me, forcing me back with his hot, hard body, his scent all male, a musky tang that played on my tongue. His eyes still held the cut of his cat, diamond pupils that dilated as he sucked in a deep breath of me. He let his chest brush against mine and damn if my nipples didn't perk up. The guy was all sex and bad news. He smirked down at me, flashing what was left of his fangs.

"Once you go cat, you never go back." He bit his bottom lip, drawing a drop of blood, his eyes sparkling, then he took a step back.

A wash of bloodlust shivered through me. *I wouldn't mind testing that theory out.*

He turned to help Amber. I was surprised, and slightly disappointed to see, he was fully clothed. His transformation must have accommodated whatever he was wearing. Worked differently depending on the shifter. The werewolves usually lost theirs, which was always fun to watch—those guys were built like brick houses in all departments. "We got lucky. Those vamps were starving. The weak ones are always starving."

I nodded as I fingered the wound on my arm. "Probably why they picked up on my scent. Would be hardly perceptible to a well-fed vamp." If I wanted to call a Strix to me, I usually had to open a vein or two and let the blood spill for a while before they took the bait.

"There are strong ones. Very strong ones. They're smart. They set traps." He nodded to the side. "We should get moving again. I'm assuming you're coming?"

"You leave the vampires behind that get ditched on the island? You save the other supernaturals, but not the vampires?" Any social setting was going to have a hierarchy. Even a prison. Strix vampires worked as gangs in the more civilized parts of the world; there was no reason to think they wouldn't set up those gangs here as well, especially if the other supernaturals wanted nothing to do with them.

"They come on a different boat usually and I don't know how the pecking order goes. I'm assuming they fight for their survival the same way we do, except we're the prey in all scenarios."

Another reason to sacrifice the humans when they landed. Brutal but it made sense. "Survival is six months normally?"

"Yeah. That's the longest anyone has been here that we know of."

I grabbed another branch and made myself a couple more stakes. "Neat." I didn't intend on staying that long.

"Like I said, they don't usually come into the forest. The smart ones wait for us to venture out. They know eventually we'll come looking for supplies." He narrowed his eyes at me. "And the forest sucks to move through. We don't take the same path twice —no trail to follow. The starved vampires aren't smart enough to navigate through the foliage. Until you came that is."

"Can we get out of here please?" Amber's gaze was locked on the dead vamps, her hand trembling as she covered her mouth. "I feel kind of sick."

"It'll be night soon. We don't light fires outside of the cavern," Jason said. "Better get moving."

Cavern? That didn't sound very comfortable. This place was getting better and better. I was not an outdoors kinda girl. I couldn't remember ever having been camping, unless a five-star hotel and room service counted. *Ugh*. Priority number one, make more weapons. Priority number two, find better sleeping accommodations, if there was such a thing in this hellhole. Or better yet, not spend too many nights here at all.

I didn't know how long I'd been on the boat—could have been days, could have been hours—but not too long ago I'd been sleeping in my own bed, exhausted beyond exhausted. I'd just come off a job that had me rounding up three wayward Strix who seemed to have missed their parole appointments in favor of a killing spree. They were likely on the island too now... That or dead. My identity probably wouldn't stay unknown for long. The humans usually paid top dollar for prisoners of war. I'd sent a lot of the inmates here, whether they knew it or not. The Dark War had made business where there hadn't been before. I had a natural gift for hide and seek and few scruples to get in the way of my bank account. So, I was public enemy number one on Vampire Island. *Good times*.

I followed Jason and Amber, keeping my senses open for any

more hungry vampires, stakes at the ready. I'd decided to take up the rear in case the witch managed to pass out. She obviously needed someone watching her back.

It only took us an hour to reach our final destination and a good thing too because twilight was quickly turning to full dark and Amber was starting to panic again.

"Did you hear that?" she hissed over her shoulder. "I think there's more vampires coming. I don't have enough power to wield right now."

I shook my head and pointed with a stake. "Not vampires, just wild animals. You're safe."

"Wild animals?" Her eyes went wider. "Not shifters."

"Shhhh," Jason growled. "If you don't shut the fuck up you might bring the vampires here yourself."

"Who's that?" A disembodied voice echoed from inside the cave, and I had to snicker.

Some sentry. *Who's that?* Really? Did they think a vampire was gonna take the time to chit-chat if they found a nest full of food?

"It's Jason, you idiot." Obviously, the feline felt the same way. He grumbled another curse under his breath as he brushed aside a few hanging vines that cascaded over the entrance. "I've got the two rescues with me."

The woman standing on guard was short, chubby and holding what appeared to be another bow. This was how they protected themselves? I wondered what kind of supernatural she was then shoved all curiosity aside when she stepped in front of me.

"Hi, I'm Fiona." She smiled brightly, her white teeth gleaming in the dying light. "Welcome to your new home."

She was bubbly. She was sweet. I hated her already.

"This is Amber and this is..." Jason frowned as he fumbled for the name I'd never given him.

"Jet," I grunted.

"Jet?" Fiona scrunched her nose. "As in the plane?"

"As in a boatload of trouble," Jason grumbled, shaking his head as he did. "Should have known with the way you look."

"So you've heard of me, then?" I snorted, ignoring Fiona and Amber's bewildered expressions.

"This way." Jason didn't bother responding, bypassing Fiona on his way into the cave.

It was wet, the walls and floor slimy, the scent...mossy. Not unpleasant unless you thought about sleeping and then it didn't seem so appealing. Jason was accustomed to the dips and turns of the tunnel we found ourselves in, leading us farther and farther into the darkness with little trouble. I could see just fine—my Dhampir senses were almost as good as a vampire's; pitch black held no mystery for me. Amber, on the other hand, was either clenching me or Jason, alternating between the two of us like we were life-vests keeping her from drowning. Helpless witches were a nuisance. If she had her powers, she could have shed some light at least. I calculated the odds of Amber surviving on her own. It seemed unlikely as long as her powers were underfed.

Light began to flicker off the cavern walls and Amber let out a sigh, her hands instantly leaving my arms as she became more confident in her footsteps. There was the crackling of a fire and soft murmurs of a few voices, the smell of some animal roasting. My mouth watered, and I licked my lips. I preferred rare, but I was ravenous and would eat just about anything.

"There's no smoke." *Enclosed area, fire burning, why are we not suffocating?*

Jason motioned up with his head. "There are vents in the stone, kinda like a natural filtration system. The smoke escapes and you can't see it. We've got it good here."

Another silent warning. In other words, you'd better not fuck it up for us. Six months wasn't a lot of time, but if it was all you had, you fought to protect it. I got it. They wouldn't have to worry about me wrecking their good thing.

I nodded. It was the only reason they were still alive.

Somehow they'd managed to stay imperceptible to the vampires, giving the predators little reason to venture into the forest. Why leave when your food was delivered by boat right to your doorstep, anyway? I didn't know much about Vampire Island other than it had once been a popular tourist destination before the Dark War blew everything to shit. High-end resorts, cruise port stop, and booming business for the humans. It had another name then, before the War had turned it into a desolate concentration camp for supernaturals.

The road I had seen earlier probably led to a port city where the Strix would set up their dens. They were the sort of creatures to prefer ruins over the unknown wilderness. Bombed out cities still offered more protection from the sun than trees and dirt. Strix were creatures of habit, with a penchant for the easy way. I'd made a lot of money off that breed of vampire in the time that I've been a mercenary, if only because they were predictable as all hell. If finding Kali became problematic, I'd be venturing into the city in search of supplies. The Strix would be hoarding them but likely not protecting them. Arrogance was another one of their many flaws.

Moments later and the tight passageway opened up to a cavern. There was a fire, a rather large one, with a spit that skewered several small animals, hovering over top. Stalagmites, stalactites—whichever, whatever—were hanging and jutting from the floor and ceiling, dipping into small pools of water. To the left was a pond, its dark blue water smelling of sulfur. The light from the fire bounced off the walls, making the minerals twinkle. It was beautiful really, for a hole in the ground.

I counted seven warm bodies—with Fiona at the entrance and the three of us arriving, eleven in total. A lot of mouths to feed. I glanced back to the spit, the grease from the animal fat sizzling as it dropped into the fire. Not enough food for everyone. I'd be hunting alone soon enough.

"Didn't think you guys were gonna make it." A tall, dark

haired woman detached herself from the group and made her way toward us. Concern written all over her face. She gave Jason a once-over; nodded when she assessed nothing was wrong, then glanced at me. "I see you finally woke up." Her tone wasn't totally friendly. She obviously didn't approve of waiting around for little ol' me.

"She's a Dhampir!" Amber said, her energy apparently rallying at the sight of food. "She saved our lives! Steph, I told you she'd be good to have around."

"A Dhampir?" Steph's lips thinned and she crossed her arms. "From what I know about Dhampir lore, the vamps will only come if you're bleeding. Is that right? We won't have a problem unless you bleed, right?"

I shrugged.

"There was a horde of them down there!" Amber's voice rose. She wasn't helping my case. "And Jet killed them!"

"Jet?" Steph laughed. "As in Jet Black?" She shared a look with Jason.

"That's right."

Steph offered her hand, her expression softening. "I've read about your clan. Your father is a very impressive man."

"Vampire." I corrected, ignoring her hand. My father was no ordinary man. "And if you knew him you wouldn't think so."

Steph smiled and nodded, withdrawing her hand to fold back across her chest. "I've studied the Dhampir for years. Worked for..." She waved her hand in dismissal. "Well, that's not important. What is important is that you're safe and we've got you here. I saw a video of you once. You were taking on five Strix vampires that must have been contracts. You kicked their asses in a glorious way. It was a long time ago and you looked a bit different then—you hair was longer, not as dark. But it was you for sure. I'd never forget those eyes. You know they glow like emeralds when it's dark? I thought you were a fucking goddess. My sire said you were death and to run if I ever saw you coming." She shrugged.

"We'd be honored if you stayed, helped us. With your training, your skills, we'd stand a better chance."

"She's trouble," Jason said before walking away.

"Hey, what do you tell me all the time? Everyone deserves a second chance?" Steph called after him, a smirk on her lips.

"Can't make any promises, but I'll do what I can for however long I can." I had no problem lying; this wasn't my reality. I was there for one purpose only. Find Kali Richards and bring her home. I nodded toward Jason. "What's his problem?"

"We'll take whatever help you can give. We'll probably all be dead soon anyway. And don't mind him. He's just a little miffed. When he got here, the crew he landed with said it was you who'd turned them in."

I frowned, narrowed my eyes in Jason's direction. I hadn't recognized him as a mark, but sometimes I did group roundups for the humans that usually made for a lot of anonymous prisoners of war. "It's possible."

"From the stories I've heard about you, probable." Steph chuckled and motioned to the fire. "But now you're here and we don't have time for grudges. Come and meet the others. The food should be almost ready. I'm sure you're hungry. Night is for the monsters. Rest and tomorrow we'll show you around the island."

I pursed my lips; the hunter in me perking up like a gauntlet had just been tossed down. Back home, nighttime equaled playtime. Vampire hunting was one of my favorite pastimes. Despite the urge to venture out in search of the enemy, I took heed of what Steph said. I didn't know the lay of the land. Tonight I would rest, get some intel; tomorrow I would hunt.

4

"So, Jet, how were things when you left? The humans been setting off nukes again?" Steph handed me a bottle of water, obviously reused. I accepted it with a nod.

"Things were...quiet."

Quiet was a relative assessment. The Dark War had almost wiped out the planet in the first few years after the initial launch. Not understanding what in the fuck was going on and suddenly faced with the reality that their fictional monsters were in fact real, the humans had nuked the hell out of key areas they thought had the highest concentration of supernaturals. Not realizing, of course, that the supernaturals were everywhere. We'd been living in the shadows, infiltrating their world and coexisting with them from the beginning of time. We were good at hiding. So the humans had nuked and the supernaturals retaliated with whatever means they had. The witch-vampire hybrids led by Cassia were the worst though. They lobbed some awful spells that made certain parts of the United States completely inhabitable due to the magic saturation. Wastelands in many coastal states.

Add to that the witches who sympathized with the humans and there was magical chaos everywhere. But blame couldn't fall only on the humans and witches or witch hybrids. There were roaming packs of werewolves that had decimated towns overnight and ghost whisperers who'd used their powers to pillage and terrorize everyone. There were also other, very dangerous, supernatural creatures with chips on their shoulders the size of boulders and a laundry list of wrongs to right. Many species had had enough with living in hiding. They'd been marginalized just by folklore for centuries and were ready to be seen, felt, and heard.

Human witch hunters had done a lot of damage too, attempting to take out the source of the problem while at the same time being hunted themselves thanks to some spell Cassia had launched. The current state of affairs was a shitstorm of gigantic proportions and there were no clear lines of division. No good guys or bad guys. Most days there was just survival.

Alliances had formed, then broken, then reformed. The war had raged on. After a few years, all sides began to realize that total annihilation was a strong possibility and, in the tenth year of battle, things seemed to have calmed down. Kind of. No more nukes, no more magical devastation. Things grew eerily quiet as the world began to settle into a new normal.

"Things were...tense. Everyone is on edge." I took a long drink from the water. It had a slight metallic taste to it. "But otherwise I doubt it's changed much in the time you've been here."

"Five months, the longest of this group." Steph shrugged. "And tense... Yeah, things were tense before I was carted off to this place. Like when you walk in on people whispering about you and you just know they aren't planning a surprise party."

"Exactly." It made me wonder about Steph's involvement in the war. Was she a sympathizer? A soldier? She'd gotten herself into some kind of trouble if she was on Vampire Island. It was the humans' method of dealing with the lawbreakers of our world. The island was rumored to be spelled by a handful of very powerful witches connected to the American Council of Witches, working in conjunction with the humans to try to stem the violence that lingered from active war. It was supposedly escape-proof.

I scoff at that because, of course, I had other plans.

Steph motioned to the group with a metal flask she'd pulled from her jacket pocket. "We've got five witches, two wolves, a handful of undeclared miscellaneous." She rolled her eyes. "A lynx and me, half-vamp. But only the good half." She laughed. "All political shit gets left at the cave door. Survival necessitates that we all get along."

I scanned the group of mismatched supernaturals. While they all ranged in size, shape, and overall degree of glowering, one thing was clear—behind their wary eyes was fear. How they'd gotten themselves onto Vampire Island was beside the point. They all knew being here meant certain death. If I had a heart, I'd probably feel some level of empathy. But I didn't. Not beyond the functioning slab of muscle that pumped blood through my body anyway.

I turned back to Steph, who was taking a swig from her flask. I detected a bloody fragrance. That wasn't water in there. Half-vampire could mean a few different things.

"Born or blooded?" I asked.

In theory, it was possible for a Dhampir to mate with a human and birth a half-vampire. It wasn't common because Dhampirs were notoriously prejudicial in their unions. Clans wouldn't accept a half anything. It was pure blood or nothing.

"Blooded." Steph smirked, a tinge of red on her lips. "I was dating a vampire when I was a teenager, didn't know. I could say I was enthralled, that he took advantage. I mean, he *was* two hundred years older than me, but that would be a lie."

We both laughed at that. Fucking vampires and their quest for youth. They always seemed to love the teenagers. "Yeah, I've heard this story many times before."

Vampire preys on innocent, or maybe not-so-innocent teenage girl, says all the right things, because he's lived several centuries and knows exactly what will make a girl melt. Bloods her so that sex is more intense and gets her addicted, but doesn't turn her. Food source as well as unrelenting lust factory all in one package. It was a survival strategy that had been used since the beginning of time with the Strix. They were like a virus, latching onto the nearest human host in hopes of surviving another century. Most times it didn't end well for the mortal. "What'd he gift you with?"

"Bad headaches mostly." Steph sighed, her perpetual grin fading a little. "I'm quick though. Can usually see things coming, good with strategy."

The Strix weren't without their skill-sets and powers. Oftentimes, they bestowed part of whatever their unique abilities were to their human blood hosts. If you were lucky and your vampire was powerful, that could mean many enhancements to your human life. At the very basic level, it meant living longer, living younger—the aging process slowed dramatically, even without the constant infusion of vampire blood. Steph could be twenty-five or she could be eighty for all I knew.

"Your vamp dead?"

"Yeah." Her smile was completely gone now. "A witch got him a few years ago."

"I'm sorry." I wasn't but I knew enough to play nice. I'd made a living killing Strix. They were nasty fuckers and their minions usually were totally brainwashed and equally as nasty. The human hosts, though, couldn't help the thrall, despite what Steph said. They were usually bonded through trickery and didn't really deserve the life they became addicted to. I did feel some level of sympathy for Steph if only because she had probably endured a lot of abusive shit from her vampire without realizing it was abuse. Most Strix vampires were fucking bastards, especially to their blooded mates. Just a little blanket belief of mine that perhaps was discriminatory but hey, fucking vampires, right?

"How do you deal with the bloodlust?" I knew what that pounding drive of the lust for blood could do to you. As an unturned Dhampir, I had a taste for the red stuff. I didn't need it. Not really. But it did give me a boost that I wouldn't turn down, ever. For her, it would be worse. Not only would her body physically crave an infusion that she was no longer getting from her vampire, but like most creatures, her mind would be desperate to secure survival. Her enhanced abilities would wax and wane as her sire's latest blood infusion slowly degraded in her system. I wasn't sure about the science of it all, but eventually, there'd be nothing left of him in her and at that point, aging and death would take hold. Drinking some kind of blood would slow the process to a degree but unless she found another vampire who was willing to share, she was pretty much screwed.

"Same way you do I'd imagine." She held up her beat-up looking flask and took another sip. "Cold." She grimaced but licked the red drops from her lips. "But it'll do."

I licked my lips too. Yeah, fresh blood, even from an animal, would work wonders on my energy levels. I glanced over at Jason, watching as he started divvying up the charred remains of the animals on the spits. The overcooked flesh wasn't appealing to me. I wouldn't mind taking a bite out of him though.

"I'd offer but I know how you Dhamps feel about the Strix." She shook the flask in my direction, making the contents splash inside.

I waved away her offer. She was right. The Dhampir had no love for the Strix. We considered ourselves the superior species— we were smarter, more powerful, died harder and, most importantly, could withstand the sun. Born as vampires, we'd always claimed the highest ranking on the vampire hierarchy. Superior not only in attitude but also historically speaking; we'd used the Strix to achieve our own interests and gains. We'd hunted them too. Ruthlessly. Enslaving them when it suited us but usually using our blood as nectar to bate and then annihilate them. It was a sport for many Dhampirs—hunting Strix just for shits and giggles.

It sounds awful to the outsider and what species doesn't have a history of violence and marginalization? But the Strix were a menace. They had threatened, on numerous occasions, the almost complete annihilation of the human race, our absolutely required blood source, due to their uncontrollable thirst for blood. Feeding frenzies alone could wipe out an entire city within hours. If left unchecked, the Strix would doom themselves as well as all Dhampir to starvation. Without humans, no vampire could survive—not for long anyway. So the Dhampir kept the Strix in line and the humans thrived, living for centuries longer than they probably would have on their own.

"You might want to consider turning," Steph said before taking a few more gulps of her bloody drink. "You'd probably stand a better chance of survival if you went full vampire."

"Ha!" I liked her boldness. It explained how she'd survived as long as she had. Interesting suggestion but not possible. I'd rejected the choice to go full vampire when I turned thirty, much to my father's disapproval. Remaining an unturned Dhampir suited me even if it left me physically weaker and slower to heal. While a Dhampir vampire was ultimately the most powerful of all vampire species, there were too many cons for me to accept. "Nah, the politics on that side of Dhampir life are intolerable." I winked.

According to the customs of my people, only the male Dhampir were permitted to blood a female Dhampir. It was the only safe way to ensure a powerful female Dhampir. Blood to blood, species insulated. It was a custom that I'd always assumed was designed to keep the males in the seat of power and the patriarchy fully entrenched. While I wasn't particularly concerned with customs, I'd be hard-pressed to find anyone willing to break the rules and risk being ousted from their clan. Turning vampire any other way for a Dhampir could have disastrous results. Despite my rebellion, I wasn't willing to take that chance and risk becoming weaker in the process. "A decision for another day, perhaps."

"Another day?" Steph chuckled then raised her voice so the others would hear. "She talks as if she's got an unlimited number of them. She's more optimistic than me!"

The others all looked over at us with varying degrees of forced laughter on their faces.

Jason motioned to me with a leg of something he'd been eating. "I'm surprised the great and powerful Jet Black is here in the first place."

I moved to a nearby boulder and leaned, making sure I could see the group, assess their reactions. Now that I had their attention. "I'm here because I'm looking for someone."

The chattered whispers stopped. My words had the desired effect; everyone was completely focused on me.

Jason had to close his gaping mouth. "Are you telling me you purposely got yourself on this island?"

With a slight snag of being weaponless and knocked out by vampire repellent. "It didn't go exactly as planned, but yes." I crossed my ankles and took a swig of water. "I planned to be here."

"You're on a job?" Steph asked, her brow furrowed deeply, her own flask disappearing into a pocket.

I nodded.

The tension ratcheted up. The hair on the back of my neck prickled. Looks were exchanged. If I was reading the room correctly, everyone was suddenly on high alert. Fingers twitched. A few words were mumbled.

"I'm looking for a witch. A powerful witch. A dark witch." I leaned toward them. "I'm looking for Kali Richards."

A collective gasp went through the cavern. Someone made a weird noise, almost like a half-choke, half-laugh.

Steph was grinning once again. "Ah shit, Jet, you should have said that to begin with." She patted her chest over her heart. "I thought you are about to go hunter on all our asses. You're looking for Kali?"

"Yeah, and I know she's here." I reached into my bodysuit and pulled out the amulet. It pulsed to life, burning brightly once again.

Steph's eyes were glued to that amulet. "Fuck yes, she's here. But we keep a wide berth. She's crazy as all hell."

"You know where she is then?" I knew this had been a good idea. The locals always had a clearer path to what I needed.

"We know where she is." Steph pulled her flask out once again before sitting on a nearby rock. She took a long drink then wiped her mouth with the back of her hand. "But you're not going to be able to get close to her. Not even within a mile."

I raised an eyebrow.

"I'm not joking. She's warded the fuck out of her lair. The animals don't even venture into her territory unless she invites them to and then it's..." She made a motion with her finger across her throat.

"Just point me in the right direction. I'll handle the rest."

"Ha, okay, yeah, sure." Steph leaned too, mimicking my stance, crossing her arms casually as well. "Kali hides herself about three miles from here."

I couldn't help my eyes from widening. So close! I could grab that witch in a few hours and be home before my stomach started to growl.

"Yeah, I see that you think it'll be easy to get to her. I've been exactly where you are, mentally speaking, once I realized who shared our island getaway with us. I thought I could appeal to her. You know, because she's supposed to be powerful as all shit and the vampires are scared of her?" Steph snorted. "She walks through the forest all the time. You know she's around because everything freezes. Like there's complete silence, everything stops moving, frozen in place. Not with magic, but with fear. She emanates this evil that is fucking terrifying. It slides through your body, down your spine, into your blood. I thought I'd be able to reason with her. Get close enough to her lair and beg for help."

Steph shook her head. "The bitch is crazy. Batshit. She's not interested in helping us. She's not interesting in anything but being left alone." Steph leaned down and rolled up her pant leg. There was a gouge out of her flesh that looked like it'd taken some muscle with it. "She killed the witches who came with me. I barely made it away alive." She dropped her pant leg. "Kali's one of the reasons we don't go out at night. It's not just the vampires you have to fear. She seems to amplify the crazy when the sun goes down. She walks out there all night doing something. Maybe reinforcing wards? Who knows? It's dangerous to get caught in her path."

"Kali Richards owes the world something, and I have a contract to bring her back." The thing with lore was that it could get carried away, fact mingling with fiction. Kali had been missing in action since almost the start of the war. She had been heralded as a savior but when it came down to it, some kind of performance anxiety had sent her running. She'd left everyone behind. Her family, her lover, a world of hopeful supernaturals who had really bought into the story that she was going to save the damn world. She'd just vanished. "She's wanted on the other side, and I never fail to deliver."

"You've got a way off the island?" Amber said, her voice hopeful. She moved toward me like she was in a trance, tears glistening in her eyes.

I nodded then slipped the amulet into my suit once again. "Kali is my way off the island."

Steph laughed, like full on belly ripping laughed. She even smacked her knee. "Good luck to you! No way that witch is getting you off the island. No way you're getting anywhere close to her either. Lady, I respect you. For real, your reputation is one badass bitch, but whoever told you you'd get off this island sold you a lie. Kali ain't going nowhere. Not with you, not with anyone. You're stuck here, just as surely as the rest of us are. And that means eventually you'll be dead too. Unless you turn vampire, then maybe you've got a chance."

5

I DIDN'T LIKE BEING LAUGHED AT. IT MADE ME FEEL LIKE I HAD something to prove. Pride was definitely my fatal flaw. It always spurred me into action, for good or bad. "Three miles, what direction?"

Steph stopped laughing abruptly. Her eyes widened. "I'm telling you—"

"West," Jason said with a finger pointed toward the back of the cave. "There's no clear path, but you'll be able to feel her magic after about a mile. It gets under your skin. And once you feel her, watch out, 'cause she could be a step away."

"Great, thanks." I shook the water bottle at Steph. "You got another one of these I can take with me?"

"You're going now?" Steph pushed herself from the rock she was still sitting on. "I told you it's dangerous at night!"

"I came here to do a job. Now that I know where my target is, I don't see any point in waiting." I shook the nearly empty bottle again. "The water was great, thanks, but anyone have a knife I could borrow?"

"I really don't think—"

"Here." Jason threw a closed pocketknife my way, followed by another bottle of water.

I caught the knife and slipped it quickly into my pocket so I could catch the water bottle. At the same time, I tossed the nearly empty water bottle I had back at him. "See ya'll in the morning...or not."

I didn't wait for any more talk. I was impatient to get hunting. The anticipation of that alone was enough to get my body zinging with adrenaline. Perhaps a bunny would cross paths with me on the way. I could use a little blood fuel. My stomach grumbled at that thought. Food would be good, but I could manage for another day or so without any ill effects.

No need to stick around and play at building relationships. I'd gotten what I needed—time to get the job done. I'd be home by midnight for sure. Showering with hot water and a foamy peach scented body wash that I could practically smell now. Clean underwear, fresh sheets, a soft bed, a blood-infused hot toddy. Ah yeah, fuck this island and the unfortunate souls on it. Not my problem.

I walked out, through the twists and turns of the cavern and bypassed Fiona the sentry.

"You leaving?" she called after me.

"Yeah, I've got places to be."

She laughed like I was joking.

Once I hit the forest, I skirted along the wall of the cavern, keeping as close to the rock as I could. I followed the wall until I was heading in the direction Jason had indicated. It was dense with shrubs and saplings but otherwise there was nothing to stop me from moving forward. The terrain appeared to slope upward beyond the cave. Mountainous, possibly a dormant volcano. Staring straight up got me some visual landmarks with star constellations. The moon wasn't yet visible, but I had enough information now to get me on track.

I snapped a few of the stronger saplings and used Jason's knife to quickly whittle a couple of crude but sturdy stakes. Not the best weapons but good enough—and deadly to a Strix. After carefully folding the knife, I then slipped it into my back-pocket. It wasn't going to do me any good as a weapon but the blade was sharp enough to shear wood and that was all I really needed.

The surrounding forest was dark as hell. Even with my enhanced vision, trekking was perilous at times. I had to hone all of my senses, and I will admit that I tripped a time or two on some sneaky logs that sprang up out of nowhere. The forest itself was active with night sounds and movements. Small animals scurried. Not fast enough, in one chubby rodent's case. He made a tasty meal for my blood-deprived throat. Was just a sampling really, but the blood did what I needed it to do. The rodent's lifeblood running through my body was enough to put a bounce in my step.

Forest living wasn't as bad as I'd thought. At least, it was fine enough to visit for a few hours. It was pleasantly warm with a nice smelling breeze that seemed to float in from the surrounding sea. There were sing-songy noises all around me too. I could picture myself swinging on a hammock, sipping a cocktail, watching Jason flex his muscles for me.

That cat, oh man, he was a hot boy, that was for sure. It was almost upsetting that I had to leave him behind. With all that hard muscle and sinew poking out of his T-shirt, he was sure to have abs upon abs, not to mention the distinctly large bulge that I'd notice in his pants. No way that was anything but what it was. I bet he was wild in bed—or against the wall, over the back of a couch. *Sigh*. Yeah, would have been a hot ride. But, alas, he was not part of the one-way ticket to civilization plan, so he'd have to stay behind. Too bad. Maybe if he'd been nicer to me... I smirked to myself.

I didn't doubt that Steph was right about Kali being crazy. I'd been warned as much before I'd accepted the job. She'd left civilization a mess, apparently, so it stood to reason that she was still a mess, probably worse off by now. Dealing with crazy supernaturals was not my favorite part of the job but I had an ace up my sleeve—or rather, down my bodysuit. One that I knew would catch her attention and bring her back to reality.

The amulet pulsed against my skin, radiating heat in waves... I was headed in the right direction.

It wasn't until I'd been hiking for at least a half-hour that I felt the first tingle of something being off, presumably Kali's dark magic rolling on the breeze. Jason was right... It slipped under my skin immediately, like a whisper that echoed just beneath the surface and made me cringe. It was a feeling of unease that caused goose bumps to rise and gave me a constant impulse to look over my shoulder.

Dark magic really sucked. Since the war had started, it seemed to be everywhere. Floating around like a toxic mist in certain places. Rumor had it that Kali owned a powerful grimoire. It was the source of her black spells and had set her on a path to darkness before she'd disappeared from the quasi-civilized world. It was also reported to be the cause of her crazy behavior. Black magic was addictive and mind-bending, from what I'd heard. It could warp even the purest witch. From all accounts, she'd become quite proficient with the spells in that book before she'd gone AWOL. So yeah, I knew she was likely using her dark magic unchecked in the time that she'd been hidden away from the world.

Something else I knew for sure was that Kali might have failed the world by not ending the Dark War, but it wasn't because she was a weak witch. Mix natural power like hers with some potent dark magic and you had a free pass to crazy town with the possibility of much devastation.

But all of that really didn't matter. I could handle crazy. The amulet was not only tuned into Kali, but once she came in contact with it, it would drag her back to the owner, along with anyone else who was holding on. Two passengers. That was the amulet's capacity. I'd been warned, explicitly, no extra passengers or there was no guarantee that we'd make it back in one piece. My plan was to find Kali, grab her, and then stick the amulet on her. Then it was bye-bye fang island and hello coffee with a pint of human blood mixed in.

"Where would a crazy witch hide?" I didn't bother to whisper —not like I was trying to be stealthy. There were no vampires around. Even with Kali's magic buzzing through me, I'd still be able to detect a bloodsucker. All I needed was to get Kali close enough that I could make a connection.

I stopped trekking as a sudden idea struck me. Why was I stumbling around in the dark when I could just call the witch to me?

"Kali Richards!" I yelled. "I know you're out here, I can feel your magic's ebb and flow. I have something to show you. Something you'll want to see. Kali Richards, I'm looking for you, witch. Show yourself."

I quickly found a spot where the trees were bunched up pretty well. Slipping my stakes into my waist belt, I freed my hands and hoisted myself up the thickest of the trees, my body angled so that I could drop down on Kali when she came into view. The power of her magic was palpable, so much so that my heart seemed to match its staccato, drumming at an irregularly fast beat. I didn't like it. My body felt like it was revving. Ready for flight or fight.

I shifted myself until I was wedged in good, my boots digging into the bark so that I could give a powerful push and launch myself at Kali as soon as I caught sight. This would be over in a few minutes. Easy peasy.

I pulled the amulet out again, letting it rest against my body-suit. The chain would make things awkward as fuck but there was no way I was going to unclasp the thing and risk losing it. It pulsed brightly as soon as it was in open air, red like blood, matching the beat that I felt in my body.

It was like Kali's footsteps echoed within the amulet, the thump of her magic rolling through me. I shook it off, trying to dislodge it from my senses. Truth be told, I wanted to run. It was taking all of my power to ignore the impulse to bolt. I chalked that up to Kali's brand of dark magic, the eerie sense that something was very wrong—more about her power signature than actual danger. At least, that's what I was telling myself anyway.

Stick to the plan. Ferret the witch out. Touch her with the amulet. Home time.

"Kali Richards, you crazy witch, show yourself!"

The forest and everything around me froze. Not like icicle frozen, more like *I'm going to shit my pants with fear* frozen. Another strong surge of adrenaline pounded through me, encouraging me to run. Jump down from the tree and get the fucking hell out of there. The bugs stopped buzzing. The night birds stopped calling. The breeze even seemed to stop blowing. It was silent and still and creepy as fuck.

Curiouser and curiouser. I gritted my teeth and pulled all of my courage into my core. Jet Black did not run from danger.

No, I just jumped right on top of it.

The power pulse got heavier, the vibration louder, and an eerie humming noise began to roll along the trees, bouncing from one trunk to the other. I picked up the amulet between my fingers, holding it so that the flat back of it was facing me. The gem needed to touch her skin—even a brush of contact should be enough.

Every muscle in my body was tense. My jaw clenched so hard it ached.

A cracking noise sounded to my left and an ethereal fog moved just beneath the tree I was in. I shifted slightly, clearing myself from the branch and using my hip to keep steady.

The humming grew louder, pounding into my skull. I wanted to close my eyes. I wanted to get the hell out of there.

Focus, Jet, you've got this.

When Kali came into view, she was not what I expected. Or maybe she was exactly what I expected. She moved like an animal, crouched low almost on hands and knees, scurrying from tree to tree, whispering as she drew invisible symbols on the bark. Her head moved like it was on a puppet string, jerking from one thing to the next, darting around like she was expecting something to attack her. Her body was covered in dirt, streaks of black mud caked her face, arms and legs. Her clothes were in tatters, woven pieces of dark materials wrapped around her chest, part of her abdomen and her lower body like a skirt. Her feet were bare. Everything about her looked primitive, native—like she belonged on the island. A wild woman from a nightmare world.

Her movements were erratic, no pattern discernible. I tracked her as best as I could, then held my breath. I clenched the amulet for dear life and made my move.

I was mid-leap when Kali rose to stand, turning on me like she'd known I was there all along. Her eyes were glaring, dark pupils that calculated quickly. I didn't stand a chance.

She swung her leg up, no magic necessary and connected with my gut, so much power that it knocked the wind out of me immediately, drilling me backward with such force that I slammed into the tree I'd been hiding in. My head cracked hard against the trunk, and the chain on the amulet broke. Luckily I still clenched it in my palm, and I didn't lose my grip.

She came at me like a wild beast, teeth bared, hissing as she launched herself. I barely had time to haul myself to my feet and block her next blow, taking the brunt of what was meant to smash my skull with my forearms instead. The skin tore open, my bones rattled, I bit my tongue, but somehow I managed to grab a hold of her hand and hang on.

"*Reverted ad me,*" I said as I slammed the amulet against her dirty skin, choking back the smell of her.

Her eyes grew wide as she looked from the amulet to me.

"No!" she hissed.

A black fog swirled around us. I felt it yank at me and knew the spell was taking hold. Kali grabbed onto my hair with her other hand and pulled me close to her lips.

"I will not return!"

She whispered something and I knew by the pulse of it that it was bad. Really bad. A burning white light flashed from the amulet, searing into my skin, stabbing down my arm. My heart screeched, twisting and turning in my chest. I screamed.

I'm dying. I'm going to die. And then I'll become a fucking vampire in the worst way.

She locked eyes with me, narrowing hers before lifting her lips into a cruel smile. "You have a black heart," she whispered. "And I know what you want from me."

She gripped my hair tighter and then I felt the twist of the muscles of my neck, my spine crackling. *Ah fuck, she's going to rip my head off.* No surviving that. Her iron-like fingers dug into the back of my head. There was a crack and then pain was nailing me through the skull. She clenched harder and I felt the popping of things coming out of alignment.

I was immobilized. As good as dead. Her triumphant smile told me so. Any second now, her fingers would be in my brain and then my head would come detached. Pain like stabbing blades went up and down my body. Excruciating. My muscles were screaming, my heart hammering with panic. White noise in my head was driving me mad.

All I could wish for was death and hope it came quickly.

A loud growl broke through the buzz, and then I was suddenly airborne again, wrenched away from Kali's grasp, the tension in my head gone.

I lay on the ground, darkness blinking in and out of my vision and watched as a giant furry cat had a showdown with a witch. *What the fuck just happened?* Pain pounded through me. It felt like my brain was seeping out of my ears.

Kali held the amulet in her hand. She smiled at me, her expression vicious, then turned her back on the cat and simply vanished.

And there I was, knocked on my ass, with no way home and owing my fucking life to a big dumb lynx.

6

"Stop licking me!"

The lynx was crouched behind me, one of its big paws holding my arm down as I attempted to swat it away. It wouldn't stop licking the back of my head. My hair was getting all gobbed up with cat spit.

"Fucking hell, Jason. I swear, if you're taste-testing me."

He snorted at that, but otherwise ignored my protests. I was losing blood and things were broken. Kali had crunched the hell out of my skull. The kitty was probably licking brain matter, taking parts of me with each swipe of his long tongue.

As annoying as it was, his saliva must have had some kind of healing agent in it. I could feel the bone mending, repairing things light years faster than my limited Dhampir healing abilities —better too, no doubt. Each lick, while gross and disgusting to listen to, was knitting up the torn and damaged muscles, tendons, and skin with some kind of pain-killing property. The pounding in my skull was gone and, after a few hundred of his rough kitty kisses, I was feeling pretty okay. Well, except for the raging blood-thirst. As ol' Drac used to say, the blood is the life—and I needed a hit something awful. I'd come close to death. Too close.

Taking blood to replace what I'd lost wouldn't turn me into a vampire, but it would go a long way toward making me right again.

I closed my eyes and let the weirdly soothing motion of his tongue lull me into a semi-sleep, willing my body to get on board with the healing and help speed things along. I kind of felt like I was floating, a soothing wash of calm settling over me.

"Hey, kitty, you got some kind of hallucinogenic in that spit of yours?" My words sounded muffled, like I was talking through a bunch of cotton balls. Sleep seemed like a good idea, and the floating sensation felt like it was going to take me away somewhere.

It wasn't until I felt the press of skin against my lips, the tangy metallic taste of blood seeping past my mouth, that there was a jolt of my own power coming into play. I snapped my eyes open to see Jason back in his human shape, looming over me, his bloody wrist was pressed hard against my mouth, his eyes blasting me with his usual anger. Or was that disdain? It was hard to tell. I'd like to ask him why he was helping me if he hated me so damn much but was too caught up in the scent of this blood bouquet.

I swallowed the first little gulp and then couldn't help myself. His blood had a kick to it, spicy heat that seared down my throat, leaving a trail of blazing want. I latched on, using my little fangs to hook into his flesh and hold him in place. I took a couple of giant pulls and let the savory nectar flow through me. I realized what I hadn't in the daze of pain and healing—I needed this if I was going to survive the damage Kali had done. There was no way I'd survive without some blood replenishment.

That was as close to death as I ever wanted to be. Jason had literally saved my life. And according to my fucking Dhampir law, I now owed him. Big time.

Fuck.

He pulled his arm away from me, prying my teeth out as he

detached himself. He lifted his open wound to his mouth so he could lick it a few times. "You good?" he grunted between licks.

I gulped. Nodded. Attempted to push myself up. Dizziness kept me down though. "Motherfucker." I whispered, my skull pounding once again. I reached up to touch the back of my head. Nothing seemed mushy, but it was tender still. My hair was wet and sticky, probably clumped with blood. I winced as I brought my arm down and examined the long cut that was there. It wasn't too deep, and my Dhampir healing abilities were kicking in, mending it slowly so that it wasn't even bleeding too much, just weeping at the deeper parts.

"You wouldn't have survived that, right?" He nodded in the direction Kali had presumably left. "If she'd ripped your head off?"

I stretched my neck, letting the muscles crinkle and crackle, my spine popping with alignment. Ouch, that was sore.

"As an unturned Dhampir? Nope." I sucked in a deep breath. "Ripping my head off would have kept me down. So yeah, I owe you my life," I mumbled.

"Why'd you stay an unturned Dhampir? If you were a vampire you'd have been able to take her." He sat back on his haunches, watching me like I was a freak show. "I've seen Dhampirs fight. Your vampire speed and strength alone would have bested her, so why keep yourself at a disadvantage?"

I grunted as I made a second attempt to sit the hell up. Weakness was not my thing. The dizziness was still there, my head still raging with pain, but somehow I managed to get myself up enough to brace against a tree. He didn't offer to help. Just sat there staring.

"Vampires only live for one thing."

"Blood?"

"Themselves," I corrected.

"Your moral code doesn't seem to be too centered around the

greater good." He snorted. "You hunt supernaturals for the highest price. What part of that isn't self-serving?"

"I never said I was any better."

"So why not turn vampire then? You could do it at any point. You die in a non-head ripping kind of way and you're reborn as a bloodsucker, right? That's what the Dhampirs get with their birthright, isn't it? You get the choice to turn. So why not give yourself the advantage?"

I gulped again, licked my lips. The taste of his blood was still there. I wanted more.

"It's not that simple." It was that simple—you die in a non-head ripping kind of way and you're reborn as a full-fledged vampire. The problem came with the process of turning. According to custom, it had to be a male Dhampir who turned the female. A male Dhampir's blood was the most powerful, ensuring that only the best possible version of Dhampir would be reborn. To do it any other way led to weakness, insanity at times...or at least, that's what we were taught. No one that I'd ever known had dared test it out. It was taboo to even think such a thing. You turned full vampire by the blood of your strongest male relative—husband, father, cousin, whomever that was in your clan. Or in my case, the love of my life.

"I was going to turn. Was all set. But then the only reason for me to become a vampire was taken away." I lifted my arm and sucked on the blood that was slipping out of my wound still. "I decided it wasn't worth living for an eternity."

"You lost someone?"

"Not *lost*. Was robbed of someone. The only one." My heart suddenly felt like it was flipping in on itself, like Kali was back to finish the job. "Everyone has had that person, haven't they? The one they would have done anything for?" I sighed and let my arm drop back to my lap. "I would have changed for him. I would have embraced my role in the clan. I was young and stupid."

"And he died?"

"He was murdered."

"I'm sorry."

"Don't be. You didn't kill him. And it was a long time ago."

"You hunt for revenge then?"

"I hunt because I like to. And I'm good at it." *And it pisses my father off.*

"You keep yourself at a disadvantage for a stupid reason. You could have been killed for real tonight." His eyes were hard once again, drilling me with judgment.

"Fuck you." I sneered.

He raised his hand. "If I hadn't come along when I did—"

"Why the hell were you following me, anyway?" I snapped, suddenly irritated that I'd been so honest with him. I thought everyone knew my story anyway. Star-crossed Jet Black and the love of her life, Julian Cross. Two enemy clans that love could have united. Or at least that's what we had told ourselves. What had really happened was bloody and awful and soul destroying.

"Wanted to see what would happen." He scratched the back of his neck. "You weren't lying about getting off the island were you? I saw a portal open."

I pushed myself up higher, grunting a little as a fresh wave of pain slid down my spine. "Nope, wasn't lying."

"And the portal is tied to that amulet?"

"Yep."

"And Kali has the amulet now?"

"Yep again." The reality of that hit me hard but I kept my face neutral. I'd made an ass of myself. Jet Black in over her head, saved by a fucking Lynx. I'm sure the way he saw things, I was weak. He was likely used to powerful women warriors. The female Lynx were notoriously brutal with their battle skills and strategies. I'd overestimated my abilities from the moment I'd arranged this mission. I'd been doomed to failure. Betrayed and stripped of weapons before I'd even gotten on the game board and now, facing Kali, I'd completely misread the situation, ignored the warnings, and had gotten my cocky ass handed to me. So not only weak, but stupid too.

"So we have to get that amulet if we're going to get off the island?"

"We?" I snapped my eyes to meet his.

"Well..." He smirked. "You do owe me your life and we Lynx have this thing about that."

I groaned. I knew a thing or two about moral codes. Despite rejecting my clan and turning my back on my father, I still felt duty bound to my culture. Dhampirs didn't take moral obligation lightly.

"I saved your life. Now you're stuck with me. Which means I'm getting off this island too."

I WAS GRUMBLY. NOT TOO INTERESTED IN TALKING ANY MORE. Stuck in my head thinking about all the ways I'd fucked things up. Home by midnight. Ha! What an arrogant ass I'd been. I was also on alert, waiting for the buzz of vamps to swell. I'd been bleeding like a sieve since Kali's attack and the scent of my blood was on the breeze. Those ferals roaming the woods would be hunting for the source of the nectar. I needed to wash up at least, dilute the scent.

Jason left to hunt us down some food. He was back quickly enough, a fat juicy rabbit in his kitty jaws. After turning back to human, he skinned it and skewered it, even managed to produce fire with some kind of human trickery that involved a flint stone and some metal. Clever cat.

The smell of roasting meat had my mouth watering and the pain subsiding enough for me to sit up without having to brace myself. My mood shifted too. Food had that effect on me.

"I thought you didn't do fires outside of the cavern." I remembered his words of warning a few hours earlier and couldn't help but think that seemed like days ago.

He cocked an eyebrow my way but otherwise ignored me.

"Why'd you do it?" I asked as he ripped the body in half, blowing a bit on the too-hot flesh before handing the meat to me. "Save my ass, I mean. Thought you hated my guts."

I took a big bite, ignoring the burn as the hot juices slid down my throat. I was famished, my stomach yowling with hunger. Injury did that to me. I could probably eat an entire horse. No joke.

"Everyone has their demons." He shrugged. "It wasn't like I was a decent guy back home. I got rounded up fair and square."

"Oh yeah." I snickered. "You're some badass that deserved a trip to Vampire Island?"

The irony of the situation was not lost on me. I'd sent hundreds, if not thousands, of inmates to V Island over the years. I'd never turned down a contract. When I'd refused to turn vampire, I'd been ousted from my clan. All the fancy cars and clothes and easy access to money, *poof*, gone. For the first time in my life I was taking care of myself. I had a talent, though. My Dhampir blood attracted Strix, and I was trained in all ways of fighting. My mother had made sure of it; her silently subversive way of preparing me for life as a female Dhampir. I was good with weapons; I was also pissed off and heart-broken. Perfect recipe for a mercenary. The contracts typically paid well, and I always delivered. My bank account would never match the wealth of my clan or my father, but I was doing okay. And it was built on the back of the supernaturals I'd sent here.

"The guys I was working with did," Jason continued between bites. "I knew better. Took a risk. The money was good. Got caught."

"Oh, give me a break! You're telling me that you're some shit-head criminal and you deserved to get caught? That you have no hard feelings that I was most likely the one to send you here?

Really?" I couldn't buy it. He wanted to help me get the amulet so that he could return home. I wasn't stupid enough to think he wouldn't betray me in the process. But, getting that amulet back was going to take some skill, and I had a feeling a Lynx would come in handy.

"I didn't say I had no hard feelings. I still think you're an asshole. But I put myself in your crosshairs the second I took the job. Working for the Strix is never advisable when you're in Jet Black territory."

"Ain't that the truth." I stripped another chunk of meat from the bone. It needed seasoning—salt, at least—but the fat was melting all into the meat and that alone was pretty delicious.

"I was with some bad dudes working on a secret plan to traffic some humans. Don't give me that look. The money was damn good and all I needed to do was keep a lookout. I was the muscle. That's it. Didn't have anything to do with the humans. But on the night it was supposed to go down, a shipment arriving at the docks, something went wrong."

I frowned. His story sounded vaguely familiar. "How long ago was this?"

"Three months or so."

"Yeah, I was on another job around then."

He scoffed. "You're just saying that because you don't want to owe me anything."

"You saved my life. I owe you no matter what." I finished the rest of my rabbit and tossed the remains into the fire. It crackled and sizzled. "I'm serious though. I was working with another Dhampir three months ago and we were close to the Canadian border, had a bunch of refugees to see to. Last time I was at the docks was on the night I arranged to get myself on the V Island shipment a few nights ago. Otherwise, I'm typically working the central. Cities are my thing."

Jason paused in his eating, his eyebrow cocked. Then he smiled a big toothy smile and continued devouring. "Well, that changes things then, I guess. Chip is no longer on my shoulder. So you're stuck with me not hating you."

"I would have taken the job though," I continued. "If I was available, I would have been the one to send you here, or maybe even possibly killed you during the roundup."

His smile faltered somewhat. He continued eating. "Everyone has their faults." He shrugged. "Can't undo what's been done. I know who you are. I know what you're all about. Right here, right now, you're my ticket off this hellhole."

"I'm obligated to get you home again." I sighed half-heartedly. I didn't think it was all that bad to have Jason around, just for the eye candy alone, but this did complicate things.

"Funny how that worked out." He finished off his half of the rabbit, licking the grease from his fingers.

I watched his tongue darting out, lapping up the rivulets of rabbit juice. His fingers were glistening and wet, his tongue sliding along each digit. Sexy as all fuck.

"Well, I guess you're stuck with me then." My voice sounded husky, and I licked my lips, suddenly parched once again.

He grinned up at me, still licking his fingers, his eyes glinting. "We'll make the most out of the alliance, I'm sure." He winked.

And I blushed like a fucking schoolgirl. "Um, yeah, sure." As if I hadn't been thinking exactly the same thing. I pushed myself up, shielding my face from his eyes as my cheeks burned brighter. *Could you be anymore awkward?* It's not like I was a virgin. I'd had men since Julian. Not many, but there had been some hot hookups. I'd never been with a shifter though.

He was at my side in an instant, his arm under mine, steadying me as I stood. "You feel strong enough to move?" He leaned in, his body pressed close, nose nestled against the back of my neck for a moment.

A shiver of lust went through me, my scalp tingling, my pussy clenching. "What are you doing?" A shiver of something else was there too. He'd been taking care of me and suddenly it felt much too intimate.

He trailed his nose along the back of my head, around to my ear. "Just making sure you're not bleeding anymore." He nipped my earlobe.

I shivered harder. Ah shit, this cat was going to get me all twisted up.

"I could lick you some more." He was grinning, his fangs glinting in the moonlight. "Take care of all your aches."

If I could melt any more I would; his voice was gruff, his cock hard and pressing into my ass. "Keep it in your pants, big boy. We've got a witch to track."

I could not believe I just said that when what I really meant was, *yes! Lick me! Lick me hard! Make me scream!* But there was something really tugging at me where Jason was concerned. A feeling that was uncomfortable and kind of unwelcome. Like I actually liked him or something. Or at least, I was intrigued enough to keep me interested.

He pulled away slightly, his body still pressed close to mine in several places. "You got a plan?"

"Yeah, but I'm going to need some weapons."

"Well then you're going to need to convince the others to help us get into the city."

"The others?"

"Yeah. We're going to need the witches to get past the traps."

"Are you serious?"

"As serious as my tongue on your puss—"

"Got it." I held my hand up, pushing him back a little. I needed to keep my head in the game. "Okay, new plan. We go back and get the witches on board."

"You going to tell them you'll take them back with us?"

I was going to make them *think* I would take them back. Truth was I didn't know how many people I could get through the portal. Two people. That was the limit, according to the owner of that amulet. Two people meaning me and Kali. But was there wiggle room on that? Not sure. I was told more would be inadvisable, not impossible.

I owed Jason my life, sure, but that could mean many things. It didn't have to mean a trip back home, at least not right away.

"Hey, first things first though. I need some water. Gotta get this blood off of me." I motioned down my body. "Otherwise I'll be a beacon for the blood suckers."

"Yeah, I shredded about a dozen headed this way while I was hunting."

I cursed silently. Another reason to owe the man. "Water?"

"Oh yeah, I've got just the thing." He winked at me, and I knew I was going to regret asking.

7

HE TOOK ME THROUGH THE FOREST, NOT TALKING MUCH beyond directing me around giant divots in the Earth which were easy to see because steam was billowing out of most of them.

"So this is a volcanic island?"

"Yep. Not dormant."

Great, another potential threat. I didn't have firsthand experience but I was pretty sure lava could obliterate all inhabitants on the island, including vampires.

"Last time it erupted was about a hundred years ago, though, so I think we're good."

"Or we're on the brink of another explosion." Never did know with Mother Nature. Witch magic had a way of amping things up as well.

"Down here." He disappeared into a wall of stone I hadn't realized was there.

I followed. Another cavern. This place was full of hiding spots. You could, in theory, survive most of the threats for a while just by staying hidden.

The cavern opened up immediately to an eerily lit pool of steaming water. It smelled of sulfur like I imagined Hell did. The water shimmered with blue and green highlights, small waves lapping at the slippery-looking rocks surrounding it.

"There's some weird little worms on the rocks under the water that glow. I wouldn't touch them—no idea of they're biters or not." He pointed to the water as he started to kick his boots off. "It's pretty warm in there. Like a hot tub." He didn't wait for me to make a move, instead he pinched his nose, winked at me, then did a feet-first dive into the pool, clothes and all.

When he surfaced, he started undressing.

"Kind of backwards don't you think?" Made me wonder if he was shy or something. Unlike most shifters, who were eager to show their naked selves to anyone who cared to see, I'd yet to see Jason bare.

"Jump in with you clothes on, scrub them as you take them off." He swam closer to the edge then whipped his shirt off, giving it a bit of a scrubbing against the nearest rock before wringing it out and laying it flat. "They'll be dry before we're done in here."

He must have been standing on a platform or something because he wasn't treading water. His chest flexed as he started to remove his pants. Lots of power in those pecs, and the hint of rippled abs down below the waterline. His arms... Yeah...big, strong, corded. I'd always had a thing for forearms, especially when pressed against my breasts, holding me in place as I'm pounded from behind.

Um...yeah... He was fit and I was gawking.

He flicked his eyes up to mine and grinned. "You said you needed to clean up. You want some privacy or something?"

Challenge accepted.

I smirked back then yanked on the zipper of my bodysuit, catching his attention as I slid it down. I liked the heat of his eyes on me as I revealed my skin. I had a kickass body made from years of honing my fighting skills. Plump in all the right places, muscle in the rest. Now he was gawking and I soaked it up, especially as I bent to peel my suit from my legs. I could see, just in my periphery, that he was lustily giving me a full-body scan.

I draped my suit over my shoulder as I snapped my eyes to meet his, then winked. "No need for privacy here."

I dove into the water, feet first just as he had.

The water was so warm, thick with something that made it soothing at the same time. I stayed underwater, keeping myself down so that all of my body could soak up the heat and the cleansing swirls of the underwater current. My remaining cuts stung for seconds before melting into the water just like the rest of me. My muscles unclenched and I let out a long sigh, a flurry of bubbles rising around me, before I kicked myself to the surface.

He was by my side when I broke water and inhaled a breath of sulfur-infused air. For a second I thought he was coming to seduce me, the glint in his eye hot as all fuck and promising dirty things to come. He got in close, the current of his body like a magnet to mine, swirling the water around my skin so I tingled. He leaned toward me, his lips brushing mine, our bodies inches away from one another. But instead of grabbing me, he grabbed my suit and then swam off back to his plateau.

I watched him do his scrubbing thing for a few minutes and then decided my time would be better spent floating. I lay back, letting the strange thickness of the water pick me up. Tits in the air, the flow of the water took me were it would.

Staring at the ceiling was mesmerizing. The roof was high of course—at least twenty feet up, with several natural air vents that showcased hundreds of stars. The ceiling itself was slick-looking as the steam rose and water droplets collected up high. I imagined that what didn't slide back down the sides of the cavern came down as rain once it built up enough. There was a constant dripping noise that was quite soothing. The air was warm; even so, my nipples puckered to hard little points of throbbing desire. I wanted him to look at me like he had a few minutes ago. I wanted him to lust for me.

I felt Jason approaching as the waves he made lapped against my breasts, covering my nipples so that they tingled and pulsed even more. I tilted my head up, watching him tread water, moving slowly in my direction. He was staring at my tits, naturally.

"Your suit is drying." He pointed to the rocks on the other side of the cavern. My suit was laid out next to his clothes. "We've got some time to kill."

He rolled over onto his back, and I had to giggle. His dick was hard, long and impressive, jutting straight up and then bobbing as he kept himself afloat.

"Oh yeah?" I waved my arms to move closer to him. We glided into one another, our skin slipping against each other in a delicious way.

I trailed my fingers up his thigh. He ran his over my collarbone. I moved mine to his hip, our bodies still floating lazily around, drawn together, bumping, then moving slightly apart. His fingers skimmed the edge of one breast, then down my ribs.

"I can think of a way we could spend our time," I said, my voice husky.

"Me too." He splashed as he lowered himself, swimming to me as I did the same.

"This could change our working relationship," he said, his eyes hooded. He pulled me into his body and I wrapped my legs round his hips, the buoyancy making my tits hit his chin.

"I can live with that." I purred as I rubbed myself down his rock-hard abs, feeling the bob of his dick against my pussy.

He leaned his head down to suck my nipple into his mouth, nipping and flicking as he did. "Me too," he said between nibbles.

It felt so damn good. The press of his lips on my skin, his dick rubbing my pussy, teasing along my clit as he tread water. His heat radiated in a different way than the heat of the water around us. His was electrifying, making my body zing.

I hooked my ankles around his back, gliding my pussy right onto his cock, and we both moaned as we sank into the water.

With our heads submerged, we found each other's lips and kissed until our breaths ran out.

He laughed when we broke to fresh air. "Come here." He grabbed my waist and pulled me toward the edge of the water, my feet touching the plateau he'd been standing on earlier. "That's better," he said as he wrapped his arms around me and pulled me back onto him. His cock slid home, deep, stretching me out, rubbing my clit roughly.

I draped my arms around his shoulders and kissed him again, liking the soft press of his lips, his tongue darting into my mouth, pumping me just like he was with his dick. His hands were on my ass, pulling me down so that he went deeper, harder, letting the water take me back up each time he thrust into me. My nipples rubbed against the hair on his chest, the abrasion doing wicked things to my sensitive skin. I loved the feel of his muscular arms, his shoulders flexing each time he moved. He was a powerful male, built differently than the Dhampirs I'd known. Everything about him was huge, but not so bulky that he wasn't fluid in fucking me. There was no awkwardness, just a slow glide that revved me up so quickly that my head was spinning. We fucked at a lazy, tranquil rhythm until the kisses got a little rougher, and the press of flesh more urgent.

He slammed me back against the wall of the pool, hard enough that I grunted into his mouth, but he didn't release my lips. His kissing was just as intoxicating as his dick. He was in me, filling me up, making me want to scream.

My climax rose swiftly, too much pleasure after too long without. He seemed to be in the same boat. We moaned together, the sound echoing around us as my climax hit in waves and his in spurts.

We collapsed into one another, chuckling as we did. My muscles felt so relaxed that I could fall asleep right then and there...and probably drown.

"I think that only killed ten minutes," he said, not letting me go, our bodies still pressed in close.

I laughed, nodding. "It's been a while."

"For me too." He gave me a sheepish grin as he wiggled his dick, the hardening girth of it letting me know round two was a likely possibility.

I raised an eyebrow. "Mmmm, that feels like a good plan."

8

I'D BEEN LIVING A SOLITARY LIFE FOR A LONG TIME. WHEN you're ousted from your clan, which means your family too, you become very hermit-like. My world revolved around work. When I had downtime, I spent it alone usually. And I preferred that. The prospect of a team approach, while likely useful in this situa- tion, was not something I was looking forward to. It meant I'd have to come to a consensus on things or risk the team splintering —a dangerous thing when you were essentially weaponless and facing hordes of hungry vampires. I had a plan and it required a team—I just wasn't too sure how much of the team would make it out alive.

Fucking Jason complicated things somewhat. I'd admit to that. But I was never that great with delayed gratification, and Jason was really hot and willing. Besides, I owed him my life so it's not like things weren't already way more serious than I'd anticipated. We'd indulged ourselves long enough for our clothes to go from wet to damp and then decided it was time to get moving.

We got back to the cavern just as the sun was starting to peek over the horizon. Everyone was already awake. Jason had retrieved some small game from the traps that were set in the forest and a few people from the group got to work skinning and prepping.

Steph was not surprised to see me back, but she did do a good job hiding her know-it-all grin behind a sleepy greeting. "Glad you didn't die out there." She yawned, stretching her arms above her head.

I nodded as I settled on a small grouping of boulders so I could stretch out my legs a bit. The trek back from the cavern had taken a lot out of me. I was winded, which was slightly concerning. Kali had really done a number on me. Add that to the soothing effects of the steam pool and a few rounds of sex and I was pretty exhausted. A bit of a catnap would do wonders, but daylight was burning and the Strix really had no defense when the sun was out. It was the best time to go hunting for supplies.

"I need to get into the city. Locate some weapons and a few other things." I grimaced a little as I rolled my shoulders back, my neck still tight as hell from near decapitation.

"You're not giving up?" Steph scoffed. "You look like you've been through a battering ram obstacle course. You still think you can convince Kali to take you home?"

"I can and I will," I said. *Just as soon as I get that damn amulet back.* "But Jason says we'll need some witches to get into the city. So I'm asking for help."

"Yeah, the witches would be good for that. But why should we help you? I mean, our life expectancy here is short—why make it shorter by venturing into enemy territory?"

"You don't have to be part of the plan. I just need the spell-casters." I wasn't going to beg. If I had to go alone, I knew I could get the job done.

That thought made me pause. I'd had a similar attitude when I'd gone hunting for Kali, and look where that had gotten me.

The expression on Jason's face was enough to tell me he was thinking the same thing. "She can get us all home," Jason said as he stepped forward, his arms crossed. "I saw her do it. She grabbed Kali and a portal opened, reeked of powerful magic. I've been through one of those things before. I know it can take us somewhere."

"Home?" Steph sounded hopeful, like all it took was a word from Jason to convince her.

"You'll take us all back?" Amber hadn't slept much; I could tell by the dark circles under her eyes and the way her body sagged. "Are you serious? You have a way?"

"She has a way, and we can all go. But we need to work as a team to get supplies from the city," Jason said.

I nodded, holding Steph's stare, daring her to challenge me again. "Yeah, I can get us back." The lie rolled easily off my tongue. "But not without the amulet that is now in Kali's possession."

"So you need to get to Kali, somehow subdue her and then activate the amulet she stole from you?" Steph crossed her arms as well, mirroring Jason's stance. "Sounds impossible. Kali is wicked powerful. What makes you think you can convince her to cooperate? Looks like the first attempt didn't go as planned."

I sighed. This bitch was a hard sell, and again I found myself wondering why I was bothering. In the end I'd have to betray them all—would be better to go it alone and skip the dramatics. "I'll admit I underestimated how fucked up Kali is. You're right, she's definitely lost her marbles. But she's still capable of coherent thought. She said some things to me." I cringed inwardly. Kali could not read minds—that wasn't her thing but it was like she knew exactly what my plan for her was. Once I got her back to the mainland, she'd go to the highest bidder. "And it was clear that she understood what was going on."

"So how do you propose subduing her then?" Steph asked.

"I worked this job once where I was rounding up some hybrids. Vampire witches who had a major case of bloodlust. Made them act insane." The hybrids could only do magic if they took blood from a witch. The power surge was temporary and left an awful craving that turned them into addicts in the worst sense. Crazed for magic. "There's a way to make a sticky kind of web that nullifies powers. Like a binding spell but in the form of a net. I need some specific ingredients—pretty common things though for the most part."

"Oh, yeah, I know the stuff you're talking about. I've seen it in action." Amber rubbed at her arms like she had the web on her, her face scrunched up. "It works well."

"It was developed by the humans to subdue supernaturals in general. I know how to make it and how to activate it," I said.

"I'm intrigued." Steph was nodding as she spoke. "We have a few powerful spell casters here that could help you with making it."

It didn't require a spell caster for the net. Like I'd said, this was a human creation so no magic required, but Steph didn't need to know that. Not yet anyway.

"And an elemental." I nodded at Amber. "If we can get Kali subdued and in the dark, we could limit her powers to some extent. She gets recharged by the sunlight. Darkness, plus the binding net and we could get her under control. Once I have the amulet, I can ignite the portal and take us all back to the U.S."

Steph narrowed her eyes. "And the weapons?"

"I'm naked here without my blades. I learned that the hard way out there with Kali. If I had my blades I would have been able to get the upper hand." Which might or might not have been true. My blades might have given me some edge with Kali but more importantly, it would give me an advantage with the group of supernaturals here. I knew I'd be the better fighter once I had some weapons. "Making crude stakes and flimsy bows isn't going to keep us safe either. We need some way to protect ourselves."

Steph didn't speak, just nodded her apparent agreement, her eyes shifting to Jason, who gave her some kind of assurance with just a look.

"Okay, we're in." Steph didn't bother to look for agreement

from the group. Obviously, she was speaking for them whether they liked it or not.

"Daylight is burning. We need to go now." I pushed myself up from the rocks, testing my strength. What I wouldn't give for another pint or two of Jason's blood and a few hours of deep hardcore sleep. But I'd worked with less before. I'd survive.

"The Strix have set up some elaborate traps." Jason unfolded his arms. "We have a general idea of where the weapons are. Not sure what other kind of ingredients you need."

"A hardware store. Or what is left of one. And some vines or ivy—any kind of climbing plant will do. There's got to be some of those around here," I said.

"We should break up into teams." Steph pointed to the others who still looked half-asleep while they waited for the food to finish roasting. "Got a couple of werewolf shifters, Doug and Bill, over there. Amber, Fiona, and Kurt are capable witches. They'll come with us. The rest of you, gather up as much vine as you can and bring it back here."

"I need you to strip the vine down. The mush from inside the vine, its guts, is what you're after. You should be able to scrape it out with some rocks," I said, then looked at Amber. "You might want to stay behind. I'm going to need you in the battle with Kali later."

"I'm a capable witch," Amber protested. "And you saved my life. I want to help you on this mission."

"I know you are; I've seen it, but I need you for later and this trip is going to be dangerous. I can't risk losing you out there." She would be a huge liability in the city. Too skittish. And it wasn't a lie. I could use her to manipulate the weather, give us some cloud cover if it was still daylight when we went after Kali. "I'll take the wolves and the other witches. You stay here and help with the vines. I need them prepped but fresh. You need to keep them moist. The insides only. And I need a lot of it. Like three or four gallons at least."

"Okay, I can do that. I guess." Amber looked resigned. She was used to following orders, to taking a back seat, but I could tell she was really unhappy about it.

"Weapons first," I said to Jason and Steph. "You got some idea of where they have the weapons hiding?"

"There's a gun store in the city. The Strix use it as an armory," Steph said.

"And are they set up with their dens? How many gangs do you think are operating?" The Strix worked in tight hierarchical structures. Each Master had a gang of vampires who'd blooded allegiance to *him*—or sometimes, but rarely, to *her*. All of the capable vampires on the island would have to join a gang if they wanted to survive. The ferals that roamed the island had obviously missed the memo or had been rejected by the gangs. Their blood craze had turned them into walking zombies, a nuisance for sure but not as dangerous as the gang members.

"There is only one gang," Steph said. "They run everything, call themselves the Outcasts."

The Strix and their gang names. I rolled my eyes. "That keeps things simple. Any idea who's running the show?" Every vampire in the Outcast gang was probably the worst of the worst. Rounded up and dumped on V Island for whatever crimes they had committed back on the mainland. I had to anticipate that this particular gang was more ruthless, more calculating than the average. And as soon as they realized I was on the island, I'd become prime target number one. Jet Black Vampire Killer was not the kind of calling card that was going to work for me here. My reputation alone could get me killed. "You've been here the longest haven't you?"

"Yeah, longest survivor left. We did some surveillance when we first got here. Me and another prisoner." She paused, gulped like those words hurt, like a memory was stabbing her brain. She closed her eyes, readjusted her stance then continued. "But I have no idea who the leader of the Outcasts is. I didn't think it would be wise to petition the gang for consideration. They don't seem to value women. Not for any other reason but food and sex anyway."

That meant that Steph and the other supernaturals knew the human women who were dumped on the island were likely raped before they were murdered. I didn't have a soft spot for humans in general—they could be as bloodthirsty as the Strix and as ruthless too. But I did have a problem with rape, no matter the species, and I knew how the Strix could brutalize women. The entire vampire species, Strix and Dhampir both, were ruthless sexists in general, undervaluing females to the extreme.

"Survival of the fittest, right?" Steph's smirk was back. "Not like we're all here because we're upstanding citizens."

"You leave those human women as decoys. Feed the Strix, keep them distracted, stop them from venturing into the woods in search of supernaturals. You know they're being raped before they're killed, right?"

"A little bit of vamp blood would have them begging for it," Steph said. "Trust me, I know."

Rage filled me. Jason laid his hand on my arm before I realized I was moving toward Steph with my fists clenched.

"We do what we have to do," Jason said, his voice softer than usual. "It's shitty, I get it, but if we didn't leave humans behind, we'd be responsible for them, for their survival. We can't be the heroes here."

"You said they'd fall prey to the ferals," I spat. Jason had said that. At the time it had seemed like an acceptable outcome. Shitty but unavoidable. Death would be quick at the fangs of those beasts. "But what you really meant is that the boatload of women I came with would be hunted come dusk, rounded up, raped and then drained by the Strix. I know gangs like this. They loathe women and treat them accordingly."

"I don't like it either, but what choice do we have?" Jason's expression looked pained. "I had to come to terms with it too.

The humans have to send food for the vampires—does it really surprise you that they would sacrifice the women?"

For a Lynx, whose people valued women, I could appreciate that it was likely a struggle for him to accept, at least.

Not something I could come to terms with. "We could take out the Master. Whoever he is." I wanted to. A bastard like that deserved to die.

"Yeah, right," Steph scoffed.

"I've taken a few out in my time," I said, venom in my tone.

"You're diverting from your mission. You need to get us off the island. To do that, you need to go up against Kali. That's your focus. Not taking out a Master vampire on an island of prisoners," Jason said. "We aren't the humans' protectors. They do this to their own kind. Let them sort it out. You get yourself and the rest of us off the island, and you can come back and take care of that Master if you want. Save all the women."

I knew he was right. We didn't have time for this, as much as I made it my personal mission to obliterate any kind of sexual predator asshole I could. There was enough of that shit running rampant in the Dhampir clans, subtle and under the guise of cultural norms, sure, but still a problem. The Strix, they fell under the thrall of whatever their Master's prerogative was. If he was a misogynist then so were the rest of the vampires. The fact that the humans knew this was happening on the island and sent boatloads of women here to feed the beasts was disgusting.

Getting Kali back to the mainland meant changing the war. Ending it, if the American Council of Witches got her. She had been, after all, foretold to save us all. If I wanted Vampire Island to cease to exist, then I needed to get Kali home and give her to the good guys.

Up until this very moment, that hadn't necessarily been on my agenda either. The highest bid for her was coming from the other side. Knowing the truth of V Island shifted my perspective a bit. Gave me something to really think about.

I cleared my throat. "They have minions, I'm assuming."

"All their minions are men. Big men," Steph added. "For the day watch. And they will be armed but not typically well-fed, so not overly strong. It's hard to keep half-blooded humans alive on this island. They require a lot of care." Steph frowned. "But they are damn dedicated. Their survival depends on steadfast loyalty."

I nodded, not at all worried about a few human minions. Big men or not, they were still human for the most part. "Okay, we need some tactical spells." I shoved my anger aside. There was nothing I could do from the island to stop the trafficking of human women. I needed to get back to the mainland and deal with it there. I addressed Fiona, who was practically bouncing as she came closer. "You got some offensive spells in your repertoire?"

"Oh yes!" Fiona bubbled. "I know a few that work well. And I've got some to help break into places. Was my specialty back home."

Fine, so she was a thief. Not exactly a great reason to be condemned to V Island, but oftentimes the other supernaturals were swept up in a raid and carted off to the prison just because of wrong place wrong time. It sucked, but it was war and war required a heavy hand to all lawbreakers.

Besides, I didn't make the rules. I'd be leaving her behind anyway so there was no room for tenderhearted ideals.

"Kurt and I can get you into wherever you need to be. Provide a distraction too," Fiona said.

Kurt moved forward, his expression grim. "I'm good with explosives." He was the antithesis to Fiona. All dark and brooding. His eyes darting around, his voice quiet.

Okay, volatile. Check. Keep an eye on that one. "And the wolves? You able to wolf out without a catalyst?"

Two tall wiry built males came out of the shadows, twins by the looks of things. Blond, skinny, not at all lethal in appearance.

"We don't need the moon if that's what you mean," Doug or Bill, wasn't sure which one, said.

They weren't alphas or betas—that was for damn sure. But a werewolf was a werewolf and the animal power could best some of the weaker Strix for sure. "You're protection. Wolf out and keep us alerted to any trouble."

The twins nodded. Unison action. It was strangely fascinating. They even stepped back into the shadows at the same time.

"We should leave now. It's going to take us a couple of hours to get to the city," Steph said.

I scanned our team. Everyone looked worn out, underfed and exhausted. If we didn't get ourselves killed out there, it'd be a miracle. I wasn't entirely confident the team approach was going to work in my favor but once I got what I needed, it was back to my usual solitary existence.

9

VAMPIRE ISLAND USED TO BE BEAUTIFUL. NOT JUST BECAUSE OF the white sandy beaches and the aqua-colored water but because it had boasted some of the most expensive resorts on the planet. I'd been there as a child with my clan. While I remembered not loving the intensity of the sun, I had loved the luxury. And five-star didn't begin to describe the decadence that had existed when Vampire Island had gone by another name. We'd mingled with the wealthy humans, wined and dined alongside them, with blood-infused food and beverage of course. Dhampirs were not unaccustomed to the best that money had to offer. As a child, I had been indulged, cherished by my family. A princess in the eyes of Clan Black and destined for great things. My father catered to my every whim.

But that was a very long time ago. Back when my innocence excused my ignorance and I had no idea what politics and heart-break lay ahead of me.

The Dark War had caused much devastation. Islands like this had been targeted by the humans if only to eliminate any perceived safe havens or perhaps just out of sheer anger that we'd been duping humans for centuries. It was senseless destruction that had taken out many popular destinations, but nothing made sense in wartime and there was no undoing it now, not even with the strongest magic.

When the time had come to lock up prisoners of war, there had been no place that would hold them on the mainlands so the humans had come up with this idea. Ship them off to the uninhabitable faraway places, set some wards—thanks to the witch allies—and let the criminals rot. It was the humans who sent prisoners to V Island. It was a human who I'd made a deal with to get here myself. So any issues I had with the island itself rested with the humans, and I'd be taking my concerns up with management once I returned.

I snorted at the idea of that. The smuggler I'd dealt with was surly not expecting to see me ever again. A thrill of excitement raced down my spine at the thought of his reaction when I paid him another visit. That was going to be at the top of my to-do list once I returned to quasi-civilization. He'd betrayed me for some reason and not because he hadn't been paid well. There would be a reckoning when I get back, that was a certainty.

Standing at the edge of the forest, I scanned the remains of the city before me.

I'd never ventured off the resort when I'd been here. Everything was always brought to me, so I didn't know what the city used to look like. What was left of it though did truly look like a war-zone. Rubble was everywhere. Piles of bricks and giant slabs of cement were strewn at impossible angles. Some of it was in large towers of haphazard building remnants. There were cars and buses that had been pillaged or torched. Fire had obviously run rampant throughout many of the shops and houses, leaving shells behind. Nothing looked safe to explore—not that that was going to stop me.

Farther in the distance, there were actually some buildings still standing and looking like they'd hardly sustained damage at all. With windows intact and only slight battering to the outer walls, they were obviously vampire strongholds.

"The windows are all blacked out. That likely means vampires are on every floor." I pointed to the large concrete building in the distance. It looked like it had once been a government office, possibly an embassy.

"Four floors plus two levels of underground parking," Steph confirmed.

"The important vamps are underground, the Master for sure." I shielded my eyes from the sun as I stepped through the last of the brush and trees. It was midday. The younger vampires were undoubtedly in a deep sleep, easy pickings. The older vamps could be awake. Holed up and confined to their darkness but not as vulnerable. If they were well-fed, they wouldn't require sleep at all.

"We don't need to go there." Jason directed me away from the vampire headquarters, pointing to the north where a strip of buildings still stood. "That's what's left of the shops. Should be a hardware store there."

"Where's the gun store?" I asked, assessing the layout of the stores. From what I could see, the road was completely impassable by vehicle. The pavement was lifted like an earthquake had wreaked havoc to shift the road into mountains and valleys of asphalt.

He pointed just to the east of the strip of buildings. "Over there. See the flag?"

I squinted, the sun making my head pound. Being unturned had some disadvantages. I was much more sensitive to heat and sunlight than I would be if I turned full Dhampir vampire. "The black one?" It was hardly a flag. Just a ragged strip of black cloth fluttering in the breeze.

"Yeah, that's it. One floor, stocked with all the weapons," Steph said. "They don't use them often, unless they're running a competition."

"What kind of competition?" My stomach twisted in that

dread-filled way when you know you're not going to like the answer you're about to get.

"They set up a maze for the humans sometimes. When the vamps get bored or when there's an unusually large shipment. Make them fight for their lives. They'll bring out the weapons then. Use them to scare the humans into compliance. For whatever reason, humans respond to guns with more flare than they do to fangs."

"They're conditioned to believe monsters aren't real," I said dryly. "You've seen this happen?" For someone who kept to the forest and the cavern, Steph seemed to know quite a bit about the workings of the Strix on the island.

Steph gave me one of her smirks. "I've lived it. Came in a shipment of over a few hundred. Ran the gauntlet. Managed to survive and escape."

"You came with another half-vampire?" She'd mentioned before that she'd had someone with her, someone who obviously had meant a lot to her.

"No. Not a half-vampire." Her smile faded.

"A full vampire?" I asked.

She cocked an eyebrow. "I told you my sire died. How do you think I survived that?"

"You found a new sire."

She nodded.

"And he's part of the Outcasts now?"

Steph nodded again. "He helped me get through the maze and escape. Then he petitioned them to join."

"You've seen him since?"

She didn't answer.

"He's still feeding you isn't he?" I pulled her arm so she was facing me again. "That's why you don't look like an addict craving a fix."

She snapped her arm away from me. "I haven't seen him in a while. A few weeks. He could be dead for all I know." Her voice caught. "You want to see me dissolve into a writhing mess of bloodlust? It's coming. Give me another few weeks and it's coming."

"Good to know."

Cracking branches had us all turning to see the twins, now in wolf form, coming out of the bush. They were a muddy brown-blond color with streaks of black running down their backs like highlights. Their eyes were golden, sparking with a wolfie kind of cunning that I'd come to expect from the beasts I'd known.

"Flank us," Jason said to the wolves then turned to me. "You ready?"

"Gun store first." I needed some weapons. That was a must. I was tired of feeling naked. My knife sheaths had the two stakes I'd made and that was it. I wanted throwing knives or whatever kind of deadly projectile I could find.

"What do you need from the hardware store? I'll go get that and meet you guys at the gun store," Steph said. "I'll take one of the wolves with me."

I narrowed my eyes at her. Was she up to something? Now that I knew she had a friend among the enemy, it made me more wary of her. Not that I trusted any of them completely but Steph hadn't been too forthcoming with me from the get-go. Why she was being honest now was a mystery. I knew a thing or two about the sire-human relationship. There wasn't much a minion wouldn't do for their master. Steph was addicted to vampire blood and her sire was on the island, presumably still alive or she'd definitely know it. That meant she'd do anything for him. Even lure the rest of us into a trap if he willed it so.

"I need glue. Or some kind of liquid adhesive," I said. "Doesn't matter if it's dried up. I can work with that. A dozen bottles will do if you can find that many."

"Glue?" Steph snorted. "Got it." She'd slung a crudely made bag over her shoulder when we left the cavern and patted it now.

"I need to grab some medical supplies. Going to hit the pharmacy as well."

"There's a pharmacy?" I glanced back at the row of stores, not really able to make out any of the signage that was still there. "You think the vamps left the medical supplies intact?"

"They don't need them. And we lost the healer we had with us a couple of months ago. We have some weaker species among our group that could use some antiseptic and stitches. Antibiotics could come in handy, too, if I can find some. If we don't succeed with Kali the first time, there might be injuries."

"We'll succeed with Kali," I said, with a determined edge. Once I got that net on her, she'd be effectively subdued. I'd head home before anyone realized that I'd left them behind. "If you needed medical supplies, why haven't you tried to get into the city before now?"

"We have tried," Jason answered, rubbing his jaw and unruly beard. "We just haven't gotten very far. But now that we've got Jet Black, notorious vampire hunter, success is within our grasp." He winked and smirked.

I rolled my eyes at him. "No seriously, why haven't you succeeded before now?"

"We were too weak. Too disorganized," Steph said with a shrug. "Too focused on survival in the forest."

"New team, new possibilities. The witches just got here a few weeks ago. Before that, we only had the wolves and some really lame hybrids of some sort. They didn't last long. Got taken out by a horde not long after arrival," Jason said. "We also have a mission to complete now and an end game that will get us home. Seems like our odds are better. Or at least our attitude is."

"What failed last time? You attempted but what went wrong?" I asked.

"The human minions roam the streets during the day. They're armed. Almost as demonic as their vampire sires when it comes to cruelty. They shoot to maim and then taunt and torment until nightfall when their vampires come out to play some more. We didn't anticipate their cunning."

"Okay, so how are we approaching?"

"I'm going to blow some shit up." Kurt was flexing his fingers and rolling his neck like he was getting ready to make a run for it. "I'll draw them out of the shadows and create a little bit of chaos. If a few of them die along the way, all the better. Fiona will get you in where you need to go."

"The dogs and cat will take out anything that comes our way." Jason added with a grin before disappearing in a swirl of body parts and fur. When it was all done, he was his usual cat self, nudging my hip with his giant head before jumping to the nearest highpoint. He made a low growling noise that sent a thud of excitement to my core and motioned us to get a move on.

Impatient feline.

"Everyone set on what we're doing?" I double-checked with the group.

"Yeah, boom, boom, boom," Fiona said as she rubbed her hands together. A sparking of magic ran over her fingers. "Kurt's good at that. And I'm good at everything else." She flung her fingers out, instantly cascading us in a wave of a spell.

"What the..." A mist of darkness covered all of us. A fog-like shield keeping us from view.

"As long as they don't look too hard in our direction and we stick to the shadows as much as possible, they won't see us. Kurt will keep them preoccupied," Fiona said.

"I'm on it." Kurt was already moving ahead, scurrying low and picking up speed as he navigated the side of the buildings.

"Let's go."

We kept to the edges of what was left of the stores, moving into the shadows so that Fiona's spell didn't seem out of place. It kind of went without saying that no one spoke. The spell might make us hard to see, but it wouldn't make our approach soundless.

Steph and one of the wolves splintered off down a side street once we made it into the center of the city. Kurt started launching his bomb spells right after they left. And I had to say, it was damn impressive.

By standing on top of one of the higher peaks of the risen pavement, he was able to lob a series of spells pretty far out. The explosions, while not causing a ton of damage, made a hell of a lot of noise.

"Just a distraction for now," he said with a grin. "I'll cause some destruction later. Just warming up."

"Sounds good to me." I shielded my eyes to see better.

His bombs made a ruckus and sure enough, the sound of boots on pavement and the shouts of surprise and anger that followed told me the human minions were coming to investigate. "Sounds like a dozen or so."

"Let's assume the guards on the armory haven't left," Fiona said, her fingers cracking with magic once again.

"Agreed." Kurt jumped down from his perch. "I'm going to go that way, keep them moving away from where you guys are headed." He pointed down a street leading in the opposite direction.

"Take a wolf," I said with a nod to the remaining shifter. "I'll take the cat."

Jason licked my hand, and I stifled a yelp.

"That's seriously gross," I hissed at him. "Quit it."

He gave me his kitty grin and took off ahead, bouncing from one pavement shelf to the next as he made his way down the street.

"He likes you." Fiona's voice came out in a singsong way that made me want to puke or punch her, maybe both. Everything she said sounded like a Disney song in the making. "Lynx mate for life you know."

"Yeah, I know, and that's not my thing."

"Was *once* your thing and it could mend your heart," Fiona said, raising her hands in defense when I snapped a glare her way. "I know about your tragic love story. Really sad that you lost your true love. Very Romeo and Juliet, minus the suicide." She gave me a sympathetic smile that seemed genuine. "Steph filled us in last night. She says you're famous."

Oh did she? I grunted in response to that. Trying not to encourage any more discussion. Yeah, two feuding vampire clans, two stupid immature young adults who had needed a serious reality check. "True love is overrated. If I could do it all over again, I'd save myself the torture and leave the love affair to someone else."

Brave words that my heart called bullshit on, but fuck if I'd admit that out loud. Problem with love was, you really couldn't control when it struck and you definitely had no say in how hard you fell. Not like my story was all that original. I'd loved, and I'd lost. The end.

"Not everyone gets a chance to experience love like that," she said, her tone wistful and full of longing. "I'd take it. Even if it was only for a short time."

"No, you wouldn't." No one would wish that on themselves. When Julian was killed, when I saw the life ebb from his body and drain from his eyes, when he was truly gone, his heart ripped out and set on fire, I felt like mine had been torched too. The agony of that loss would never leave me. Its residue tainted everything I'd done moving forward. And there were many days that I wished I'd died alongside him. There were days that I'd been so reckless in the years after that I almost had followed him into death.

Silence lasted for maybe a minute before Fiona was yammering again.

"But still, Jason, he's a good male. Worthy for a second chance love affair." She resumed her giddy bouncing as we moved down the side of the stores. The sound of shouts as another blast rocked in the distance had us moving a bit quicker into the next bank of shadows. "You guys could get a romance started and then, when we leave here, you'd be the love affair that conquered Vampire Island."

Where did this girl get her imagination from? Sheesh. "He's a good distraction." I corrected. "Now shut up before you get us caught."

I will never love again. I reminded myself, my daily mantra since Julian had died so many years ago. And after what I was about to do—namely leave the bunch of them stranded on the island, possibly even Jason—I doubted he would be able to think about Jet Black, notorious vampire hunter, without wanting to kill me.

10

THERE WERE TWO GUARDS POSTED AT THE DOOR. THEY HADN'T moved to investigate Kurt's bombs. They looked freaked out and ready for attack but not ready enough to handle Jason the cat pouncing on them.

Fiona and I had just gotten to the bottom of the street, directly across from the gun store, when Jason came barreling from the side. He took out guard number one with a clawed swipe to the chest that opened the human up like a tin can, then moved to the next guard and slammed him against the wall, snapping his neck with the force of it.

Both guards dropped to the ground, and I was left a little in awe. That was fucking awesome! I'd seen him battle vampires and he'd managed to get Kali to back the fuck off, this was something different. The pure animalistic efficiency of his kill was truly like watching a predator in the wild. Calculated, deadly—those humans hadn't stood a chance. It actually made me wet. Not that I wanted to have sex with a cat, but seriously, the man side of him had to be just as formidable, and I already knew that his body fit mine in all the right ways.

Jason sat on his haunches, idly licking the blood from his paw, looking smug. I swear he even winked at me.

"Uh, we've got a problem," Fiona said as we got closer to the main doors.

I patted Jason's head as we walked past. He ducked down in an attempt to escape. "Not a huge problem once we get in."

I could feel the vampires inside. It was a zing against my nerves, warning me of their proximity. I pulled a stake from my waist sheath. The windows on the double doors were blacked out with paint and metal shutters covered what I assumed was a bank of glass. Vampire den. Made sense. There weren't that many buildings left standing and what better way to protect your assets than to load a structure up with built-in security? When it came to starved feral vampires, sunlight would make them sleepy but the promise of blood would trump that. It was a clever and calculated way to give intruders a second thought about breaking in. Made me realize that the human minions had really been just for show. "Don't forget who I am."

Fiona gave a knowing smile. "Right, badass vampire hunter."

"You get me inside, I'll do the rest."

Jason gave a kitty growl at my side, which I took as agreement. Between the two of us, we'd kick some vampire ass.

"Stand back." Fiona's magic shimmered along her fingers. In the distance, more bombs were going off. Kurt was keeping the humans on the run, no doubt. "Three, two...." She zapped the lock and in a matter of seconds, it had melted into a puddle.

No alarm sounded when we opened the door. "Maybe we should keep this open. A little sunlight might help," Fiona said as she peered inside the dark store, sounding a little more than hesitant.

"See if you can work a spell to lift those shutters. They have padlocks along the bottom. Burn those off and get these things up. We'll get to work inside."

"Might make a lot of noise," Fiona said as she rattled the nearest shutter.

I rolled my eyes. "So do something about that. You're supposed to be a powerful witch, right? Figure it out." I lifted the other stake from my belt and braced myself. "We need knives; leave the guns. Projectiles that don't require gunpowder are best. Quiet weapons. Crossbows if you can find them," I said. "At some point, I'm going to need you as a human, Jason. Your hands will be more valuable than your paws when it comes to getting weapons." I paused as he gave me one of those looks that said we were on the same page. Or fuck you. Could have been either. "Once we get inside, I'm going to open a vein." Jason nodded his big furry head. "It'll draw the vamps to me like they're in a trance. Makes them easier to kill. You ready?"

Jason nodded and snorted. I took that as a yes.

He moved ahead of me, very chivalrous. Fiona moved to the side, crouching to inspect the locks on the shutters, mumbling to herself.

I swung into the darkness, moving through the door and jumping up to stand on the turnstile that blocked the entrance.

The store was stocked, all right. Weapons of all shapes and sizes, caliber and accessories lined the back wall and were encased in display cabinets. A swirl of dust danced in the beam of sunlight from the open door. The stench of vampire was everywhere and, I sensed movement immediately. That zing of electrical impulse that gave me a heads up whenever a vampire was near jolted up a few notches, making my body tingle in a way that fuelled my vampire-killing rage.

I lifted my wrist to my mouth and used my little fangs to open my flesh. Blood poured against my lips and I took a swallow before turning my wrist outward for the vampires to smell. "Here you go, monsters, take a whiff of this."

Jason was crouching low.

The vampires moved quickly, rising from their sleeping positions on the floor. Not underfed, not starving. Not ferals. These vampires were ready for a fight and there were a lot of them, at least three dozen, maybe more. My blood was calling to them, waking them from their day sleep, their eyes zeroing in on me, black dots of bloodlust that became totally fixated. That was the power of my unturned Dhampir DNA. Within minutes the bloodsuckers would be...

"Ah shit..." At the back of the vampire crowd, in leashes that appeared to be chained to the wall were big, nasty looking werewolves. "They've got beasts on the wall, angry as fuck!" I yelled.

Whether Jason registered what I said was up for debate—he definitely had to feel my tension spike. He sprang up from his crouch; the power in his legs sending him barreling to the first line of vampires and then it was a blood frenzy all around. The werewolves at the back were foaming at the mouth, growling and scratching at the floor, rattling their leashes in a way that sounded like the chains wouldn't last long. They'd been starved—that was evident in their visible rib cages and sallow faces, and it would keep them submissive and permanently in their werewolf form. Their bodies would be constantly trying to heal, which usually happened faster as the beast. Whatever the vampires were doing to them had made them wild, vicious, and only few hard yanks away from being free.

I needed to clear the room of vampires if I was going to have a shot at the werewolves. My blood did wonders to sedate the fangs as they surged en mass. A horde of them coming at us in a way that made my heart sing. I could tell the moment my blood hit their senses. Drawn to me like flies to a flytrap. They were not powerful enough to fight against my thrall.

I smiled. *Too easy.*

I jumped from the turnstile and started to clear the horde.

Strix vampires smelling Dhampir blood became sluggish, uncoordinated. It was nothing compared to what would happen if they decided to take a bite. One sip—even a tiny drop on their tongue—would cause paralysis in a matter of minutes. A vulnerability for any vampire that was allergic to sun and stakes. Not that I had any desire for fangs puncturing my skin but still, it was nice to know that a drop of my blood would be the last thing they tasted.

One after another, I slammed them with my stakes, splintering the wood, taking each one down with a stab to the heart. A quick strike so that I wasn't giving up my crude but efficient weapons. Strix were easy as hell to kill. One slash to the heart, or even partial decapitation would end them. Another way Dhampirs were superior—as vampires, we were hard as fuck to kill. Highly guarded secret though. There were very few supernaturals outside of the Dhampir species who knew how to kill one. Even though I remained an unturned Dhampir, I never dared share that weakness of my kind with anyone.

The vampires smelled horrid but not as bad as the werewolves. I battled, splattering my blood all over them as I worked and tried not to gag on the stench.

I could hear Jason making his way through the mass of fangs on the other side of me. It was strangely comforting to know I had a big cat watching my back. One perk to the team approach. And I didn't hate it. I liked the sound of his claws ripping and teeth shredding. The cat was powerful and possibly a better vampire killer. Nah, scratch that. No one was better than me at fang disposal. I had a body count in the thousands, but Jason was damn efficient.

Just as we seemed to clear a path, more vampires poured in, coming up from a basement or cellar by the looks of things. *What the fuck?* Hadn't Steph said this place was one floor?

They were stronger, faster, and didn't yet feel the effects of my blood. I used my teeth to rip open both of my wrists and let the blood flow fresh, pumping from my body and sending that intoxicating scent out to meet my prey.

One of the vampires released the beasts chained to the wall, setting them loose in the store to wreak havoc. Major complication. Glass display cases shattered, weapons and stock went flying. The werewolves were so incensed that they attacked the vampires around them, knocking them to the ground and ripping heads off with one bite. I grimaced. Things had just escalated to a shitshow times a hundred.

"Fuck me!" Time to upgrade the weapons. I used the opportunity to snag some large hunting knives from a broken case, arming myself with those to take on the werewolves. I looked over the crowd, trying to locate Jason in the chaos but couldn't see him anywhere. For a second, I had a sinking feeling that maybe he had fallen under a pile of vampires, and fuck if my heart didn't twist at the thought. Then I heard a clicking noise and looked behind me to see him in human form arming a crossbow, his bulging biceps coated in sweat as he locked the cable in place and then loaded a bolt. We were definitely outnumbered, too many vampires, even with my blood messing with their heads, and now the beasts. Yeah, totally screwed. *Shit.*

Jason started shooting, the thunk of bolts impaling vamps oddly pleasant. He cleared the ones crowding me and gave me room to do some damage. I did a front roll into the horde and came up stabbing. The beasts were working the room from the other side, all growly and pissed off, roaring and spitting like wild animals do. Because I happened to inhale through my mouth, their toxic scent turned into a nasty taste that hit me at the back of the throat. Gross.

With the werewolves pressing forward, the vampires were crowding all around me again, closing in—getting too close, actually. It was harder and harder to maneuver my blades. Jason was shooting from above but it was slow going. Not like crossbows were rapid fire.

One of the fangs got close enough to draw blood, latch onto my back and scrape his teeth against my jugular. Panic took hold along with anger. *How dare this vile thing touch me!* I reached over my shoulder to wrench the vampire away but he was big, and the angle was awkward so I hacked away at his neck until he stopped moving. With a disgusted grunt, I let the thing fall, then reached up to touch my throat, wincing as I traced the wound. Fucker got me good.

I snapped my gaze to the shutters, the distinct sound of metal moving catching my ears. In that instant they sprang open all at once, and *bam!* The vampires started to get toasty.

There were screams and grunts and attempts to escape the light. The sun immediately turned the odds in our favor. Fiona made her way inside and started shooting off little fireballs, effectively taking the vampires out with a contained little flame to add to the scorching sunlight.

The werewolves came at us now that the path was clear. They were fierce and terrifying with their gigantic malformed bodies and frothing mouths full of pointy teeth descending like a freight train on us. I nailed one in the chest with my giant knife, leaving the blade embedded while I gutted another beast with my other knife. His putrid intestines spilled to the floor in a grotesque heap. Jason took out the second one with two back to back arrows. One to the heart, one to the head. Beastly threats nullified.

"Holy shit, that was intense!" Jason shouted, not at all sounding like he'd had a bad time. "Did you see all those vampires? There had to be at least fifty." He was bouncing.

"Yeah, can you imagine how many are in that four-story building?" I wiped my hand over my neck, wincing again at the bite that was still there. It irritated me that I'd let that vampire get so close. Typically my attacks were well planned and every contingency accounted for. This had been madness. Vampire anarchy. If I hadn't had a team with me, I'd be dead for sure. And that didn't sit well now that I was reflecting on all the ways it could have gone wrong. Not to mention that Steph had given us inaccurate information. Something to take up with her later.

"Fiona, there are duffle bags over there. Grab two and let's get loading." Jason glanced at me like he was concerned. "Injured?" He kept his voice low.

I shifted my hand away, knowing that by now there'd be little more than a scratch on my flesh. My wrists were already healed from where I'd opened the veins. "Nah, I'm good."

"You got bit." He leaned closer, his breath hot on my skin.

"If you lick me I will rip your tongue out," I growled.

"That's not what you were saying earlier." He grinned as he pulled away.

Ignoring him, I moved to grab a bag as well, then started loading up all the knives I could find, taking the time to sheath every single empty holster on my belt at the same time. No more crude stakes for me. Steel could kill a Strix just as well as wood.

A tension I hadn't realized I'd been carrying started to dissolve as I loaded myself up with weapons. Time to get this party started. I was tired of the surprises on this island and ready to go home. Now that I was armed once again, I felt back in control.

"You're a lot like my sister," Jason said as he dumped packs of crossbow bolts into his duffle bag.

I cocked an eyebrow, wondering just where he was going with this.

"Not like that," he scoffed. "My sister, she's the alpha designate in our pack. My grandmother has been battling some kind of mystery illness for years, so my sister leads the pack in her place."

"I'd heard that about Lynx packs, the women run the show." Not many shifter species had that particular feature. I'd always liked the idea of cat shifters because of it. Dhampirs had a very rigid understanding of leadership. Men were considered the strongest and smartest of the species, a legacy of misogyny that hadn't changed despite the humans making huge strides in women's rights. The women were mastered by the Lord of the clan, and obeyed their rule in all instances. It wasn't because we were weaker or stupid—the reality was, when it came to the transformation, the females of our species were forced to submit to a bonding with the strongest males in the clan. And once bonded, you were under their command.

There was some room for defiance. The strongest females

could overcome the will of their Lord to some degree. My mother had been one. Her quiet fury at being collared was something she'd used to benefit me. She'd ensured that I was trained in all forms of battle from the time that I was a child. My father, if he'd known, hadn't posed any resistance. I'm sure he'd felt my training would benefit him in the end. Obviously, I hadn't fulfilled my destiny where that was concerned.

"Yeah, well, she's a tough kitty." He smiled "And she likes to take risks. She thinks she's invincible." He raised his hand when I opened my mouth to argue. "I'm not saying that as a criticism. She's tenacious. Fierce. That part of you reminds me of her. And that's the *only* part that reminds me of her." He gave me one of his sultry looks, a full on body scan that made me kind of want to jump him right there and fuck his brains out, my body already amped up from battle. Being wanted by someone, even if it was a temporary thing, was dangerously intoxicating, I was realizing. "You've got my back, like she does. Tough as hell and on my side. What's not to like?" He said the last bit almost under his breath, like I wasn't supposed to hear it.

I brushed the comment off because it made me uncomfortable. I didn't have his back. Not really. I was fully prepared to leave him on the island if the amulet only had room for me and Kali. So what did that make him? Gullible? A poor judge of character? Too trusting for sure. "Fierce, yeah, that's me. Watch out, I bite."

He chuckled. "So do I." He winked then zipped up his bag. "I'm loaded up. You ready?"

I threw some rope and a few other things into my bag then zipped it up too. "Yep, Fiona?"

"I'm ready." She snapped her fingers and her bag zipped on its own.

Show off.

"Kurt's keeping the humans running by the sound of his explosions. I'm going to send him a signal that we're good to go," Fiona said as she heaved her bag up. "Time to put the bastards out of their misery."

"He'll kill them with the explosions?" Jason sounded surprised. "I thought his spells were more about the noise than the damage."

"Kurt likes to play with his prey." Fiona's smile wasn't a nice one. In fact, her usual bubbly self had taken on a hard edge since we'd gotten down to business, her face kind of contorted in a way that was part terrifying, part impressive. It actually made me respect her a bit more. "We leave them alive, the vamps know what happened."

"The vampires are going to know what happened no matter what." I waved my hand around. Not that I had any problem with taking out some minions, but knowing Fiona wasn't just good at breaking in—she was likely a murderer too—had me questioning her loyalty all around. *Remember where you are, Jet. These assholes are on the island for a reason.*

"Not if I have anything to do with it." Fiona flicked her hand up then mumbled something under her breath, a string of nonsense that I couldn't make out.

But I didn't need to know what she was saying, because I could feel the result. Her spell swirled around us, creating a dust storm. The vampire's bodies were disintegrating right before our eyes.

Actually *in* our eyes, up our noses. Both Jason and I started coughing.

"Yeah, you might want to get outside. Things will get a bit nasty in a few minutes." Fiona tossed her bag over the turnstile and then leapt over it herself. Leaving Jason and me to stare after her.

"What the fuck?" Jason was covering his mouth. "A little warning maybe?"

I picked up my bag, keeping my eyes shielded. I'd experienced many disgusting things in my hunts, but this one was by far the worst. Inhaling vampire guts was so not cool.

By the time we made it outside, the sun was hanging lower and mid-afternoon was upon us. I squinted, my eyes sore from the vampire dust and the intensity of the sun.

Fiona had walked off a bit, fingers of one hand pressed to her ear. If she was communicating with Kurt, she was doing it with another spell.

"She's more powerful than she let on." I nodded toward Fiona.

"They've only been here for a few weeks but yeah, she definitely came off as a bit of a lightweight. Didn't show off or give us any hint that she had this kind of power. Or at least, she didn't show me. It's possible Steph knew." He scratched his face along the edge of his beard. "Definitely changing my assessment of her though. She'll be good when we go up against Kali."

I nodded, but I didn't know if I agreed. Fiona was powerful, sure, but it was possible she was suddenly whipping out the impressive spells because she'd come into contact with whatever boosted her magic. "She ever mention what fuelled her? Like Amber, she needs red meat. Kali needs sunlight. What fuels Fiona and Kurt?"

"Ah, right, that's a good point. Could be that she was deprived of whatever it is that jolts her. I'll see if I can figure it out before tonight."

Loud bangs shook the ground. Kurt was laying his bomb spells. Taking out the enemy. I braced myself against the vibration. The explosions were close by—within at least a few hundred feet.

"Good idea, I'm not a huge fan of enigmas." I glanced at the position of the sun again. Jason seemed tight with Steph. I wasn't entirely sure how close they were, so I wasn't keen on sharing my suspicions of her with him at the moment. I needed time to suss out their relationship. Steph was definitely one puzzle that made me uneasy. "We need to get moving."

"That looks like Steph in the distance." Jason pointed toward a side street.

Sure enough, the half-vampire was making her way quickly down the side of the road, keeping to the shadows as if she was still shielded by Fiona's spell from earlier.

"Looks like her bag is full."

"Anyone else getting that weird vibe or is it just me?" I watched Steph as she moved, trying to detect anything out of the ordinary. Her bag looked stuffed with things, she didn't appear to be injured and yet... "Where's the wolf?"

Before anyone could say anything, a series of explosions rocked the ground around us, shifting my center of gravity just before all of the windows in the store blew out. I shielded myself from the onslaught. Tiny shards of glass embedded into my skin and stuck in my hair. I crouched low to the ground, searching for the source. My ears were ringing.

Fiona was still standing. A safe distance away from the blast, she turned toward us with concern on her face, but otherwise didn't look overly bothered by the explosion.

"What the fuck?" I shouted, my voice sounding muffled in my head.

Fiona opened her mouth to say something.

"Sorry!" Kurt came out from behind a building with his hands raised. "My bad."

His voice came in waves of volume, pockets of sound in-between the buzz of white noise in my ears. I shook my head, trying to clear the clutter.

"'My bad'?" Jason growled. "You could have killed us."

Fiona tossed her duffle to Kurt, who caught it easily.

"Yeah, sometimes I lose control over my spells. Didn't mean to send that one your way," he said.

I slowly rose, shaking the glass bits from my hair. I could smell blood, *my blood* oozing from the many cuts the glass had made. *Fuck.* Luckily it wasn't nighttime or we'd be swarmed by feral vampires. As it was, by the time the cuts healed, I'd have left a pretty distinct scent trail for them to follow once we hit the forest.

Jason sniffed my arm and looked at me with concern. "You're bleeding."

"No way you can lick them all closed." Not unless I wanted to strip down and get lathered from head to toe. No time for that now anyway. "Where are the guards?"

"I trapped them under some rubble a few blocks over. Most of them are dead. The ones who aren't won't make it to nightfall. I was listening to the screams when Fiona reached out to contact me." Kurt was smirking.

He liked to play. Torment his prey. Not really my thing but okay, wasn't like I was going to be hanging out with the dude beyond the next few hours. Good to know who the monsters were though.

"And you thought we needed a blast?" Jason was still clearly furious, his fangs visible and eyes streaked with silver.

"I got spooked okay? Thought I saw something." Kurt shrugged.

"Where are the wolves?" The noise from the blast finally cleared from my ears. "One had gone with you, one with Steph. So where are they?"

"Don't know," Kurt said. "Lost track of mine when I started playing."

Steph made it to us finally, her breathing strained as she panted through her first words. "You see Doug or Bill anywhere?" Her chest was heaving and she was covered in sweat.

Missing werewolves. Not good. Everyone shook their heads.

"I went into the pharmacy and when I came out, he was gone." Steph patted her bag. "I got the glue and some first aid kit stuff. Couldn't find any antibiotics, but I did get some painkillers, just in case."

I scanned the group, trying to sort out who was lying. Had something happened to the wolves? Had they taken off for some reason? Headed back to camp? Got distracted by a little bunny or two? Nah, none of that felt right. "We need to get back to camp."

I had a bad feeling, *a very bad* feeling about things and started calculating how much time it would take to mix up the net for Kali. Sun would set in a few hours and vamps would come looking for us. I had to get the fuck off the island tonight or things were going to get really messy.

No further discussion needed. Everyone started walking, moving quickly despite being loaded down with bags and weapons. There was an urgency that you could feel, like everyone knew the shitstorm we'd created. And the missing wolves, yeah, that didn't sit well either.

"I don't like it," Jason mumbled to me, moving closer as we trekked through the forest.

I'd left some distance open between me and the rest of the group so I could think. The witches were a mystery. Powerful and secretive, but were they conspiring? Fiona was walking with Steph, bopping along like she had a song in her head, and babbling about nonsense things, all trace of the powerful, calculating witch gone. Kurt was off on his own, weaving around trees, his hand trailing along the trunks, plucking at leaves here and there, mumbling to himself.

Jason had slowed down, falling back until he was in line with me.

"What?" But I knew what. It was the reason I was gnawing on my bottom lip, studying the witches and Steph from behind.

"I haven't been here that long, but I've talked a lot with those guys. The twins. We shared battle stories and shit."

"You mean cats and dogs get along?"

"Fuck off," he grumbled. "I'm serious. Shifters have a kind of code, you know. Respect."

It wasn't the same with vampires. The Strix and Dhampir did not defer to mutual anything.

"Anyway, I talked a lot with those guys. They were scouts from a large Northern pack that had been sent out to gather information for their alpha. Got caught up in a raid and sent here. Not bad guys, kinda naive, but overall they didn't give off the vibe of being malicious or deceitful. And wolves, man... When they have a job to do, they fucking do it. They don't stray. They would have identified you as the alpha of this mission. You told them to go with Kurt and Steph—that's what they would have done. No matter what."

"So you think something happened to them?"

"I think something is up, yes. Not sure what."

"What do you know about Steph?" I asked. "She ever talk about her vampire buddy?"

"Nope. First I heard about it was when you did." Jason nodded toward Fiona. "She isn't what I thought either."

"I'm pretty sure everyone here is hiding something."

"Not me." He nudged me with his duffle bag. "I'm an open book."

"Ha! No man is an open book."

"You know what I want from you. You're my ticket home. And I want to go home. My family needs me," he said, his tone serious once again. "You know that I'm into you, even if you're an asshole most of the time." He winked.

"I'm on a mission." I had no time to be anything but an asshole. "And this island...fuck..."

He laughed. "Like I said, you remind me of my sister. You're a tough lady, exactly what I'm used to." He touched my arm. "You can trust me."

I winced at his words, but turned my head away so he wouldn't see. What was with all the guilt I was feeling for this man? Not like I'd never acted in my own self-interests before. He'd saved my life, and I owed him one. There was no time limit on that debt. I could go through the portal and send someone back for him. I knew a few black magic dealers who could rig some way to fetch him, I was sure.

"I think we should figure out a way to separate from the others. You know, when it's time to head home," he said, his voice lowered even more.

I raised my eyebrows at him, suddenly gaining a new appreciation. "You'd abandon your pals?"

"Like I said, I don't like it. Something's not sitting right in my gut. And I know how portals work. Better to keep the number going through small so you don't send everyone off course. Three is probably enough."

Here's hoping. For Jason's sake, anyway because suddenly I got the feeling that if I left him behind, he wouldn't last long enough for me to save him.

❧ 12 ❧

"HEY AMBER, YOU KNOW ANYTHING ABOUT FIONA'S POWERS?" I kept my voice low as we worked, huddled together, pouring the glue out of the bottles that Steph had found. The glue had been almost completely coagulated but with a little water and some vigorous shaking—and also, I suspected, some help from Amber's elemental magic—it was flowing from the bottles into the palm leaf-lined hole the others had created for our mixing purposes.

Amber glanced up, her brow furrowed. "Fiona has powers?" She glanced over to where Fiona was working with Jason to scrape more of the vine guts into the palm leaves laid out along the ground.

"You've never seen her cast a spell?" I tossed the empty bottle I'd been draining into the pile. There were no more bottles, and the amount of glue we had was probably overkill. I sat back, wiping my arm over my forehead. It was getting close to nightfall; I could feel it. The pressure to wrap this up and get the plan in play weighed on me.

"Nothing beyond a simple enchantment to clean out some water bottles." She tossed her empty bottle to the pile. "I mean, I haven't been here long, but she doesn't seem like she's all that powerful. That's why I couldn't understand why Steph wanted to take her into the city. I figured she must be good at fighting or something."

"She whipped out some fucking powerful spells. Kurt too, while we were there. You think her power source is something to do with the city?"

"It's possible, sure. I've heard of some weird things activating a witch's powers."

I was watching Jason work. He'd taken his shirt off, and his muscles were flexing with each pass he made against the vine's insides, scraping out the guts in a fluid motion. The dark brush of hair on his chest glistened with sweat. It was enough to make my insides melt. I'd always liked the furry ones. So very different from my first and only love.

Julian had been fair, even for a Dhampir, with auburn hair and freckles. He hadn't been able to grow much beyond a bit of stubble every few days at most. We'd been young, sure, but he had definitely been softer than what I preferred nowadays. It wasn't the fair ones who turned my head anymore. It was the ones who looked powerful, dangerous, deadly even. And Jason fit all of those: hard, hairy, and strong. Incredibly enticing.

Julian's body had been lithe, like a swimmer, solid but smooth. He'd danced beautifully at the many balls we were forced to endure. That's what had caught my eye at first.

I was there, standing next to my father, who played court to his many alliances. I was a trophy on display and bored out of my wits with of all the political talk. But then I'd seen Julian dancing with an older woman—his mother, I would later learn—and I'd just fallen in love with the image of him. He wasn't very different than the other unturned Dhampirs our age. We were all so innocent. We didn't really understand the undercurrent of rivalry that existed between the clans.

I'd had no idea just how much my father loathed the Cross clan until I spent the evening dancing with Julian, only to be reprimanded severely later by my father's right-hand man, Luke. Father, of course, would never muddy our cherished father-daughter relationship by showing his anger outright. He always sent his henchmen. Even when it came to killing Julian. While it was my father's order, it had not been by his mouth that I'd learned of my love's fate.

Luke, the most trusted of my father's men, and the most brutal, thought I was a spoiled brat and never missed a chance to set me straight.

My punishment that night, the night I'd first danced with Julian, had been a violent reminder of how little power I truly had over my own life in that clan. Luke had ripped chunks of my hair out. He'd punched my body until I couldn't even stand. He'd whispered horrid things as he did it. Things he'd like to do to me if only my father would allow it. He'd own me; teach me the proper way of the Dhampir woman. He'd show me how to give respect. He told me that I was useless. That I was evil. That I was a waste of life and a disappointment to my clan. I always loathed Luke, but that night he reminded me that even a solider for my father had more control over my world than I did, simply because he was a man.

I had been left black and blue, broken in so many ways. Mostly though I felt the sharpest pain from my clan's betrayal. My clan, the ones who were supposed to cherish me, honor me, protect me, had turned their back on me, had witnessed my brutal beating and had taken it as a lesson not to displease my father. He, of course, had not been in the room while it happened, but he had sanctioned it before he left.

I blinked away a sudden jolt of pain and anger that the memory caused. The subtle abuse was so constant from birth that it was the norm. While little rebellions happened often enough, there was usually some form of punishment to follow. Often, it was nothing more than a sharp reprimand and removal of some kind of privilege. The men from my clan knew what we were doing at all times—even my mother's attempt to train me was only a partial defiance. The quiet warnings she'd whisper to me were her true rebellion. She'd been subversively building me up to turn against my father, challenging me to turn my back on him, though I didn't realize it completely until the day she was killed.

I shook my head, looking down at the cavern floor so that I could clear my thoughts. If I let the rage consume me, or the sadness sweep over me, I'd be useless.

A grunt had me refocusing on Jason as he moved rhythmically to do as I asked. Cleaning those vines as effectively and quickly as possible. He was all masculine power but not in the same way that my clan demanded. There was nothing about him that suggested violence or misogyny. Jason was all animal, sure, including the magnetism, but I knew, somehow, that he'd never abuse that in the name of taking control away from someone else—from me or from any woman.

I realized that Amber had stopped talking and was looking at me with a frown. I winced, shaking my head to snap out of my thoughts. "Sorry. So what kind of weird things can activate a witch's power? Give me some examples."

Amber glanced over at Jason, then smiled a bit when she turned back to me. "Weird like eating broccoli or biting nails, plucking out hair, sex, that kind of thing." Amber wiped her hands on her pants. "If Fiona showed you a lot of skill in the city, then she definitely was triggered by something there."

"Like a thing? Something in the air?"

"Maybe, but more like something she ingested or touched. Could be a feeling too. Like excitement or fear. Would have to be extreme to have that much of an impact though."

"The promise of mayhem and murder?" It would make sense. She seemed to have a lust for violence.

"Yeah, could be. Witches are strange. What fuels us usually shapes us though. If she needs mayhem to show her stuff, then I'd imagine she's a pretty violent kind of witch."

"I don't think she's a stranger to murder. I'd watch your back." And why I'd warned Amber I would never know. Not like I gave a shit if she survived or not. Not like I could take her back through the portal with me.

Fuck.

The island was definitely messing with my long honed ability to not give a shit. Part of me wondered if being sleep-deprived was making me soft.

"What do you mean—"

"I think we're done here. You guys ready for mixing?" Jason jumped up from his latest vine, ready to drag the palm leaves closer to the hole.

"Yeah, slide it over and dump it in." I nodded toward Amber, ignoring the concerned glances she was shooting Fiona. I shouldn't have said anything to her. Her fear was written all over her face. "Amber," I snapped at her, forcing her to look back at me. "Can you go grab a branch or something we can use to stir?"

"I don't need a branch," Amber chirped, back to business. She said a word, sounded like *motus* or something, and suddenly the glue and vine guts were swirling gently, mixing before my eyes.

"Impressive." And it was. Amber's powers were nowhere near as deadly as Fiona's or Kurt's had been, but the practicality of her magic was very handy. It made me wonder what the fuck she'd done to get herself on the island.

She blushed. "Not sure how much help I'll be when we go out after Kali though. I haven't eaten since this morning."

"Good point," Jason said. "I can take care of that." He pointed at a few of the other guys. "Go out and check the traps like I showed you." He'd started to walk away when I grabbed his arm.

"Hey, before you go." I slipped a knife from my belt and handed it to him. "I need some of your blood."

His eyes sparkled, a smile spreading on his lips. "Oh yeah, sure no prob—"

"Not for that," I snapped before addressing the others. "I

need blood from a few of you. Supernatural blood is the catalyst for this recipe. Just a few drops."

"Interesting," Steph drawled, her hand already reaching for her own knife. "Even half vampires?"

"Full vamps would be better," I said, not caring if I was offending her. Bottom line was she hadn't been turned, so she wasn't as good as the real thing, but neither was I. "Yeah, yours will do."

She grunted something in my direction but didn't argue. Blood drops from Amber, Jason, Steph and a few of the others had my mixture bubbling like I'd known it would. It didn't take much of the secret ingredient to ignite the brew. It was weird, sure, and you had to wonder how the humans had figured it out, but it worked without fail every time I'd seen it used. It would work on Kali too.

"That's all it needed." I watched as Amber's stir-spell kept the concoction from boiling over.

"Cool," Jason said before turning to exit the cavern. "Be back in a few with meat." The other guys followed him.

"So what do we do with that?" Steph asked. "How are we going to get it to Kali?"

I grimaced as I looked around and cursed myself for not thinking of that earlier.

"What about the glue bottles? Can we use those?" Amber held up one of the empty bottles.

"Yes, brilliant," I said, my mind working out the logistics. "A good squeeze should send out a string of it if we open up the tops a little wider." I glanced around the cavern, spotting some left-over palm leaves. "But I think we can also use some other methods." If we rigged up some leaf balls, we could toss them up and then explode them over Kali with a well-timed arrow or blade.

"What are you thinking?" Steph followed my gaze, walking over to the leaves.

I walked over as well, picking up one of the waxy leaves and folded it to create an empty pocket. "Yeah, this will work." I motioned to my duffle bag. "I got some rope from the gun store. We can strip it into twine and use it to tie some of these up."

"Good plan, I'm on it."

And so we worked. Fast. And by the time Jason and the others came back with food, we were ready. And starving.

"Sun is setting. I figure we've got an hour, maybe, to eat and get on the hunt."

"I hope everyone likes their meat raw." Steph joked as she took the rabbits from the guys.

Jason had a larger animal draped across his shoulders. Looked like some kind of deer.

"If you guys aren't opposed to a witch-fire-cooked meal, I could have those edible in about twenty minutes," Amber said, impressing me once again.

"We'll get skinning," Steph said as she ripped the fur straight off the back of a rabbit.

I nodded then moved to the cavern tunnel, wanting to get some fresh air and also a sense of the vampires. My blood trail would lead scouts, followed by the strongest of them, right to us as soon as the sun set. I hadn't told anyone about it because I figured we could handle it, but that didn't mean I wanted to be taken by surprise.

The forest was quiet—not eerily quiet like it got when Kali was around, but peaceful quiet. Like it was settling into night slumber. Once again, I found myself thinking that it would be nice to sling a hammock and just relax out there, listen to the hum of the night bugs and relax under the warm breeze. It was a kind of paradise... Well, except for the vampires.

I heaved out a deep breath then walked around the side of the cavern, trailing into the trees a bit in the direction of the city. I closed my eyes and stretched out my vampire sensors. Working like an echo locator, I sent a signal that bounced back to give me an idea of distance between me and the fangs. It was pretty accurate; I'd spent much of my lifetime honing that skill so I could nail it to within in tens of feet. It came in handy when you were surrounded by males who were stealthy as shit and could turn on you at any moment.

"You're not hungry?" Jason startled me out of my vampire-tracking zone.

I cursed under my breath, hating that he had the ability to sneak up on me. "How do you do that?"

He chuckled. "A cat never tells."

I grumbled some swear words in his direction but closed my eyes once again. "Shut up, I'm trying to track the vamps."

"You think they'll be hunting?"

"It's likely they will." I waved my arm toward him. My body-suit was cut up pretty good from the shards of glass. "My blood could lead them right to us."

"Fuck."

"Exactly. It's not for sure though." I sighed. "I didn't bleed buckets, and it's stopped now. Depends on how sensitive the vamps are. If they have a tracker among them. How powerful they are. If the Master is willing to venture into the woods. All the same, we should be ready for an attack. Now, be quiet." I mumbled, forcing myself to block him out for the few minutes I needed to home in on the vampires.

It hit me like a soft whisper. Just a blip that was barely detectable. The vampires were stirring. Did that mean they were on their way? Maybe. It could also mean they were just starting to get that restless jittering they got as the sun was releasing them from their day prisons. It's as if I could feel their excitement bubbling as the sun slowly descended, soon to give them access to the outside world once again. I would hate to be so confined, but I'd lived long enough under the rule of my father to understand that everyone had their own prisons to deal with.

I opened my eyes, ran my hand through my hair.

"How long do we have?"

"We have some time." I winced as I tugged on a tender spot on my scalp where a cut was still healing.

"You're still hurt?" Jason touched my arm, then ignored my flinch and attempt to get away. He pulled me closer so he could inspect my wound, parting my hair with a soft touch. "Oh yeah, looks deep."

"I'm fine," I snapped but without the venom. I was tired. Feeling worn out and suddenly, desperately wanting him to touch me...so naturally I was pushing him away.

We'd have to fight the vampires before we could go after Kali. I realized that now. I didn't want to risk engaging the witch with the city vamps on their way. I moved over to a soft-looking spot in the grass and sat down. "I could use some blood," I admitted wearily, looking up at him.

"That must have been really hard for you to say." He wasn't smiling in his usual playful way. His eyes said he knew exactly what asking for help had cost me.

"It was." And I wasn't going to ask again.

He got the message.

He lifted his wrist to his lips as he walked toward me. He crouched in front of me, then offered his blood. A waft of it made my heart flutter and my stomach moan. I locked eyes with him, silently giving thanks as I guided his wrist toward me, running my tongue along the wound. The taste of his blood jolted me like a hit of caffeine. I licked, long lazy strokes that I knew were revving him up. It was intentional. I wanted him. All of him. His eyes drooped, lids half-closed as he bit down on his bottom lip and stared at me with lust blasting.

I lifted my mouth, blood wetting my lips. "I have a better idea." I pushed myself forward and moved close, very close, practically climbing onto his lap. I nuzzled his neck, nipping playfully, feeling the hard press of his cock as I nestled closer. I brushed my lips along his jugular. My fangs were sharp enough to cut through. My heart hammered at the fluttering pulse I felt there.

"Mmmm," he moaned, his hand on my back, nudging me closer. "Yeah, do that."

I paused, glanced up at him. His eyes were closed, a faint smile on his lips. We were stuck on a hellish paradise island, and chances were only one of us was getting off. Getting off the *island*. Right now, right here, I was determined to get both of us off.

I lifted my hand to his chest, bracing myself, my fingers molding to his muscles. Pecs that could make you weep. And then I opened my mouth and bit him. A jet of his blood hit the back of my throat, a groan vibrated through him, his chest rumbling under my hand as I started to suck and swallow.

✣ 13 ✣

I'D BEEN WITH MEN SINCE JULIAN. HOT, QUICK FUCKS IN THE back of trucks. Blowjobs in the shower. Forgotten hotel rooms in forgotten cities, or what was left of them, with easily forgotten guys. They'd scratched an itch and that was it.

Jason could have been one of those guys too. Could have if I hadn't tasted his blood. Could have if I hadn't felt his heart thundering under my hand, or felt the press of his cock rubbing against my crotch, making me moan for so many different reasons. Could have if I didn't owe him my life. As much as I wanted to brush the cat off, escape the island without him and be done with it, never to think of him again, I was Dhampir and I felt the driving pulse of obligation to the man. It was a loyalty that I hadn't felt toward anyone in a very long time.

But I wasn't fucking him because I owed him one. I was fucking him because of the *reason* I owed him one. He'd saved my life, not because he'd had to but because he'd wanted to. He had followed me, perhaps out of curiosity, but he had intervened because he was *that* guy. The hero. And he gave a shit. When he said he had my back, deep down in my gut, I knew he meant it. So I could give him my body again. I could let him get inside my heart, just a little, so that I gave a shit too. I was a tough girl; I could handle a little of his warmth, this attraction and even his affection. I owed him that at least.

I realized what it meant; I was soft for Jason. The damn cat had gotten to me. Despite the discomfort that came with that admission, I wasn't going to reject it. I couldn't. I wanted him too much.

As his blood coursed through me, I felt all of my senses zing, a super punch of power from a lethal predator. I wanted to suck until my stomach ached, until my body felt so full of him that I couldn't move. But there were other ways to get that. My fangs secreted a healing agent that would plug the twin holes I'd made so he didn't bleed profusely. As much as I would have loved to take more, his hands on my tits had me wanting something else entirely, more urgently than his blood.

"You're dangerous," he whispered, his lips latching onto mine, teeth scraping along my tongue before letting me inside to tangle and thrust and probe. His blood was still in my mouth, the taste of it mixing with his saliva. I wanted to devour him completely.

I'm dangerous? My thoughts were so lust muddled that all I could do in response was bite back, sliding my teeth down to nip at his bottom lip.

He hissed, and not in a kitty way, then pushed me back, unlatching our lips on a whoosh of breath. With fingers on the zipper of my suit, he peeled it open, baring me completely. I didn't wear a bra or underwear when I was in lycra, no need. The damn suit was like a second skin. Being out of it, with tits bared and the warm tropical air brushing against my skin, I felt hypersensitive and craved his touch.

On my back, my flesh exposed, he ran his fingers gently down the middle of my torso, between my breasts, circling my navel, straight down to my pussy. I didn't close my eyes. I watched as he devoured me with a look alone. His lust like a beast all on its own. Impatient and wanting to be fucked in the worst way, I slipped my arms out of my suit and then slithered it over my hips. He helped me take the rest off so I was completely naked and he was not.

"I want to see some skin, kitty," I purred at him, smiling as I ran my fingers over my breasts and squeezed. "Show me those great big muscles of yours." Under water I'd felt him more than seen him; now I could feast on his entire body and I was eager to do so.

But instead of complying, he opened my legs, hands under my knees, eyes glued to my wet folds and then slowly, like he was cherishing every taste, he licked his way down my inner thigh. I wanted to scream from the torture of it. Between his feather light kisses and his tongue licking in gentle strokes, by the time he reached my pussy I was dripping wet. My clit was throbbing. My back arched. Anticipation almost killing me.

I pinched my nipples, twisting and flicking, a little pain with the pleasure was never a bad thing. "I think you're the dangerous one."

He smiled at me then, a lazy kind of smirk that said, *oh hell yeah I am*, and then his mouth was on me, licking, sucking, stroking, biting, making me want to come immediately, making me want to kick him away because it was too much...too much... And then his fingers were inside of me, pumping me up higher, hooking so that he was hitting that exact spot that make me squirt.

Faster, harder, longer, the sucking made me arch into each draw, made my movements frantic as I chased that orgasm. One for the record books. Man, the cat could lick.

My climax rose, uncontrollable. It rose and burst, and I was coming all over his face, squirting against his mouth. He was licking and sucking still, making me cry out and moan until I didn't have a voice to make a sound. Until he'd rung every last whimper out of me and my body buzzed so hard that I almost saw stars.

And when he was done and I felt like my limbs were made of mush, he finally showed me his muscles. Standing over me while I watched with hooded eyes, he stripped. First his shirt, up over his head, his muscles flexing, chest, arms, abs, all moving in fluid motion. He tossed the shirt aside then snapped open the button on his fatigues; flip, zip and his pants were down. Going commando as well, I noted. His huge cock sprung free. Once again, it did not disappoint. Rock hard and jutting with a slight curve that I knew would hit me just the right way, his balls hanging but not overly so. His dark hair surrounding it all. With one hand on his cock, he stroked, watching me, waiting for me.

Now it was my turn.

I pushed myself to my knees and hooked my hands under his legs, coaxing him down so that he was sitting with his back propped up against a tree. His cock nudged my face as he moved so that he could get comfortable. All the while he was watching me, reaching for me, releasing his cock so he could palm my tits. I smiled as I licked him from base to tip, circled his head with my tongue before sucking him down, past the gate of my throat, taking him all in until my lips touched his base. And then I squeezed with my mouth, pushing and pulling with every muscle I had, lips tight, cheeks sucking in. I fucked him, pumping slowly as I stared into his eyes, watching as he lost control, listening to his groans, feeling them vibrate through his body with each stroke I made. Up, down, up down. His precum seeped out, salty and slick, mingling with my spit and hitting the back of my throat. I swallowed it all, loving how he tasted, how he sounded, how he felt. I fondled his balls, cupping, rubbing, gently squeezing. I knew I was good. Really good. I could make him spew and be done with it. But as much as I loved to suck a big cock, what I really wanted was that giant dick inside of my pussy, to be filled and made to feel like there was nothing else going on in the world —like I was not going to betray him the second I had the chance.

I was a horrible, selfish person, and I didn't need a man to fulfill me. I sure as shit loved a good, hard fuck and I damn well would make sure he had a good time while we were together.

As his eyes nearly closed, his back torqueing up, I released him, letting his dick bob freely before climbing on top and sheathing myself, pussy lips to cock base. He snapped his eyes open at the sudden change, bewildered for a moment before realizing that I was going to pump him again. That my slick pussy was going to wring him dry. I rolled my hips, adjusting until I found the sweet spot, where the friction hit me just right. And that's all I needed. Perfect fit.

He played with my tits. Cupping, pinching, flicking, driving me wild with his fingers, scraping his nails, twisting so I cried out at the pain. All the while I rode him, my hands in his hair, gripping, clenching, stroking, pumping us both. My climax came fast and hard, barreling into me once again without much warning. I let it rise as high as I could, milked it for every shudder it gave, loved the feel of his orgasm as he sputtered and spent deep inside of me.

I could screw this man all damn night and not get tired of it. I could screw this man for many nights and not get tired of it.

No, wait. Those were dangerous thoughts.

I was going to slip off of him, quietly get dressed, suggest we head back to the cavern and mobilize the group. I was going to do those things, but then I was on my back again and he had my one leg over his shoulder. He was drilling me hard and fast so the forest floor dug into my skin, and I felt the pounding of his balls against my ass. I wanted to laugh out loud from the sheer pleasure of it all.

"Ohhh, yes!" I moaned, because fuck, that's what I needed. I needed to have my brains fucked right out to get rid of these haunting thoughts. Thoughts about him, about staying with him, about finding a way... Dangerous, impossible thoughts.

His eyes were fierce, cat eyes, staring down at me. He bit his bottom lip, sweat dripped into his eyes. He had his hands on my hips as he pulled me into him, thumping me harder and harder so my boobs nearly hit my chin and I wanted to laugh and scream and cry from the intensity.

I didn't realize I could come again. I didn't think it was possible to do it over and over but there it was, a wisp of another orgasm gripping my insides, making my clit throb to the point of pain.

This man. This shifter. Holy fuck.

His grunting was hot. The sweat dripping onto my body was hot. The musky smell he gave off was hot. And the way he used his body to pound me good was so fucking hot that I could barely stand it.

"You're a wicked woman," he growled, letting my legs drop so he could lie on me, his weight flattening my breasts, his body covering mine. His chest hair scratched in a delicious way, rubbing against my nipples. He scooped me up, held me so close, his lips on mine, kissing away my screams as the orgasm took us both over the edge again.

We didn't speak. There was nothing to say. We just lay there, our sweat-soaked bodies tangled together, his cock still inside of me, our breaths coming out like pants. Hearts racing together.

I could get used to this. I liked having his arms around me. I liked it way too much.

I closed my eyes, my arms around him, my lips pressed to his neck, my heart thudding hard, fast, painfully.

I could get used to this, but I didn't want to. There was no room in my life for a man like Jason. And that was the end of that.

❦ 14 ❦

"WHAT ARE YOU GOING TO DO WITH KALI ONCE YOU GET HER back?" Jason was dressing on one side of the small clearing. I was dressing on the other.

We had our backs to each other in some weird post-sex awkwardness that I couldn't really explain because it hadn't happened after the first time. Maybe it was all those thoughts I kept having. The dangerous ones that made me feel like there had to be a way to get him off the island.

"Huh?" I'd heard him—I just didn't want to answer. I didn't think he'd understand. I was a mercenary. I worked for the highest bidder. I didn't value supernaturals' lives as much as I probably should, or at least as much as people thought I should.

He moved in behind me just as I was zipping my suit back up and slipped his hand in before I could. He cupped my breast, flattening his palm over my heart.

"What are you going to do with Kali, Jet?" His words were whispered against my ear in a way that made me shiver, the dark undertones delicious and deadly.

"What do you care?" I whispered back, gripping his wrist, the bones there crunching a little.

"She's supposed to save the world," he said. "Who's on the other side of that portal?"

I forced his hand out then finished zipping my suit. "The vampires are coming. I can feel them."

"Don't change the subject," he growled. "*Reverted ad me.* Return to me. That's what you said when you ignited the amulet. That's the spell to open the portal."

Fuck. I cringed. Anyone could use that spell to open the portal with the right words. I turned on him, glaring. "There were multiple contracts up when I left. A mutual friend gave me the amulet."

"Whose interests does the amulet serve?" He was staring at me, his eyes burning a hole in my conscience...or at least whatever was left of my conscience.

"You know the answer to that." I dusted the front of my suit off, breaking eye contact long enough to reassert my control. He had the Latin. He could activate the portal. He could leave me behind. Now I had another unfamiliar feeling in my gut. Panic. I could not stay on this island. I had to get back.

"The highest bidder, right?" And the look he gave me would have withered a lesser person.

I didn't answer. Instead, I moved into the trees, walking toward the cavern.

"She is supposed to save the world. If the hybrids get her, they'll kill her. She'll be dead, done, no more chance at ending this war for good."

Only partly true. If the hybrids paid the highest, Kali would become their blood slave until Cassia, ruler of the hybrids and ultimate world fuckerer supreme, drained her dry and stole her powers. *Then* Kali would be dead.

"She was *supposed* to save the world. She had her chance. She failed. Now she goes to the highest bidder."

The prophecy was legend now. A mythic kind of story that got told to little kids like a warning. If expectations are too high, you're going to fail. Kali Richards was destined to end the war but she hadn't. End of story.

"And you feel no guilt about that?" He was right behind me, almost on my heels.

"No. Why should I? The world is the world. No one can change what's happened and Kali is just a witch who failed. Prophecies are bullshit anyway, and I like money. Accept the reality of our circumstances and quit acting like you've got some self-righteous mission to fix what's wrong with the world."

"This is an opportunity to be a hero, Jet. To redeem yourself of any wrong you've done in your life." He pulled up next to me, falling in stride even though I was making it hard for him to, cutting into the forest so he had to fall back once again. "You can't deny that you don't feel some guilt. We've both done shitty things. Things we could make up for if we thought about others instead of ourselves."

So that was what he was after—forgiveness, redemption. "That's not my style. I have nothing to beg forgiveness for." Yet. "Everyone I have ever hurt had it coming, and I'm not just saying that. They did something that deserved a punishment and everyone eventually has to pay their dues, including Kali."

He didn't respond and his silence made me want to turn around and look at him in the same withering way he liked to look at me, but I didn't. He knew who I was and what I was capable of. If he was smart, he would assume that I'd betray him too. And maybe he had assumed that. Maybe he would try to steal the amulet from me. Maybe he would try to open the portal and leave me behind. But if he did, the person on the other end of that portal would kill him. I was the only one authorized to use it. If I wasn't in tow, Jason wouldn't know what hit him.

"I'm going to change your mind," Jason said with a cocky twang to his voice. "I'm going to convince you to give Kali another chance."

"No, you're not."

"Everyone deserves a second chance."

"That's bullshit." Fuck, this was tiring. Why I was bothering to indulge the conversation was beyond me. Normally I'd just tell him to go fuc—

"Jet!" someone yelled.

"Hey, you two! There you are! It's getting dark. We need to go, right?" Amber was waiting for us at the edge of the cavern, wringing her hands and looking frazzled.

Steph came up from the other side of the forest like she'd been scouting. "I've been looking everywhere for you two!"

Luckily not in the clearing a few yards away. I eyed her suspiciously for a few seconds but she refused to look at me.

"Vampires are coming," I stated as I pushed past Amber, the high I'd felt from my glorious fuckfest pretty much gone and a shitty mood firmly in place. Fuck Jason and his moral high horse.

"What!" Amber was right behind me, almost tripping me up as we navigated the tight passageway.

I cursed myself for lashing out at Amber. I hadn't meant to tell her that way. But the reality was we had about an hour, tops, before the vamps got to us. Super speed would make their journey from the city quicker than ours had been. We were going to have to battle before we could get to Kali. It was a delay that I had hoped to avoid but one that I knew was inevitable. Vampires first, Kali second. That made my mood dip dangerously.

If I could figure out a way to ditch this crew and find Kali myself... But yeah, who was I kidding? That hadn't worked out too well the first time.

"Jet, what do you mean the vampires are coming?" Amber's voice carried into the cavern and echoed off the walls just as we stepped out of the tunnel.

All eyes were on us.

Fiona was holding green balls of wrapped-up palm leaves, her eyes wide.

Fuck! Not the kind of announcement I'd planned on. I could practically feel the panic rise around us.

"We have to prepare for an attack." I confirmed, making eye contact with everyone in the space. "The vampires are on their way. They'll find us in about thirty minutes." I tightened the time-line so that everyone would feel that sense of urgency that would fuel their fight response...hopefully. I walked toward the weapons, reaching out to grab a crossbow. "Is everything ready?"

"You knew the vampires were coming and you guys decided to detour outside for a little private time?" Steph yelled as she entered the cavern as well.

"We can handle it," I growled.

"Don't be stupid, Jet!" Steph growled back.

Fiona dropped the ball she was holding, sending the liquid spraying everywhere as it burst open. She jumped back to avoid being hit. I scowled at her. What a waste.

"If they send a horde, we're done! No way can we fight that with what we have here," Steph said.

"We don't have to fight," Kurt said he sidled up next to Fiona. He had a small animal bone in his hand that he'd clearly been gnawing on. He nudged the busted-up ball with his foot. "If we find Kali, Fiona can echo her powers and send out her presence for about a mile."

Fiona was nodding. "Steph, you said the vamps don't like Kali's powers, right? That's why they won't come into the forest."

Steph cursed under her breath, mumbling something as she glared at Fiona and Kurt. "They don't come into the forest for a lot of reasons. But now they know Jet's here, they can smell her blood, right?" She waved up and down my body. "All those cuts on your suit, you've been bleeding, haven't you? That's going to bring them right to us, isn't it? Kali be damned, your Dhampir blood will bring them all if only to get a piece of you."

"Are the vamps scared of Kali, Steph?" I asked, crossing my arms. "Your vampire sire tell you that? Where were you just now?

Not looking for us, right? You'd have found us in a few minutes. We weren't far."

Steph let out an angry breath. "I don't know what you're talking about."

I snorted, cocked an eyebrow. "You knew the vampires were coming too, didn't you? Someone told you. Your sire, right? That's who you were scouting for. You're trying to deflect the attention to me for some reason."

She opened her mouth like she was going to argue but then all the fire seemed to drain from her. "I left him a message. I was looking for him, but I didn't know the vampires were coming. I can't feel them like you can."

"You left him a message about what?" Jason snapped as he walked toward us.

She shifted her eyes to him, looking guilty. "I told him we had a way home."

"Did you do something to the wolves?" I asked. If she was working for the other side, she might have been trying to sabotage our plans, and it might have started with the wolves.

Her eyes went wide. "What? No! I told you, I went inside the store and he just disappeared."

"What about the basement in the armory? You told us that it was one floor and yet a stream of blood suckers came up from below."

Steph's shook her head. "I didn't know! I've never been in there so how would I? I scouted the area months ago and didn't see any evidence of a sublevel. I told you what I knew."

"There are vampires coming," I said. I could feel them like a slither down my spine.

"Because of your blood!" Steph yelled.

"Or because of your message," I countered. I rotated my arms. "My blood scent is powerful but these are just scratches. I haven't shed enough to really pull them in. But that doesn't matter because the vampires are coming. So, I'm going to ask you again, are they scared of Kali or what?"

Steph's eyes flashed. It looked like she was calculating her lies. "Yeah, fine, whoever the Master vamp is down there. He knows who Kali is and that she can wipe him out if she wants. He doesn't venture into the forest."

"So the vamps I'm feeling are likely lieutenants. Not as strong. And if Fiona mimics Kali's magic signature so everything freezes like it does when she's around, they'll get freaked out and stay back?"

"Yeah, they steer clear when Kali is roaming," Steph said. "I'd imagine if Fiona's magic works, she'll keep the vamps away."

Including her sire? I held Steph's stare until she looked away. Defeated? I had no idea what her plans were and how they involved her sire. Was he bringing a horde of vampires straight to them? Did she think she could access the portal without me? I shifted a curious glance to Jason. Had he told her the spell? Were they in this together? What wasn't I seeing?

"Your loyalties are torn," I said as I shifted my gaze from him to Steph, lifting my hand to keep her from arguing. I didn't want to hear it anyway. "We leave now, ahead of the vampires." I was so done with this shit. "We find Kali, subdue her. Stick to the plan."

"Your plan or Steph's?" Jason's voice was rough, a quiet anger still under his words.

I ignored him. These people were criminals. Untrustworthy. Even Jason. "Everyone load up. Grab as many containers or balls of net as you can and let's get the witch." I didn't care what happened after I left. I just needed to get to Kali and that damn amulet. "If we don't get to Kali in the next thirty minutes, everyone needs to be ready to fight the vamps."

"Sounds like a reckless plan," Jason said as he grabbed a crossbow for himself. He leaned closer to me so the others wouldn't hear. "Almost sounds like you're intentionally pushing our luck. Vampires attack, chaos ensues, some of this crew gets killed... Fewer people you have to take through the portal."

I didn't let his words affect me. Vampires added a layer of chaos that would help with my plans, yes. But I could control how quickly they found us. I could open a vein at just the right moment and they would ignore everything else, even an echo of Kali's powers, to get to me. Steph was right about that. My blood was like a drug to an addict. They would stop at nothing to get to it.

So that was my plan. I would take the power back in this fucked up situation. I'd call the vamps to me at the right moment, the rest of the group would have to engage in battle. All I needed was enough of a distraction to get to Kali myself, find the amulet and use it. Easy right? Even I knew the plan was a long shot. But if it worked, well fuck, I'd be home in a couple of hours, tops.

"It's a reckless plan, sure, but if you've got a better one, let's hear it." I slipped a quiver over my shoulder then motioned to Amber. "Grab those sacks of palm balls. Everyone make sure you have a few bottles of glue as well. As soon as you see Kali, you hit her with everything you've got. We need to get enough on her to bind her powers."

"And then what, Jet?" Jason hissed.

"And then it's home time," I hissed back. For me and Kali. It was the safest plan. That's the way it had to be, I realized. Take care of myself first, bring Kali back, and as soon as my feet hit home turf, I'd pull the strings that needed pulling to get Jason off the island too.

Unless he dies in the time it takes you to do that.

I looked at him. Like really looked. He was pissed at me. Jamming his bolts into his quiver. He wasn't sharing his suspicions with anyone else. He could expose me and turn the group against me—they were already pretty much there, distrusting how I was leading them. But he wasn't saying a word. His lips were a tight line of disapproval, but he was seething silently. Damn his loyalty.

If I left during a battle, the vampires could take him down. They might kill him in the chaos.

Once I crossed through the portal, it would take me some time to get back to Jason. Days at least. Maybe longer. He was a fierce fighter, but could he survive long enough for me to get back?

It all seemed too risky and his loyalty to me was making me think that it wasn't worth taking that chance. I owed him. Fuck. I owed him.

We could take our chances and I could bring him with me into the portal, risk being torn apart on the journey.

Hey, every plan had its flaws.

"Everyone ready?" Steph asked as she heaved a bag full of palm balls over her shoulder. "No time like now to get this show going." She was still glaring at me. Whatever her plans had been, I'd effectively fucked them up.

There were a few grunts, but there were no words. Everyone was ready. Or as ready as they were going to be.

"Let the witch hunt begin," I mumbled as I passed Jason. He grabbed my upper arm, halting me mid-step and yanking me back so he could growl at me again.

"No matter what happens, Jet. I'm stuck to you." He pulled me even closer, his hot breath rolling over my face. "Watching your back."

This time his words didn't sound like he was talking about my protection. This time it was a threat.

I yanked my arm away. "Your funeral."

15

AND THEN THINGS WENT TO SHIT.

I WAS RUNNING. OUT OF BREATH. OUT OF BOLTS. IN THE DARK. Pitch black dark and my eyesight was flickering like it did when I'd lost too much blood. I was still running though, my legs sore, exhaustion burning through my lungs.

I could feel them closing in, the blood dripping from my neck like a homing beacon, leading the Strix straight to me. I hadn't been the one to open myself up. This chase was not deliberate or welcome. That in itself was terrifying.

One minute we were stalking Kali, getting closer by the feel of the eerie silence, and the next a blade had been against my throat, slicing deep. A stealth attack by an unknown hand. Could have been any of them. Steph, Fiona, Kurt, Jason...

Then the vampires had been there, everywhere, coming for me. Uncontrolled chaos. That many vampires, they'd drain me dry no matter the risk to their lives. I would die. And then I'd be reborn as the thing I loathed above all others. Dhampir vampire. But a monstrous thing, like the ferals, blood deprived and lusting for it. Susceptible to the first vampire who blooded me. I'd be begging for it, and then I'd be bonded to that vampire for eternity.

I crashed through the foliage, banging myself off of trees like an out-of-control pinball, my brain fuzzy from loss of blood and something else, something seeping through my veins, making me burn again. I remember feeling a snap against my neck, just before the blade had sliced. Similar to what I'd felt on the boat. Like someone had dosed me with that fucking poison they seemed to enjoy injecting around here. My gushing blood had purged most of it away almost immediately but enough had gotten in and it was fucking me up something awful. I felt drunk. I kinda just wanted to sleep or at least stop and rest. But I'd be swarmed within minutes. Had to keep moving.

My mind cycled back to what troubled me the most. Who had dosed me and then cut me? Jason had been at my back the whole damn time. So close I could practically feel him up against me. I strained my memory, trying to recall—no, he hadn't been behind me when I was attacked. He'd been in front of me for some reason... He'd moved forward...ahead of the group because...

I stumbled into a tree, almost knocking myself out by a low hanging branch. There was no time for unconsciousness. Not if I wanted to stay alive.

There were at least two dozen vampires, maybe more, tracking me. Some of them crazy, starved and manic, others smarter, cunning, cutting me off and laughing when I swore and swerved. I had my knife in hand to slash them back before running in a new direction.

They vibrated through me, those vampires, my Dhampir awareness sending jolts every second, revving me up, cranking my body to the point of total distraction, making it harder to run and not take myself out by fallen logs or hanging branches.

I was in trouble. Big trouble. And running out of energy. I needed a better plan than this, a way to distract them somehow.

I crashed through a line of small trees, and where the ground should have been was a drop. And I dropped, hard, managing to do a neck-saving roll that landed me on my ass instead of my head. And then there was sand. The smell of seawater hit me on the breeze. I snapped my head up, scanning the horizon. The ocean was ten yards in front of me, waves slowly lapping. The beach spanned in either direction. It ended fifty or so yards to the west at a rock face. To the east it ended at a dock where there was a warehouse, brightly lit and calling to me like a beacon.

I knew where I was.

Trouble didn't even begin to describe my situation. I was fucked.

I stood, made a move to head back into the trees, at least to grab a branch, arm myself with something big I could swing, when I was slammed with the feeling of vampires en masse, a jolt that rocked me to the core. My feet did the retreating, beating backwards until I was sinking into the soft sand that marked where the tide was washing in.

I glanced to my right... Rock, no chance of climbing with my neck bleeding like a sieve. Warehouse it would have to be. I sprinted left, the wet packed sand making it easier to run and—injury or no—I was determined to get my ass off that beach. Too much wide open space, too easy to be overtaken and literally consumed.

I didn't have to look behind me to know they were coming. I heard them crash through the trees, the pulse of their proximity intoxicating; they were practically biting at my ass, making me move faster. Being Dhampir meant that I had almost the same speed as a starved vampire; I just hoped that I was more motivated to get away than they were to get a meal.

Heart hammering, feet moving, breath nothing more than pants, I ran for my life.

I almost got there. Almost.

Slamming me from the side, a vampire who came out of

nowhere took me down, rolling with me to the water. My knife went flying and I couldn't reach my belt for a new one. I dug my fingers into his eyes, blinding him as I felt his eyeballs pop, the ooze of blood and whatever else dripping onto my face. I punched him in the ear then gripped his upper and lower jaw, curling my fingers into his mouth and wrenched his jaw open until I heard a crack. The fucker screamed and rolled off of me. I scrambled free but it was way too late—the others closed in, and I was suddenly surrounded. The dock, maybe a hundred feet behind me, might as well have been a million miles away.

I braced myself for attack, pulling a blade in each hand. Ready to defend myself until those fuckers drained me dry. It was not the way I'd envisioned my death necessarily, but I'd always known I would die violently.

The manic vampires were all fangs, hands out, trying to cage me, like they had enough sense left to attempt to lull me into some kind of peaceful acceptance of my fate, not realizing that I was Dhampir. The vampires who knew better hung back, presumably to watch the show.

As one stepped forward, another would push back, hissing and snarling like rabid animals unwilling to share their catch.

For the first time in my life, fear licked down my spine as I envisioned my limbs being torn in an effort to quench their thirst. I had no doubt that this was gonna hurt. It was possible that they could end it for me permanently. If they did enough damage. I was at the point where I wished that would be so. It would be better if they ripped my head off and drained me dry. Then at least I would know peace.

Another one stepped toward me. I met him halfway, punching him back with a quick jab to the jaw and a kick to the gut. He fell into the group, knocking down a few of the others. The collective rage rose around me. There were too many. They crowded in.

I fought.

Hard.

Fangs tore at my flesh, hands grappled for a grip. They tried to get me down.

I screamed my fury, kicking, punching, even using my teeth, wanting to puke at the taste of dirty skin. My legs buckled, but I fought to stay upright.

And just when the sheer number threatened to overwhelm me I was suddenly yanked up and out of the melee, like the hand of some god had dropped down and pulled me free. Arms encircled my chest, pulling me back and out of the fray. The vampires started to fall, blood gushing from chest wounds, heads ripped from bodies. The ones that weren't insane realized what was going on and took off toward the trees only to be hit with arrows in the back. Within seconds all were dead and I was fighting out of the embrace of my savior, kicking backward and using my head to knock myself free. Whoever had me let go.

I spun, unsteady on my legs, dizzy from blood loss and whatever else.

I was surrounded by vampires again. Not the crazed feral ones from the beach. No, these ones—at least twenty this time—were calm, collected, still dangerous as fuck. There was only so much one hunter could take. My head was pounding. I dropped to my knees.

"Giving up already, Bridget?" A smooth voice echoed in my muddled brain. "You've changed."

I snapped my gaze up to the dock, the bright glare from the warehouse overhead lights making it difficult to see clearly. But I didn't need to see a face to know that voice. A voice I never thought I'd ever hear again. So it couldn't be. I was dead, right? This was just a flash of my afterlife? Or a blissful dream as the vampires sucked me dry on the beach.

"Even blood soaked and dirty, you are still a striking woman," the silky smooth voice said. "I've missed you."

No. It couldn't be. The love of my life. The man who owned my heart. He was here.

"Julian?" His name stuck in my throat like a lump. Tears filled my eyes, unstoppable as they rolled down my cheeks. "You're alive?"

"In a manner of speaking." He laughed that warm laugh that always made me melt when I was with him.

I reached up to touch him but he was so far away. How could this be?

The one who had taken me out of the vampire swarm trapped me in his arms again, pulling me back from Julian, subduing me like I was nothing more than a rag doll.

I bit his arm then slammed my head back again. I saw stars but it worked—the vamp dropped me to the sand and I stumbled forward, fists raised. Nothing and nobody would keep me from Julian.

"Calm down, would you, darling?" Julian pointed at my neck. "You're bleeding still. Every vampire on the island is on their way here, Strix and Dhampir alike, and I bet you're buzzing so hard right about now you wouldn't even notice."

The brute behind me shoved my shoulder. My knees buckled immediately, and I struggled to keep upright. "I don't understand. There are Dhampirs here?" It made no sense what he was saying. It made no sense that he was even here. "I saw you die."

"I know, sweetheart, it's very confusing." He snapped his fingers and then motioned for me to be lifted up to the deck. "I'll explain everything to you.'

Strong hands grabbed me by the waist and hoisted me up. I didn't fight this time. Julian held his hand out to me and I grasped it as my feet touched the dock. He immediately pulled me into him, wrapping his arms around me as he nuzzled my neck, licking at my wound so that it would heal faster. My legs gave way but he held me up. I couldn't think. Julian was here, his arms around me, his tongue touching me, his body protecting me. I never thought I'd feel this again. I was overwhelmed, my heart bursting with disbelieving joy.

"I watched you today." His lips were pressed against my ear, his voice a whisper. "What a fighter you've become. Sacrificing those vampires was worth it to see you fight."

"You were watching me?" My voice sounded hazy, my lips dry, tongue-tied. All I wanted was to curl up with Julian and sleep.

"I sent for you, sweetheart. Finally, after all this time, I could and I did and here you are." He pulled me back so he could look down at me. "But I lost track of you when you arrived on the island. And then there you were, attacking my armory and you were glorious, darling. Truly. I was mesmerized. So much so that you escaped again. You and your friends. But I knew I'd catch up with you eventually. This island isn't so big that you could disappear forever."

"What?" What was he saying? I screwed up my face, my thoughts clearing. "You brought me here?" I pushed on his chest, wanting some distance from his scent, his intoxicating embrace.

He held on firm, caging me in his strong arms. "I've been waiting a long time for this, Bridget, and now you're here and we'll finally be together forever."

I had no power of my own to fight him, hardly able to stay on my feet. Too much blood lost, too much shock. I looked at him feeling like my brain was fizzling.

Something snapped around my throat, tight, almost to the point of choking. Stabbing pain cutting into my neck as it locked into place and tore into my flesh.

I cried out and he pulled me close to lick away the blood that dripped from my new wounds.

He'd collared me. *Oh fuck.* An ancient Dhampir blood-letting device. I would slowly bleed to death. It was the most humane method of killing an unturned Dhampir. After I died, he would feed me with his blood to bring me back. Then I would be his vampire, devoted to him. Bonded in a way that I'd always wanted to be. And yet...and yet...

"Not like this." My voice was wobbly, tears streaming down my face. "Please, Julian, not like this."

He pulled me close so I was staring into his eyes, shining with an intensity that hurt. His eyes were the vibrant blue like I remembered, ringed with black, mesmerizing, so blue that I could swim in them. Despite the pain. Despite his actions, I still felt that pounding beat of love for him, a rush of excitement that he was alive.

"Once upon a time you vowed to be my partner for eternity. You vowed to become my bonded Lady and rule a clan with me. Remember that?"

I couldn't move, I couldn't speak. I had vowed that. I had wanted that. Desperately. Thinking I could escape my father. Control my destiny.

He lifted his finger to brush against my face. "I've built an empire here, sweetheart, and together we will rule my clan, never to be parted again."

❧ 16 ❧

HE KISSED MY LIPS TENDERLY. "I AM SORRY THAT WE WERE parted for so long, but I needed you to grow stronger, to become the formidable woman you are now. Worthy to rule by my side."

Worthy? Now I was worthy?

My head hurt too much. My body slumped further. I was so tired. Worn out. Defeated... Wait...no...Julian was here. Alive. All this time... I opened my lips to speak but the collar dug in deeper, making me moan with pain, the feel of my blood oozing down my neck, a reminder of what was going to happen. I was going to die and be reborn, my loyalties attached to him. No choice. The decision had been made for me.

He kissed me again, just a brush of his lips on mine and then he held my face and locked eyes with me. "I will explain everything to you soon, Bridget. I promise. The most important thing is that you're with me now and soon we will be together as we once were, eternally bonded."

I could get lost in those eyes. So blue. So clear but for that dark ring. The ring of utter blackness that looked like it was swirling. Tears welled in mine, making everything blurry. "Julian... I don't want..."

I moaned as darkness came to take me under.

୫

I MUST HAVE PASSED OUT. OR HE'D HYPNOTIZED ME, WHICH WAS possible. Dhampir vampires often developed special abilities after turning. The power of suggestion was a common one that many vampires inherited to some degree. Usually harmless. There were, on rare occasions, intensely powerful hypnotic abilities that came with the change, and it typically ran in families. Julian's mother had been renowned for her gift. And she'd always, as far as I knew, used it judiciously.

She'd explained to me once that it wasn't a violation of someone's will but merely a manipulation of something that was already there. She could never force someone to do something that went against their moral fiber for example, but she could, with the right wording, convince someone to do something that they had only briefly considered. Suggestion only worked if the intent was already there. Considering the weird disorientation I felt, and the complete lack of memory as to how I'd gone from the dock to a plush, four-poster bed, I had a feeling Julian's mesmerizing baby blues had put me there. I'd wanted to curl up with him and sleep, he had merely encouraged me to do so.

No violation. Right?

I felt the burn of my heart intensifying as tears bubbled to my eyes. How had I gotten here? To this moment where suddenly my long lost love was alive and in our reunion, I was violated, collared against my will and left to bleed out. Alone. Weak. Dying.

I scoffed, then groaned. *Suck it up, Jet.*

But how to you go from mourning to this? Any other circumstances and I'd be overjoyed. Right in this moment, I'm confused, angry, disappointed, hurt...ah fuck, I'm hurting so bad that it feels like I could die just from the way my heart feels. I'd never stopped loving him even if I'd come to accept that he was dead.

His memory was one of the reasons I'd never turned full vampire. I knew, in my line of work, that one day I'd be ripped apart, and I'd die a true death. I knew that one day I'd be reunited with him in the afterlife. I'd hoped, at least, for that.

I sucked in a gentle breath and tested the strength left in my body. I couldn't stay here. I could think straight enough to know that staying here would make me a victim. A victim to the one person I never saw coming. The one person who I'd trusted without any doubts. Julian was alive, and here. He'd collared me without consent and betrayed me in every way possible.

He was as good as dead to me now. In fact, if given the chance, I'd kill him myself.

Wincing, I reached up to finger the collar. Someone had wrapped a bundle of fabric around my neck, cushioning the collar and collecting my blood. It had been recently changed by the dry feel of the cloth.

I was still fully clothed and laying on a soft duvet. The room was dark but I could make out the silhouette of big bulky furniture. My body hurt, my neck in particular. I could only guess by my lethargy how long I'd been unconscious and bleeding. Death would come for me soon if I didn't do something about it.

The collar kept the wounds open and bleeding so I needed to get it off. As soon as my throat was free of the blades, my body would regenerate tissue to heal the wounds.

Unless I was past the point of healing and then I was totally fucked.

Julian had been dead for fifteen years and it would have been better if he'd stayed that way. He'd been watching me? Waiting for me to grow more powerful? *Worthy,* he'd said. And he'd *fetched* me? Like I was some kind of pet? His words rolled through my head.iHi

He'd manipulated my smuggler and put me on that boat, weaponless. He'd watched me struggle to get new weapons by battling a horde of vampires. And now he was once again derailing my plans to capture Kali and get the hell off of Vampire Island. All in the name of love.

Yeah, fuck him. That sounded more like possession. I would be owned by no man. Not my father and not Julian.

The fact that he'd faked his death wasn't lost on me either. It meant that he and my father were likely in collusion since it was my father who had not only ordered the kill but who had orchestrated the show for me to see. I'd watched Julian be decapitated by Luke, my father's number one henchman. I'd watched Julian's heart get ripped out and set on fire. A true Dhampir death. I'd watched him die. Or so I'd thought. What a naive woman I had been.

Time to get the fuck outta here.

But I didn't move. Not an inch. Not as tears rolled down my face. Not as my body shook with heart-pulverizing sobs. What had I ever done to deserve any of this? Why did these men in my life think that I was nothing more than a puppet for their amusement? Hadn't I shown how strong I was? Hadn't I proven that I could live without either of them?

I closed my eyes tight and willed myself to stop.

Not all of the men in your life think this of you. Jason sees your strength. He respects your power.

Not that it matters because Jet Black is a badass bitch. *Stop. Crying. Get. Up. You will not die like this.*

I ran my fingers over the cloth, fumbling to find a place to loosen it. I felt like I was underwater, slow motion, clumsy. I needed to get the collar off. Now. I'd spent enough time being vulnerable and enough time wallowing.

Reaching both hands around the back of my neck, which was awkward and painful, proved to be the best strategy. The cloth was looped in a bow like closure. I tugged hard to unravel the knot then pulled the cloth free. The air on my skin made me shiver...and then it felt like I wouldn't stop shivering. Cold...I was so damn cold. A shudder ran through me, then a convulsion.

Stop wasting time.

I took in a deep breath and willed my body to stop shaking.

With fumbling fingers, I found the clasp of the collar and prayed that it didn't require a key or code. Thankfully, it was old fashioned and clicked open when I pressed on both sides of the clasp.

I sucked in a shallow breath, bracing myself for the inevitable pain, then yanked the collar free.

Razor sharp blades pulled at my skin as I tore them free, leaving behind searing pain that jolted me from neck to toe.

I quickly replaced the cloth, holding my neck tight with both hands, breathing through the pain, willing the slits in my flesh to knit up and stop the blood flow.

If they didn't close, if I was too far gone, then what? Not lay here and die. Not wait for Julian to come back and claim me as his. That wasn't my way. Not anymore.

Find another vampire to sire you. Feed from whoever you get your hands on. Survive. Then you can bring Julian a reckoning. Then you can find out what the fuck is going on.

My mind jumped to the obvious realities.

Julian was clearly in charge, which meant he was likely the warden of Vampire Island. He'd had a clan of Dhampirs at his back on the dock. His family? Perhaps. Plus other Dhampirs who had pledged allegiance to Clan Cross. The Strix were his to command. He'd use them to do all the dirty work on the island. Manipulate them with blood deprivation, control their loyalty and make them work for him. It all made so much sense. Except for why he would let the supernaturals live in the cavern. He had to know they existed and that they posed a threat to his weapons cache, among other things.

So had Steph been telling the truth? Was Julian and his clan terrified of Kali and what she could do to him with her powers?

That was something I could leverage. If I didn't die right here on this bed.

I nudged my fingers into the most tender parts of my throat, feeling for the gaping wounds. The cloth was wet with my blood but it didn't feel sopping. Fingers crossed that my flesh was actually knitting back together.

The door opened quietly, just a *whoosh* of sound and a slight change in light as someone slipped into the room. I moved the collar under the pillow next to me then ran my hand slowly down to my belt, my fingers brushed against cool metal. I could have laughed with triumph. I had one blade left. I moved my hand away just as the intruder got to the side of the bed.

"Your blood is flowing well, my dear."

That was not the voice I'd expected to hear.

Mariana Cross, Julian's mother.

She moved to the other side of the room and opened a wide bank of windows that I hadn't realized were there. The light from the moon streamed into the room, illuminating everything in its ghostly glow. She stood looking out for a moment. The picture of her, standing like that, framed by the window and basking in the glow of the moon, was like fifteen years hadn't passed. Everything about her was the same, as it should be, since she was eternally youthful. Forever thirty years old. She wore her red hair to her waist, the beautiful tresses curling in giant waves that were braided into intricate designs at her crown Her body, slim, her clothes, just as she'd always preferred—sleek black pants and a white cascading blouse that covered her almost to the knees. She had on high heels that seemed so inappropriate on Vampire Island. Not that I expected that she had anything to do with the wild and dangerous life outside of the compound.

"You're probably wondering what on earth is going on." Her voice was soft, with a hint of an accent from her home country of Romania. Her union into Clan Cross had been prearranged at her birth. Just as my mother's had been. The ways of the old world.

Before Julian's death, I'd adored this woman. Idolized her. Despite the feud between our families, I'd still managed to find ways to spend time with Clan Cross. Not only were there monthly events that called all of the powerful clans together for socializing and political moves, but our estates had been within the same gated community. Acres and acres separated us but that hadn't stopped me or Julian from seeing each other. It was a friendship that Mariana Cross had never discouraged. It was a quiet alliance that I had so badly needed after my mother's death.

"I'd so wished this could have been done differently," she said as she turned toward me. Her face was angelic, her eyes dark, almost black, to contrast her son's blue. Her lips were painted red, her makeup as extravagant as ever. I had to wonder what life was like for her on the island. What delusion she'd wrapped around herself to make this all more palatable. "It's wonderful to see you again, Bridget."

I didn't speak. She wouldn't expect I could with the collar cutting into me. I let my other hand shift from where I'd been holding the cloth to my neck, satisfied that my wounds were indeed starting to heal. I felt it like a tingle, so subtle that it was almost imperceptible. The coagulation of blood was enough to give me a boost of energy. My body would rebound...slowly yes, but eventually I would have enough strength to get the hell off the bed. Hope pulsed through me.

She moved to sit down in a chair next to a large dresser, crossing her legs, her hands, nails long and manicured, entwined at her knee. She was leaning forward, studying me. I shifted my eyes slightly so that I wasn't looking at her directly, not at all interested in her brand of mind manipulation.

"We came here not long after the war started. Julian had been building this stronghold before that though." She leaned forward a bit more. "I know how awful it must have been for you these past fifteen years, thinking that he was gone, but we wouldn't reach out to you sooner. It wasn't safe and you weren't ready."

I frowned.

"I know that's of little consolation. We are sorry, dear, please believe that." She cleared her throat when I turned my head away. Clan women had very little control over their lives unless they were the head of the family, not something that happened very often. I could have given her a pass, let her play the innocent party, but I didn't really want to. She'd had the luxury of knowing Julian was alive and during that time I had felt like I'd died, my heart ripped out over and over again.

That ever-present feeling of being in mourning, a feeling I'd carried with me like a heavy weight on my back, had suddenly been replaced by pure, unadulterated rage. I'd been lied to by more than just Julian. I'd been betrayed and ultimately had walked around like a fucking fool, not knowing how orchestrated it all was.

"Anyway, I found out just after the war started that Julian wasn't dead. He sent for me, brought me here to safety where he'd built this magnificent mansion." She waved her elegant hand around. "You'll see once you are better. It's stunning, Bridget, truly. A masterpiece."

I closed my eyes as a surprising jolt of emotion spiked through me. Tears once again burned behind my eyelids. Self-pitying thoughts pounding in my head. How could they...have done this to me? To be living, carrying on while the war raged, keeping me in the dark about—

I felt the weight shift on the bed. Felt her cool fingers wrap around mine.

"It was done out of love," she whispered. "Your father..."

I opened my eyes to glare at her, almost breaking my charade of compliance. I wanted to blurt, "My father what?" But I kept my lips sealed tight.

For fifteen years I'd thought my father had killed the love of my life. For fifteen years I had lived with revenge driving me. I could never kill my father, I wasn't strong enough as an unturned Dhampir, but I could shame him by being a hunter, by being a mercenary. By making a name for myself that ensured he would always know where I was and what I was doing. A black mark on his reputation. Each kill I made was a knife strike at him.

"Your father forced this on Julian." Her fingers tightened around mine. "Forced him to agree to exile after learning of your plans to bond. He was incensed. The fury of that man..." Her other hand drifted to her throat while mine drifted back to my knife, unnoticed. "My Stephan was dead for only a matter of weeks before your father began making moves to take over Clan Cross, Julian thought by uniting the families it would put an end to that."

I froze, my eyes wide. It had all been a power play? The love affair? It had all been an attempt to keep my father from obliterating Clan Cross? Julian's father had died just before we'd met. Just as my mother had. A strange and horrible coincidence. Julian had been so distraught, until he met me...or so he'd said. The sudden realization of the depth of the betrayal was almost too much to bear. What a fool I'd been.

"Oh no, dear, don't think it was a rouse. Julian loved you from the first moment he saw you." She laughed like we were having a silly misunderstanding. Like I was just being a foolish girl. "But uniting our clans would ensure a measure of safety for Clan Cross." She sighed heavily. "You remember the night it was supposed to happen?"

I nodded, mainly to divert her attention as I slipped my knife slowly, inch by inch from its sheath. Rage burned through me, giving me a rush of adrenaline. Would it be enough to overpower a vampire? Mariana had never been a fighter, and the element of surprise would put her at a disadvantage. I would at least be able to subdue her enough so that I could escape.

"Your father had already known about it, he'd already threatened Julian. Forcing him to go through with the plans so that you'd be most shamed. That brutal man." Her words carried an edge of venom that I was accustomed to where my father was concerned. "He wanted you to suffer the most. Julian did die that night, on the night you two had set for your bonding. He died. But his heart had not been burned. That, the vision of that, had been directed by your father."

My father's sinister power. His was not able to manipulate one's thoughts. He couldn't make someone do something, intention or not. But he could conjure your worst nightmare. Make you see something so horrifying that it left your mind in tatters.

That's what he had done to me that night. Made me believe I was witnessing the death of my love. And I had never doubted what I saw. Why would I? My father had shown me already what he was capable of. To hurt me in this way was not an unbelievable thing. He'd shown me my worst nightmare and I'd accepted it as truth.

If Julian had bled out that night, who'd brought him back? My father?

That was too grotesque to even think about.

"Julian was reborn in the most agonizing way and then exiled. Here. But my dear son had a plan. He had allies. Even though your father took control over Clan Cross, Julian was here building a new clan. Slowly mounting his power. Waiting for the day to come when he could match your father in strength. But then the Dark War happened." She sighed again, her fingers leaving mine so that she could twist a lock of her hair. "And it was chaos. It took us years to find you. You were such a formidable warrior. Julian saw immediately what you were doing to your father. Weakening him with your actions. And we both knew that with time you would turn yourself into a woman so hardened that you could fight alongside Julian to defeat the man who had taken it all away from both of you. This is what your mother would have wanted for you."

The manipulation knew no bounds. I was a pawn in Julian's silent war against my father. All this time, I had been an unsuspecting player, my rage simmering, wallowing in grief, honing my skills, yes, but not to be used in someone else's game.

"He has never stopped pining for you, Bridget." She reached out to pat my hand. I grabbed her wrist instead, pulling her toward me as I moved closer to her.

"Don't you dare speak of my mother."

I used all of my available strength to pound my blade into her chest, angling it so that it pierced her heart. Her eyes were wide, pain tearing through her beautiful face. Her mouth gaped, twisting into a horrible grimace. I left the blade there and pushed her away, letting her slide to the floor in a heap.

That had taken almost all of my strength. I closed my eyes for a moment, bracing myself so I didn't fall backward, pooling what little reserves I had left.

The knife in her heart wouldn't kill her like it would a Strix, but it would slow her down, especially if I left it embedded. She'd have to take it out first before her heart could heal itself. That would take a lot of courage and energy. Easier for her if someone found her and helped.

I ripped the cloth away from my neck and felt the wounds that remained. The blood had stopped oozing, my flesh was tender, but I wasn't going to die any time soon. I moved from the bed. My whole body ached, but there was no time for being a wuss.

Mariana's eyes were still wide, unblinking as she tracked me. She opened her mouth but no sound came out. The shock of such a wound had a silencing effect—trust me, I had intimate experience with that. All the same, I grabbed one of the pillows and ripped the cover off then shoved it deep into her mouth, effectively gagging her. I shifted her legs out so she was stretched into a line then shoved her under the bed. The knife hilt knocked against the wood frame, essentially wedging itself between the bed and her heart. She moaned pathetically. Tears streamed from her eyes. Her hands were fluttering at her sides, as if she could lift them to her chest to yank the knife out.

"Good luck with that."

The ruffles of the overhang would conceal her for a little while. The blade in her chest would keep her in place. I let the overhang drop then lifted it again so I could look at her one more time. I reached in and swiped a few drops of her blood, bringing to my lips. Her taste was like Julian's. It gave me a jolt. I closed my eyes to savor. Then I opened them again and glared at her.

"I will never forgive what you did, what Julian did. Please tell your son that if he comes after me again, I will kill him." I leaned closer. "That's a bona fide guarantee from Jet Black, Vampire Hunter."

❧ 17 ❧

I COULD NOT GO OUT THE BEDROOM DOOR AND HOPE TO MAKE it through the house to the outside. I was in no shape to take on Julian or his henchmen.

I moved to the bank of windows, inspecting them for a means to scale the wall to the ground below. It didn't look good. There was no balcony, nothing jutting that would serve as footholds and it had to be at least forty feet up. Jumping would most definitely break something in my body. I didn't have enough strength to mend the damage that would cause, not immediately anyway.

I glanced back at the bed. There were sheets... Tying them was perhaps an option.

Or...

Something thumped against the bedroom door, shaking it against the frame. I detected the faintest sound of...growling?

I picked up a hefty-looking statue, dismayed somewhat by how much strength it took to hold it, and moved along the wall to the door. Listening for whatever was making that sound. I could hear a slight snapping noise, like bone grinding against bone. With my hand on the knob, I slowly, quietly, opened the door.

Orbs of green blinked up at me in the darkened hallway. A

muzzle coated in blood. The metallic smell of so much red stuff made my stomach growl.

The werewolf was in a beastly form—not animal, not human in shape but somewhere in between—straddling a prone vampire, face down. The beast was gnawing on the vamp's spine which, with a snap of the were's head, became detached from the vampire's body.

"Bill or Doug?" Fuck, I hoped it was one of them...and that there wasn't any plan to remove my spine from my body.

The beast version of a shifter was a more intelligent and communicative form than when in the wolf form. It was also the most violent version that a shifter could take. It looked at me like it wanted to devour me. Contemplating my body as if assessing prime rib on sale all the while gnawing away on the vampire's bones...crunching them to bits. No worries there...obviously at the apex of the predatory hierarchy.

I lifted the statue, thinking it might do some damage if I threw it hard enough. Maybe it would buy me some time so I could make a run for it. My arms quivered under its weight. The beast followed my movement, seemingly amused...and then it dropped the bones from its mouth and rose to its full height of around seven feet, standing upright on two paws instead of four. It was a monstrous thing to behold. I got a waft of nasty beast smell but held my ground. Now that I was toe-to-toe, running was out of the question.

It loomed over me, studying me, inhaling me. Its fangs were dripping a mixture of blood and saliva. Sad to say, I was so deprived of blood that my mouth was actually watering at the sight.

The beast licked its snout, slopping saliva in a spray, then bared its teeth. It did not seem like a friendly gesture.

I wanted to glance over my shoulder, thinking that maybe pulling Mariana out from under the bed might tempt the stinky beast enough to distract him. Seemed like a good enough plan. Yeah, sacrifice the ex-mother-in-law to be. Solid idea.

I was ready to bolt backward, my hand still on the door so I could fling it closed when the beast abruptly pushed past me, knocking me to the side and into the wall. So much for that plan. Fuck, I was pathetic. Blood was definitely a top priority. I needed my strength back.

It moved to the bed, glanced down at where Mariana was making mewing noises, then glanced back at me with a wolf-like smirk. Shaking its head as if it was denying itself a treat, the beast moved to the windows and, with both fists to the glass, pounded...one...two... three times, until the bank of windows shattered around him.

"I could have done that, big guy," I said weakly, wondering whether or not I actually could have broken the window with my limited energy. "I guess you're not going to tell me what the hell is going on."

The beast didn't want to eat me. Okay. Good. At least not at the moment anyway. The urge to run slid out of me as I leaned against the wall...my energy waning completely, my legs trembling. I glanced toward the open doorway, past the prone body of the spineless vampire and wondered why the hell the alarms hadn't been raised. I squinted. There was a weird fog seeping through the halls. It smelled funny...and it made me tingle.

I kicked the door closed with my foot. *Something witchy this way comes.* The beast had brought a spell with him. Or a spell caster.

I looked to the window. "What's the plan, big guy?"

He ignored me.

Seconds later a rope appeared, a grappling hook latching onto the edge of the window frame. The beast secured it and then it came at me, stalking in a way that made me feel helpless and defeated. There was no gentle approach from a monster like that, no other way to perceive it than, *holy shit I'm going to die.*

Muffled shouts sounded down the hallway. Whatever head-start we had was slipping away. No spell caster then...just a bit of magic. Made me wonder who was on my side. Jason? Amber? Steph? Who was staging the rescue attempt?

The beast bore down on me, its chest at eye level. All I could see was fur.

With a shrug, I shoved my marble weapon aside and slid myself up the wall. Might as well get this over with, right? Best to play the damsel until I could get some liquid nourishment.

He grunted something unintelligible then grabbed me around the waist and hoisted me up and over his shoulder, pinning my legs down so that I was locked on tight. His fur was as coarse as I'd expected and his smell didn't get any better up close. I gathered some fur in my hand and tried to flatten myself as much as possible against his body.

He didn't hesitate. Instead, he moved to the window, gripped the rope that was there and flung us both over the side. The descent was quick, and a little terrifying. He held the rope between his forearm and other hand, moving us down to the ground so that we thudded within seconds. He flipped me over in a maneuver so quick that I hardly had time to react. I ended up on his back, my arms wrapped around his neck. He grunted at me in a beastly way that was clearly an order to hang on and then he ran...with me literally bouncing, trying not to fly off.

I gripped his fur so tightly that I was afraid I might take a chunk of flesh with each jolt forward. He moved fast...jumping some shrubs, diverting from a straight line, loping with as much stealth as you would expect from a seven foot tall monster. In other words, zero stealth but all efficiency.

A cinder block wall loomed ahead and just as I expected to be dropped down and boosted up and over, the beast made an impossible jump, scaling the eight-foot wall with little trouble. I glanced back at the mansion just as we reached the top of the wall and gaped. Julian had built a beautiful compound. It looked like a castle in some ways with two turrets at the sides and hundreds of windows lining gray brick walls, balconies and green grass, surrounded the building. Lights were blasting all over the property, sweeping around in search of us. Another wolf was running in between the lights, making the sensors go haywire as it bolted from one end of the property to the other. Bill or Doug? I still wasn't sure whose back I was on or who was now distracting the vampires while we escaped. Shouts came from the building, commands ordered, nothing I could really make out but it was clear my absence had been discovered. It was chaos.

The beast I was riding jumped down to the other side of the wall, cutting off my view of Julian's home and the other wolf. The landing was more jarring that I expected, and I slipped a bit from my perch on his back.

"I can walk," I said, thumping the beast on the chest to let him know it was time to drop me.

He gripped my arms instead, hoisting me up higher and then locked my hands in one of his. A powerful grip keeping me in place. Our ride wasn't over, it seemed. I felt the *whoosh* of something sweep by me and heard the thunk of an arrow embedding into a tree just in front. I ducked lower, the beast grunted, slouched somewhat and then started to run once again.

We went straight into the forest, jumping over logs, under branches, missing obstacles in a way that was truly awe-inspiring. He weaved and dodged, not taking a direct path and the forest was pitch black, not a glimmer of light penetrating. I had to trust that wherever we were going was not into the hands of a new enemy.

We ran for an hour. At least, I mean, it seemed like an hour bouncing around on his back, fighting to stay put, my legs straining to hold on. His fur was soaked with sweat, which didn't improve the smell. It was so far up my nose that I could taste it.

There were times when I felt the buzz of Strix around but whenever the buzz happened, the beast would veer, changing course until that feeling went away, almost as it if was attuned to the vampires in the same way I was.

When it was time to stop, the beast gave no warning. One minute I was on its back, the next I was being flung in an arc to crash into a tree so hard my breath whooshed out of me. I was too stunned to react at first. My head throbbed, and my body hurt. I struggled to move, trying to get a leverage my boots against the tree roots beneath me.

The beast looked hungry again, green eyes cold, calculating as he panted hard, his whole body heaving, staring at me like he was trying to figure out how the hell I'd gotten on his back.

"What the fuck, dude?" What I wouldn't give for a knife right about now.

He bared his fangs, lifting his upper lip to show me how long they were. Both impressive and terrifying. I had no doubt that he could rip my throat out with one bite. He tilted his head and roared, a sound that vibrated through me with a chilling rush.

I am so fucked.

Something came crashing into the clearing. A flash of gray fur I recognized, a familiar cat-like shape stood between me and the beast. I couldn't see a damn thing. I moved my feet around to get myself off the roots that were tangling me up and shifted to the side, trying to get a better view.

"He can only stay in beast form for so long before he loses all links to his humanity." Amber peeked at me from the side of the tree. "I cast on him so he would hang on longer, with his permission of course."

Her sudden appearance startled me and I raised my fist to punch her out.

"Holy shit, a little warning!"

She reached out to grip my hand, folding her palm over my fist. "He told us that if he started going feral to knock him out."

I didn't know a lot about werewolf shifters other than how to recognize their transition states. Wolves followed the traits and behaviors of their natural counterparts, more predictable, less dangerous, but only because they were driven by needs more than wants. In beast form, all bets were off. Natural tendencies were more berserker than wolf.

I shook her hand off and leaned back against the tree for support. "And the cat is going to attempt to do that?"

Knock out a feral beast? *Yeah, right.*

I craned to see over Jason's body, angling as much as I could. Both animals were locked in an eye staring contest that seemed unbreakable, moving from side to side. It was obvious that the beast wanted to get closer to me and Amber, but Jason was having none of it.

The beast was clenching and unclenching its clawed fists, foaming at the mouth while Jason, in his cat form, growled a low, dark and deep sound that could not be mistaken as anything but a warning.

The odds didn't seem fair for the cat, if I was going to be honest.

And then suddenly another wolf came barreling into the clearing, tawny fur, green eyes, facing off with his brother in a mass of growling, fangy aggression.

The tension spiked, the beast roared, and I thought for sure someone was about to die. Amber whispered something. There was a crack, a giant one. Leaves rustled and a branch the size of a two-by-four crashed down straight on the beast's head.

Everyone stopped. All sound ceased. The beast wavered for a second, its eyes rolling back so all we could see was white, and then it crumbled to the ground in a thundering crash.

"Fuck me!" I breathed.

"Wasn't sure if that would work," Amber said.

I shot a look her way. "Remind me not to get on your bad side," I mumbled. I pressed myself harder against the bark, calculating how far I'd get if I bolted into the woods. I couldn't forget that someone had sliced my throat earlier, and I still didn't know who had done it.

Once again, I found myself weaponless and surrounded by the unknown. Could I trust these people? Unlikely.

"Take my blood." Jason thrust his forearm into my face, a wound already oozing, blood there for me to suck.

I turned my head, forcing myself to look away. "No." Hardest thing I've ever had to do. My body was screaming for liquid, my throat raw.

"Jet, you need blood. Your body is weak, your skin pale... Well, paler than usual. I saw what he did to you, that vampire, I know what those collars do. Drink my blood." He shoved his arm toward me.

I snapped my eyes to his. "Someone tried to kill me. Opened my throat from here to here." I motioned where the knife had cut me, my skin still tender. "How do I know it wasn't you?"

He pulled his arm back, his eyes just as fierce as mine felt. "I was in front of you, moron."

I blinked. Oh yeah. I'd already remembered that, too. That he was in front of me. I knew that.

Jason held my stare. "I saw a wolf moving between the trees. It seemed like he was trying to catch my attention so I moved forward to intercept and then all fucking hell broke loose. I'm not totally sure, because I didn't see it with my own eyes, but Steph was right behind you."

"It was Steph," Amber said over her shoulder. She'd moved to the center of the clearing without me noticing and had started a small fire. "She's the one who cut you."

"Why the fuck—"

"She thinks she knows the spell to unlock the amulet," Jason said. "I gave her some Latin so that she thought she was in the loop. Keep her off my back. Never trusted that woman."

"Good plan," I drawled.

"I didn't expect her to do something so damn stupid." Jason

rubbed his hand over his face. "Doug told us she trapped him in the city. Somehow got him to fall down a deep crater. Took everything Bill had to get his brother out of there before the vampires got to them."

"I knew she was up to something," I grumbled.

"Her lover, the vampire, he was there with her," Amber said. "You were right about that. He'd been tracking us with some other vampires." She shrugged as everyone looked at her. "I used a spell to camouflage into a tree when everyone else scrambled. The vampires were after you, Jet, but somehow Steph's sire managed to keep himself from falling into your blood's thrall. Once it was clear, Steph and her sire moved off together with the netting bags so I followed them."

The wolf was sitting by his brother, the beast, his muzzle resting on his paws as he seemed to listen to Amber's story.

"They figured they had enough power between the two of them to take Kali out and use the amulet. Everyone knows those things have a limited capacity for transporting bodies," Amber continued.

Yeah, very limited. I kept my face neutral. "So what happened? Did they find Kali?"

"Oh yeah, they found her all right...or more like she found them." Amber winced. "They lasted longer than I thought they would. Kali's wearing the amulet, but she's got it wrapped in some kind of spell so it isn't touching her skin. I know how those things work—so does she, it seems. It's a summoning stone... It can pull anyone in contact with it to the owner as long as the correct spell is being used and the target is touching it in some way. Kali's amulet glows for her so it's easy to see laying against her skin."

Yeah, I knew that—it's how I'd found her in the first place. "So they saw she was wearing the amulet and then what?" I asked.

"Steph and her vampire managed to get a few nets onto Kali. It weakened her enough for them to get close. Steph tried to use the spell, but since she didn't have the right one..." Amber shrugged.

"She had it coming," Jason grunted. "Betrayers always get what they deserve."

I felt his words like a slap. I knew he was directing them at me. I reached out and grabbed his arm, biting down before he could stop me. The second his blood hit my mouth, I moaned. Yes, I needed it. Fuck, I needed it. He didn't resist, just closed his eyes while I sucked and licked and pulled his blood into my mouth, each swallow revitalizing me. Giving me energy. Power. Zinging through me like a gallon of caffeine. Even if I couldn't trust these assholes, at least I could take what they had to offer.

By the time I finished, I felt like I could climb a tree right to the top without breaking a sweat.

"So Steph is dead?" I asked as I wiped my mouth with the back of my arm.

"Quite." Amber nodded.

"And the other witches? Kurt and Fiona?"

"I didn't see where they went. Everyone scattered once your blood was flowing. There were at least a dozen vampires that seemed to come out of nowhere."

I nodded. I'd run too. Dropped all of my weapons and run. What I remembered was chaos, my fingers gripping my throat, trying to close the wound, while I maneuvered through the trees. The witches could be dead or they could be up to their own plan.

"And Kali is bound?"

"Somewhat," Amber said. "The netting was only partially covering her. She was weakened, that's for sure, but not stuck in place or anything. I followed her for a bit, watching as she moved slowly through the forest. I know where her lair is."

"So why didn't you try to open the portal?"

"I didn't know the spell. And when I found Jason, he was set on rescuing you."

I refused to look at him. His eyes would remind me that I

owed him. Over and over again, I owed him. What was with this loyalty? This devotion?

"We all wanted to rescue you," Jason corrected.

Amber lowered her head a bit.

So I knew she'd voiced an opinion otherwise. Fair enough. I would have done the same. Like she said, there was limited capacity for the portal to carry people. The fewer in the group that needed rescuing, the better. She would have left me behind, just as I would leave her behind when the time came.

Heartless right? After all that they'd done to save me? But life wasn't fair, I'd seen that firsthand today. There was nothing I could do about Julian's betrayal. As much as I wanted to go back and storm his stronghold, challenge him to a fight, I knew I would never win. He was a full vampire now, so I needed a better plan if I was going to go after him.

But first, I had to get the hell off the island.

"I tracked you to the beach. Got there just in time to see you being collared and taken." Jason motioned behind him. "I knew I didn't stand a chance against that gang of vampires."

Not a gang, a clan, with Julian in the lead. I forced down a lump in my throat and pushed back on the lingering pain those thoughts caused.

"They're Dhampir," I said, noting the look of surprise on everyone's faces...well, except for the wolf who didn't really have the capacity for surprise on his face. "So they'll be able to follow us during the day. I was collared to be bonded and, I doubt they'll let me live without following through. So I appreciate the breakout. Not too interested in that kind of eternity." I pushed myself up from the tree, brushing my pants in a stupid attempt to get them dirt free. "We're going to need to get moving soon. Stay ahead of the vampires."

They'd be coming for me for sure. Julian would never let me go now that he had me here. His possessive nature had hooked me when we were younger. Now I saw it for what it was. Not romantic. Controlling. The kind of guy that would collar you for death and then eternal life without your consent.

"They won't be able to find us for a while," Amber said, her tone smug. "I worked a spell before you got here. The fog is like pea soup down there and it's sticky too... It'll freak them out."

She smiled in a way that was kind of creepy.

"Buys us time." I nodded. "I need to think."

Nobody said anything as I walked to the other side of the clearing. I could smell fresh water and hear the faint sound of a waterfall. Time to soak the dirt off of me.

"We need to do something about food. Amber needs some fresh meat," Jason said as I continued to walk away.

"If you catch something, I'll cook it." Amber hadn't looked up from her fire stoking as I walked past her.

"I'm going to go get cleaned up." I looked over my shoulder to make eye contact with Jason. "I do not want company."

❧ 18 ❧

HE DIDN'T FOLLOW ME. AND THAT WAS FINE. IT'S WHAT I wanted. Let him go hunt for food for the witch. I needed quiet time with some fresh water and my thoughts. My dark and deadly thoughts.

The waterfall turned out to be small, maybe three feet high falling into more of a babbling brook than a pond, but it was good enough for me and deep enough for a soak. I unzipped my suit and peeled it off my grimy skin. Sweat, blood and dirt had all worked its way down my suit. I loathed the idea of putting it back on, but it's not like I had a choice. Hopefully I'd be back home in a few hours. For now, though, I'd do my best to scrub the worst of it off, knowing that, no matter what, I'd still smell like beast and dirt..

I thought about Julian's mansion and the likelihood of a wardrobe full of snug, expensive clothes waiting for me there. He'd been planning for my arrival. He would have had every comfort available. He would have created a world to cater to my needs. To keep me there, satiated and content while he planned his war against my father. If I had been the Bridget he'd last seen —the young, naive, desperately in love woman he'd left behind—

then that would have worked. But I wasn't that woman anymore. I'd hardened. Grown calloused. Become a killer with no regret. If he'd been watching me all this time, he'd know that. There was no taming the wild beast I'd become. It'd been foolish of him to think he could. Even if he'd managed to turn me to full vampire, I would never have abided his rule.

"Fuck, Julian," I whispered, wrapping my arms around myself to ward off a shiver. My traitorous heart ached, my thoughts painful, like knives sliding in deep. I'd loved him so much. All of me had been wrapped up into him. I'd been blind to his faults. Part of me mourned that kind of innocence. How much simpler life had been. Grief could turn to anger, that was an easy switch to flip. And I *was* angry. How dare he manipulate me into thinking he was dead? How dare he act as though he was doing it all for me? How dare he think that he had blanket consent for a promise I'd made over a decade ago? I was furious with him.

But my heart felt like it was shredding all over again. I'd longed for him for all that time. I'd never truly moved past the trauma of seeing him die. Not really. And now to find out that his death had been manufactured. That it hadn't happened the way I thought it had. A true mind-fuck if I'd ever known one.

I thought I would never love like that again. And now I was here, knowing that he'd sold me a lie and forced me to live with it.

Once I was crossed, I never, ever, gave a second chance. But I couldn't bear the thought of revenge and that felt like defeat. Uncharacteristically, what I really craved was to just get the hell away. Go back home, take care of those who had betrayed me there and then move on with my life. My solitary life.

And yet, if I was being honest, a part of me ached to go back to him. To listen to him explain, to give me a reason to forgive him. When you spend so much time in mourning, it's hard to turn it off completely. Strangely there was clarity in this kind of confusing revelation. The fog of mourning lifted. The knowledge that Julian had been plotting and scheming from the very start, that he'd abused my trust and manipulated my emotions, brought with it a balm to the pain of losing him so many years before.

I had no doubt that he was capable of worse abuse, especially when he didn't get his way. His mother was a cowed woman, totally subservient to her Lord. First to her husband, who had been killed when we were young and now to her son, who had taken on that role. The great provider. Taking care of all of her needs, and mine too if I would only behave. I had no delusion about who Julian was now.

Even though I would have never imagined this, I felt total acceptance. No need for revenge. I'd spent too long dwelling, carrying the weight of grief for years. It was time to move on. I had a mission to complete. Get Kali back to the mainland.

My thoughts drifted to Jason. The strange shifter who'd vowed to watch my back and who had followed through at every opportunity so far. What was his deal? What was his plan? Why didn't he just abandon me?

The confusing feelings I had revolved around the cat and only the cat. I wanted to crack him open and figure him out. I wanted to do right by him.

I sighed and shook it off. Feelings only caused problems on a job.

I poked a toe into the small brook. "Fuuuuuuck...that's cold."

"That amulet will only take you and Kali back, won't it?" Amber slid out from the trees, her steps silent and stealthy.

I tried not to jump, scowling at her instead. "I said I didn't want company."

She didn't look at me and her cheeks were red, presumably because I was stark naked standing there. I'd always been comfortable in my skin and didn't really care who saw me. It clearly bothered Amber, though, making me wonder why the hell she'd searched me out in the first place.

She bypassed where I was standing and crouched down at the water's edge, shifting her hand under the surface for a few seconds. "There." She pulled her hand out and shook the water off. "I warmed it up for you." Still not looking at me, she sat back a little.

I softened my expression and dipped my toe in again. "Wow! You did!" The water was heated to a comfortable temperature. I didn't hesitate to walk in, moving to the deepest part which only came up to my knees. "Thanks," I said over my shoulder.

"If you use some of those flowers with some of the pebbles, you'll get the worst of the dirt off your skin." She was pointing to a patch small yellow blooms that collected on the other side of the brook.

I moved toward them and gathered up a few, bringing them to my nose for a sniff. Pleasant, sweet, like honeysuckle. I gathered a few more and then sat down, my ass resting against the coarse bed of the brook. It lapped just under my tits, tickling me in a way that ramped me up. Suddenly, the idea of fingering myself sounded way better than sitting here talking to the witch.

"You going to watch me wash myself?" I scooped up some small pebbles from the side of the water and wrapped the flowers up among them. "I'm not against a little voyeurism but I'm not going to promise I'll keep things PG in a few minutes." I needed a little pleasure for all the pain I'd just endured.

Amber cleared her throat, ignoring my teasing. "I need you to tell me, the amulet... It's a ticket for two, isn't it?" She'd crossed her arms and finally raised her gaze to meet mine.

"I don't know for sure." I shrugged while rubbing the pebbles and flowers against my skin, scrubbing the grit and blood away. My neck was still tender to touch but nothing was bleeding. "I was told how to use it. I was told it would be a limited window and not to resist the pull."

"Those amulets are usually very restricted on travellers," she said. "And that one in particular is very small. You're planning on leaving us here, aren't you? That's the only thing that makes sense."

I thought about lying but decided against. She knew what was going on—no sense in continuing the charade. "So I go through with Kali and then I send help back." It sounded lame even to me.

The look she gave me said she felt the same way. "Does Jason know?"

I shook my head. "I appreciate what you did for me. Jason keeps saving my life. I'm indebted to him. I will not leave you here. You have my word on that."

"And what happens if we die before you can get back? What if you can't send someone for us because something happens to you? The journey through the portal itself could kill you if you land the wrong way."

All valid arguments. It was a calculated risk that I was willing to take.

"I have to get Kali home and nothing will stop me from doing that."

"If you break the amulet, I could amplify the portal and get us all back," Amber said, her tone suggesting some doubt.

"Break the amulet?" I was shaking my head as I continued to scrub. "You break that amulet and I have no chance of getting back."

"Breaking the amulet will release enough power to bolster this spell I know. I can get us all back."

"Oh yeah?" I scrubbed harder, getting annoyed that this conversation was even happening. I wasn't breaking the amulet. That was for sure. "You don't sound too certain of that."

"Jet, I can do this. I can get us back. *All* of us." She nailed me with a look of utter confidence.

And for a minute, just a flash, I actually believed her. And then I looked down and saw her wringing her hands and I knew she couldn't promise me anything.

"Sure, okay, we'll figure it out once we find Kali," I lied then I lay back to soak my body, dunking my head all the way in to rinse the makeshift soap off of my skin. "Now go away. I want some peace so I can think."

I dunked my head back, letting the water swirl my hair, then pulled my head back up so I could use some of the flowers there too.

"We need to talk."

I snapped my gaze up to where Amber had been standing to find Jason there instead. He had blood on his hands.

"Caught a deer." He crouched to rinse his hands in the water, scooping up some of the pebbles to scrub away the blood.

I scanned the tree line looking for any sign of Amber, but she was gone. "You see the witch?"

"Yeah, she was mumbling something about something. Doesn't sound like she's a big fan of yours at the moment. I told her the meat was ready for prep." He reached farther into the water and tugged on my ankle. "We've got some time to ourselves."

I didn't say anything. I didn't have to. I just leaned back on my elbows, my hair soaking in the rippling water, feeling the sluice of it glide over and between my breasts, my nipples puckered and throbbing. This guy...this shifter, was exactly what I needed right now. He was a distraction, and I wanted to get lost.

"You have no self respect." I murmured with a half-smile on my lips.

"When I see a naked, hot Dhampir soaking in the water? Oh hell no, I don't."

He slipped his shirt off, kicked his boots to the side and unwrapped his generous cock from his pants. He stood there naked, giving me a good few seconds to appreciate the beauty of his body...those muscles, that sinew, flexing as he moved toward me. He crossed into the brook then sat across from me, the water reaching his waist. "Warmer than I expected."

"Witch magic," I muttered.

He grunted something, his eyes on my tits, tongue darting to lick his bottom lip. So fucking sexy. He wrapped his hands around my ankles again and tugged hard enough to pull me on top of him, gliding over his thighs, the hair there tickling my ass, and then straight onto his jutting cock.

I gasped as he filled me, his dick pulsing inside, then wrapped my arms around his shoulders, my lips against his neck. I bit him, sinking my little fangs into his flesh to draw more blood while he pumped deep inside of me. Rolling his hips slowly, rubbing my clit deliciously.

His blood ran down my throat, lighting a fire in my belly that made me moan, sparking every nerve ending as it spread throughout my body.

"I thought I'd lost you," Jason whispered against my ear. He stilled his movement, his cock buried deep.

I pulled my lips away from his throat, planning on ignoring him, his words too tender. Too intimate. He gripped the back of my head, fingers entwined in my hair, and pulled my head back to lock me in place so I had to look at him.

"There was no consent there," he said roughly. "When you were collared. You had no choice."

I shook my head.

"You knew him, that vampire, didn't you?" His words were edged with possession, like he already knew the answer.

I could feel my heart shredding, an unexpected response. Jason knew just how to touch that part of my heart that I'd walled up completely. I didn't want to talk about this with him. Or with anyone ever. I just wanted to bury it.

I rolled my hips, nudging him to keep me high on sex. To keep me distracted. He stilled my movement with another tug on my hair.

"Jet," his voice was guttural.

I sighed. "Yes, I knew him."

I rolled my hips.

He grunted.

"We'll talk later," I whispered, trying to keep the emotion out of my voice. I leaned in to kiss him but he stopped me with his firm grip in my hair.

"Later? Like when you go through that portal with Kali and leave me behind?"

A chill ran down my spine. I snapped my eyes to his. What I saw there was not pain, or hurt, or even surprise, just understanding and acceptance.

"The witch has a way to get us all back." His voice was gruff. "I know it's in your nature to think only of yourself, Jet. I know you've spent a long time alone and hurting. But things are going to change. I've got your back, and I'm sticking to it from this point on. You aren't leaving me behind."

I can't even say I wanted to get up and leave. I couldn't even say that his words made me angry, because he wasn't wrong and I liked where I was sitting. I liked the way his body made me feel, how he gave me a warm buzz that banished all of the darkness from my thoughts.

"I would have come back for you," I said, all fight gone from my voice. "I wouldn't have left you here for long. I need to get Kali back. I should have gotten her back by now."

"Who are you working for?"

But I shook my head, lowered my lips to his and kissed him. Ignoring the small protest as he tried to speak, instead taking advantage of his open mouth and plunging my tongue in to stroke his. I rolled my hips again, urging him on, to fill me up, to drive me to the peak of satisfaction and take me over the edge.

It didn't take longer than a few seconds to get his head back in the game. His hands left my hair and gripped my ass, digging in as he pushed me toward him, grinding against my clit with a rough stroke that bordered on pain. We kissed the entire time, our lips never parting, the taste of his blood flowing between us. I could get lost in this man.

My orgasm crashed like a wave against rocks, knocking me

over with its intensity. I pressed myself closer to him, holding him hard, our slippery bodies making movement fluid. I moaned as my climax went on and on, shattering the disappointment that had so far marked my day, the trauma of seeing a ghost and the obliteration of my entire understanding of the world. I was reeling from it all. Too much vulnerability. Tears burned my eyes. I pressed my face into his neck, breathing him in.

He roared as he pumped his cum into me. I felt the hot jets spurt deeply, and I finally unlatched myself from him. The high was crashing, reality looming.

"Why are you sticking with me, Jason? You knew I was planning on leaving you here, so what is this? Just sex?" I hated that it sounded like I was asking for more. I wasn't. I just didn't understand Jason's loyalty. "I'm not looking for love."

Jason chuckled, the rumble of it vibrating my chest. He pulled back to look at me again. "There's something about you I guess"—he lifted his hand to my hair, brushing some strands away from my face—"that I can't get enough of. I'm not looking for love either." His fingers tugged on my bottom lip. "But I like you, and I believe that in the end, you'll do the right thing. You're not as hard as you want everyone to believe."

I gulped, shifted my eyes away, uncomfortable with his certainty. "I wouldn't count on that."

He chuckled again. "Ah, Jet, you're a stubborn woman, but I sure do like your pussy. If I'm gonna die on this island I'd rather have another fuck before you leave me behind."

I snapped my gaze back to his, surprised by his tone, but his eyes were sparkling like this was all some great joke, and then he dipped his head low, captured my nipple and sucked me into mindless oblivion once again.

19

"HERE'S THE DEAL," I SAID AS EVERYONE, MINUS THE GIANT werewolf that was still taking a nap, ate their various chunks of witch-cooked deer. "That Dhampir who tried to claim me is someone I used to have very strong feelings for. Someone I thought was dead."

Jason glanced up at me, a question there that he didn't dare voice. He knew enough to piece it together. I held his stare for a heartbeat longer, conveying to him that this was not something I wanted to discuss further but that he was right to think it was Julian.

"As it turns out, he's alive and he's determined to make me his for eternity. So that means he's going to be coming for me."

"It also means he can withstand the sunlight," Amber said.

Doug had turned himself back to human form and was gnawing on a giant leg, grease dripping down his face. "They got a pretty big army too. Those Dhampirs, they don't die easy."

"No, they don't. You can get them down with any kind of substantial hit to the heart, neck or brain. You can decapitate them as well. But they won't die." I gulped. "To kill them, I mean *really* kill them, you have to take out the heart and burn it."

The whole group understood the gravity of what I was revealing to them. How to kill a Dhampir vampire was not common knowledge. It was a highly coveted secret, one that centuries of our species had fought to protect.

There was a full minute of silence as they absorbed the information.

"Any kind of fire?" Amber asked.

"Any kind, but magic-infused is usually the most effective and the quickest. As with most things related to my species, the heart doesn't want to die so intense flame is needed," I confirmed.

"Okay, that's good to know." And the way she looked at me said that I'd maybe earned some loyalty points. "So we're going to be under attack at some point is what you're saying and you want us to watch your back."

I wasn't sure if that was a supportive comment or not so I decided to ignore it. The witch was definitely throwing attitude my way. Long gone was the meek and compliant scaredy-cat I'd seen when we first arrived. I kinda wanted to remind her that I'd saved her life on that ship, but with the way my tally was going, it felt like I owed everyone more than they owed me.

"The vampires are scared of Kali, right? So I think we should leave now, before the sun breaks the horizon and find her. I know that everyone is going on very little sleep at this point but time is really slipping here. I'm not sure if I'm a temptation worth risking an encounter with Kali as far as the vampires are concerned, I'd like to think that I'm not that big a deal, but knowing this particular vamp like I do, I have a feeling he'll come looking for me or at least send some of his minions to. And I don't really have much of an interest in becoming a vampire concubine or a vampire at all. I also don't want to stay on this island any longer than I have to. So if you want on the train that's taking us back home, we leave now."

"Once we find Kali, we break the amulet?" Amber said.

"Tell me more about that." I watched her hands, her expression, I wanted to know for sure if this was possible, that she was truly capable...

"I'm an elemental and the amulet is a precious gem. This is my domain." Amber set her food aside, not a tremor to be seen. Her tone was all confidence. "I've been thinking about it since I saw it, since I realized what it was. A summoning stone can be harnessed in many ways."

"It's been cast upon to latch onto Kali though."

"That's why I need to break it. It's attuned to Kali, but the summoning stone, at the very core is designed for one thing."

"Opening a portal?"

"No, a power disruption." Amber shifted back on her heels. "I know a spell that will allow us all to travel to a destination but I need the power from the summoning spell to do it."

"And you think you can manage that?" Jason spoke up, leaning forward as he tossed a bone into the fire.

"To get us all home?" Amber nodded. There was no hesitation in her expression, her movements, her voice. "I know I can."

"You in or what?" Jason turned to me, his stare challenging.

So this is what I had to do, right? I sighed. Saving these people who had sacrificed in order to save me...

I nodded. Something had happened to me. My heart felt like it was beating for the first time in over a decade. The callousness I wore like armor was slipping. For all Jason's jokes about leaving him behind, I just couldn't do it. Not anymore. Not knowing that Julian was here and what he'd do if he found out that Jason and I had been intimate. Obviously my ex had some serious issues with possession. And Amber, yeah, she wouldn't last a week. Even if she was becoming more assertive, that wouldn't translate into survival. I was surprised as hell she'd made it this far. The wolves, they were just too loyal to toss aside.

I'd been living with a self-centered moral code for so long that I'd forgotten what it felt like to have a mostly solid team behind me. I didn't hate that feeling, and that's how I knew I was making the right choice.

"We'll do whatever you think necessary to get us all home." I'd eaten my fill, which wasn't much, already and nodded toward what was left of the animal and then at Amber. "Eat up. You're going to need the strength to tackle Kali."

"I know where she was ambushed but we have few weapons between us," Amber said as she tossed aside what was left of her food.

I looked around. The shifters had their own innate abilities to help—the witch had her spells. I was really the most useless one of the group. "I'm going to head back to the cavern while you are all finishing up. I'll grab what weapons were left behind and meet you—"

"Like hell!" Jason snorted, his eyes darting to mine with incredulity.

I flinched, immediately understanding the problem. "I'm not going to leave without you." *Fuckhead. I'd just made this profound decision, and he was assuming the worst of me already?*

"You aren't going to that cavern alone. Are you nuts? You've got a Dhampir hunting for you and who knows where Fiona and Kurt are. I doubt they're dead though. And I don't trust their motives in anything."

Oh. So he was worried about me. I closed my eyes briefly and sucked in a deep breath. Working with partners was challenging. Baby steps. I opened my eyes and looked at him, trying to say sorry without actually having to say sorry. He nodded, his eyes never leaving mine.

"When your throat was cut, everyone dropped what they were carrying and scrambled. I left my crossbow when I shifted, the net balls were left behind. We'll all go back to that location as a starting point and then move to Kali's lair from there." He tossed another bone into the fire then wiped his hands on the grass. "She has wards around her lair that are meant to confuse and injure," Amber said. "Super high-pitched sounds that will burst your ear drums. I know a counter spell but it will only work for a few seconds at most. If we can all breech the wards in that time though, they become null and should stop."

"Should?" Doug barked a laugh. "Sounds convincing."

"Unless we can lure her out of her lair," Amber said, her voice taking on a tone that was harder than her normal. That strange assertiveness that hadn't existed the day before was somewhat unnerving. "You have a way to convince a partially bound witch to venture outside of her safety zone?"

"We can get her out for you," Fiona slid from the shadows, a wide smile on her face.

I glanced toward Jason, wondering, just as he probably was, if she'd heard us speaking about her and Kurt.

"Good to see you're alive. We were just talking about what might have happened to you." Jason finished wiping his hands then stood, casual as ever. "Where's Kurt?"

Fiona glanced over her shoulder. "He's watching Kali's lair. Making sure she doesn't go anywhere."

"And you have a way to get her out?" I asked, noting that she had a crossbow slung on her back.

She nodded, then slipped the crossbow from her shoulder, holding it out to me. "Here, take it. I can practically feel the burn of your glare." She unlatched a bag from her other side. "I've got some net glue bottles in here and a few knives. I don't need the weapons but they were just lying around. Thought I should gather them up."

"What happened to you when the vampires came?" I walked toward her, taking the crossbow once I'd closed the distance. There was a bolt loaded already and four more attached to the frame.

"Oh, we're not stupid. When the shit hit the fan, we climbed up a tree." She was smirking as she said it. "I'm no hero."

"Brilliant, really," Jason said as he approached, his hand

outstretched to take the bag. "You have a great tactical advantage up high."

"For sure." Fiona didn't hesitate to give him what he wanted, freeing herself from carrying anything.

He opened the bag and gave a cursory inspection. "Good haul. This will help shave some time. We don't have to detour to the attack site. We can head straight to Kali's lair."

"And you have a way to get her out," Amber repeated my question, her tone full of disbelief.

"Yeah, tried it already to see if it would work." Fiona's smile was all ego. "You know who Wyatt Steel is?"

"Isn't that Kali's husband? Partner? Something?" Amber said. "Didn't he die ten years ago? She killed him, I thought. That's the story floating around anyway."

I'd heard that version too. Kali had accidentally killed the love of her life in her attempt to end the war and had exiled herself in her grief. It wasn't the only story surrounding her disappearance and it certainly wasn't the most wild, but it was the one that most people believed.

Fiona nodded as Amber spoke, her smile growing wider. "That's right and I know how to mimic his voice. It's something I can just do after I meet someone."

Lovely. So she could impersonate anyone? What other secret talents did she have? "You met Wyatt?"

Fiona nodded. "Back at the Academy. His family is a really big deal at the American Council of Witches, and he's like a golden boy of theirs. I met him when I was a kid doing a tour of the place. Picked up his voice then." She shrugged like her skill was no big deal. "I can pull Kali out of her lair by using Wyatt's voice." She flung her hands up. "The witch is already batshit crazy anyway. She thinks she's hearing voices as it is, dwelling on the past, and that voice in particular gets her moving." She pointed at Jason. "I get her out, you hit her with the net, we do what we need to do after that."

"By tormenting her?" Jason sounded like he didn't approve. Like this was a cruelty that he couldn't abide. "Don't you think that's... Oh, I don't know, awful to do to someone? Using the ghost of someone she loved? Seems gross to me."

Fiona was about to respond when I cut her off. "He's not dead," I said.

Everyone looked at me, eyes wide. Amber seemed most shocked of all, her mouth actually hanging open.

"He's not dead," I repeated. "So it's not cruel and unusual punishment."

"How do you know that for sure?" Amber asked, shaking her head like she just couldn't accept what I was saying. "I heard this story from a reliable source. Kali killed Wyatt and then went insane."

"Well, I hate to break it to you, your source is wrong." I adjusted the crossbow on my back. "Wyatt Steel was the one who gave me the amulet. He's the one who the portal leads to. He wants Kali back."

And he's quite the fucking bastard if you ask me. He was unwilling to pay anything upfront and an overall ass in general when I was dealing with him. He'd had no respect for my skills or my species and made it very clear that I was the last resort. He made such a big deal about finding her and bringing her to him that I'd decided, almost immediately, I would be selling Kali to the highest bidder. He wanted her; he was going to have to pay.

"Why does he want her back? Because he loves her?" Jason asked. "Or because he's pissed that she didn't stop the war?"

Good questions. "Don't know. The guy is a prick. He said he'd give me information on a need to know basis. Gave me the amulet and told me to fetch." While there were not a whole lot of inter-species alliances going on, especially with the witches, I'd come to expect a little bit more respect that what he'd given me. I was the best woman for the job, even if he wouldn't admit it. He had said I'd come highly recommended...but he'd said it like he was chewing on glass. "Said he'd been looking for her for the last ten years but had been called to some battle front and needed to focus his efforts there now."

"The West Wall," Fiona said. "The witches have been fighting there almost from the beginning. They've got some kind of sanctuary, somewhere in the north protecting the most magically unique witches so that Cassia can't get her hands on them. If she manages to break through their defenses there and gets those witches, there will be no stopping her and her hybrids. They'll drain those witches dry and take their powers...and some of those witches... Well, it's rumors only, but they can do some crazy shit. If they're calling Wyatt there, it must be pretty bad. Especially if he gave up searching for Kali."

"So things are dire for the witches? And Wyatt presumably wants Kali back to do what?" Jason asked.

"Help fight? Fulfill her prophecy to end the war?" I suggested. "Who knows? All I can say is that the man is a fucker."

"If we do the spell like I want to," Amber started, "it won't lead back to him at all. I can direct us wherever I want."

"Sounds good to me," I said, ignoring a hard look from Jason. Better than my plan had been. The amulet led back to Wyatt, so I was going to play dirty and use his distraction at seeing his long lost love to take him out...temporarily, so I could squirrel Kali away for a while. Get a bidding war happening and see how high it would reach. My plan, which I realize was tremendously flawed, was built on my ego...which had taken a serious hit in the last few hours. No way I'd get Kali anywhere once Wyatt had her. "Would give us a chance to assess what they want her for at least." Finding Kali was a huge boon; I could make enough money on her alone to retire from vampire killing. Or at least pursue it as a hobby more than a career. After this trip to Vampire Island, I was thinking it might be time for a long overdue vacation from all things.

"And break your contract with the man? Surly that's not how you operate," Jason said.

"I didn't have a contract with him. He threw some numbers at me when I pushed the issue. Made a vow to pay me what I deserved once I brought Kali back. If you ask me, that in itself sounds untrustworthy."

"We get her back, you sell her to the highest bidder, we all get a cut," Fiona said with a shrug.

"Like hell!" I snapped. And damn, she had me all figured out. Had to give her some credit for that.

"You need us for this to work, Jet. You're going to have to pay up one way or another," Fiona said.

True. "We'll negotiate the terms once we've successfully captured Kali. Alive. If you kill her, even by accident, we are shit out of luck."

"Vow it," Fiona pushed.

"Fine, I vow to all of you that once we get back, I will set up a bidding war so we can all profit from Kali's return. But you all will need to help me keep her safe until the deal goes through, and I don't want to hear any squawking about moral obligations."

"How much money are we talking here?" Jason asked, his arms crossed.

"Last I heard, the going rate for Kali was two hundred million and blanket immunity," Fiona said. "But that's just a rumor and we might have a bidder who'd be willing to go higher."

I cocked an eyebrow. *Now* I was intrigued.

A chorus of swearing disbelief rose up from the group.

"A witch who wants Kali?" I asked.

Fiona shrugged. "Not a witch and not someone I have direct access to, but with your reputation, I could make contact."

"How much more do you think?" Jason asked.

"Half a billion from what I've heard." Fiona tossed the number out like it was nothing.

Jason and Amber both gaped. The wolf grunted.

"So..." I scanned the group. "Are we all in or do any of you have some moral compass that needs adjusting?"

Nobody spoke. Nobody complained. Not even Jason. So I guess that old saying was true after all. Everyone, most certainly, had a price.

20

IT TOOK US THIRTY MINUTES TO HIKE TO KALI'S LAIR. THEN Fiona climbed a tree, claiming that that was the best position to lure Kali out.

The rest of us hid in the surrounding forest. Doug and Bill were both in wolf form, no harm done to Bill's head, although he had been a bit grumbly when he'd first roused from his impromptu nap. They were both prowling the perimeter, looking out for vampires.

Kali's lair was what you'd expect from a crazy witch. A cave cut into the rock face of a mountain, surrounded by dead things. Bleached out bones of various animals hung from the trees and were strewn around the premises like a dragon had been feeding. The trees next to the cave entrance looked dead, but not the normal kind of dead. Instead, they were withered and black, like they'd petrified and turned into granite or something. It didn't smell all that great either. Like sulfur was lingering on everything.

"That's her ward," Kurt said in his slow drawl. "Curses like that smell like Hell. Literally I guess." And then he chuckled at his own joke and moved off to the tree Fiona had climbed, craning his next to see her through the foliage. "Hey, babe, you about ready to get this show going?"

She didn't bother to answer him. Instead she started calling Kali, quietly at first. The sound of Wyatt's voice coming from the top of a tree actually gave me chills. Her ability to mimic was uncanny. It wasn't a perfect match—there was something off about it, like she was talking into a can. Distortion made it sound strange. It was creepy. I didn't like it.

I looked over at Jason, who was cringing as he glanced up toward Fiona. He didn't seem to like it either.

The sound of something shuffling along the cave mouth had me swiveling my gaze that way, kind of awestruck that this was actually going to work. I held up my glue bottle, ready to squeeze out what was there. Once the mixture hit air, it would expand and drift, coating whoever was in its path.

A chill touched me, like a freezing cold breath running down the back of my neck. I shivered, readjusted my grip on the bottle. The ground at the cave entrance turned frosty, a white coating that made the leaves and vines sound like they were crackling and dying. It explained the state of the trees around the cave entrance.

When Kali came into view, I was shocked all over again. I'd seen photos of her, of course. She was infamous, beautiful, young, strong. She'd looked crazy when I'd first tried to trap her, hunched over and shuffling as she moved like an old woman; nothing had changed in her appearance since then. She was so filthy, her skin looked like it was coated in soot, streaks of apparent tear tracks lined her cheeks, what was left of her clothes barely covered her. I could see the binding net that had hit her already. It wasn't much. Maybe a few strands. Certainly not enough to hobble her powers. No wonder Steph and her vampire had been obliterated when they'd tried to capture Kali earlier. *Idiots.*

The state of Kali made me angry. How could this happen to a witch who was supposed to save the world? She looked vulnerable in a way that made me uncomfortable. I shifted my eyes briefly to Jason; his influence was making me give a shit and that, too, was uncomfortable.

I turned my head back to Kali. I could also see the amulet. It was hanging from her neck, shifting in such a way that it looked like it was surrounded by some kind of invisible bubble. Definitely not touching her skin.

She was mumbling as she moved, her gaze sweeping, her fingers twitching at her sides. She had power still, a lot of it, and it was sparking there along her fingers, over her hands, pulses of blue and purple, ready to launch and strike whoever was a threat.

"You're not really here." Her shaky voice was barely more than a whisper. "I know you're not really here."

Kurt shifted around the other side of the tree, looking like he was going to try to take her from behind.

Fiona called out to Kali again, Wyatt's tin can voice muffled a little. "Kali, sweetheart, I am here."

Kali stopped walking. She stopped moving. Even her eyes stopped sweeping the area. She tilted her head, listening. I held my breath. She was steps away from the supposed wards but not close enough for me to get the net on her.

Her lips curled into a snarling smile. She raised her hand at the same time as she directed her gaze up, exactly to where Fiona was positioned. "You're not here," she growled. And then she yanked down, effectively removing Fiona from her tree.

There was a gasp, a bit of a cry, and then Fiona tumbled out. Not gracefully or gently. No time for her to land on her feet, that was for sure. She fell in a heap, her body crunching as bones broke, her leg at an impossible angle once she hit the ground. I cringed, bit my lip to keep from making a sound. Kali lifted both hands, her face twisted into rage, magic snapping along her fingertips, ready to finish Fiona off, no doubt.

Kurt came flying out of his hiding space, a ball of power circling in his hands. Kali didn't even look at him, she flung her hand to the side, just a flip of her palm, and Kurt flew back and slammed against the wall of her cave with a sickening crunch. He didn't move after that.

Fuck it. I launched my glue, forcing out a giant arc of it, hoping like hell that it would fly far enough.

The second it passed through her ward, a high-pitched scream began drilling into my ears like it was going to split my head open. Everything slowed, my eyes teared and I slid to my knees, dropping the glue bottle in a vain attempt to block the sound.

In that split second, when the glue was slowly spreading, arcing in the air and moving toward the witch, Kali locked eyes with me, her expression telling me that I was going to die. She opened her mouth, time sped up, her fingers flexed, magic sparked.

And then, thank fuck, the glue spread into the net like it was supposed to and landed on her, coating her evenly and effectively taking her out. The ward silenced.

I whooshed out a breath of relief, my body vibrating from a mixture of pain and adrenaline. I swayed on my knees, fighting to stay upright.

Kali shrieked, and batted at the stickiness that coated her. With each movement the glue got tighter, binding her so that she lost mobility with every passing second.

Her eyes bulged, fury there. The pulse of her magic ebbed to nothing. Even the trees seemed to sigh with relief. The tension that was alive in the air, dying to a whisper. It was like she was frozen in place. Her stance exactly as if she was about to launch an attack. She looked like a menacing statue but the glue did what it was supposed to do; it nulled her magic.

"Check to make sure Fiona's okay," I directed at Amber. Fiona hadn't stirred since falling from the tree, her body twisted in a way that didn't look good.

Amber pushed herself from the forest floor, blood trickling from her ears. She nodded once, her movements stiff.

I moved to Kali's side and lifted the amulet.

Because Kali's magic was bound, the amulet no longer had the protective bubble around it. I could lay it on her skin and mutter those words, then I'd be back home. One second, that's all it would take. The thought actually made my gut twist. Damn Jason and his moral conscience. It was infectious, it seemed.

"Don't," Kali whispered, her eyes on mine, a blink of sanity clearly there. She looked scared, yet defiant.

I held her gaze for a few heartbeats. Was that a one off? Was she lucid all of a sudden? Or was she trying to trick me? I glanced over at the others. Jason and Amber were tending to the fallen witches. No one was paying attention to me. The wolves were presumably too far out. I could be gone, with Kali, before anyone realized what I'd done. I'd deal with the consequences of that later.

The spell rolled through my head. *Reverted ad me. Return to me.* I opened my mouth.

"Don't take me back to him." Kali's voice was so low, I almost didn't catch the words.

I pushed the amulet, gem down, against her skin. A pulse of magic sparked. We both sucked in a breath.

"Do what you must, but don't take me back to him," Kali said, her voice bordering on pleading. "Please."

"He's your lost love. I thought you'd want to go back to him." The thought of that, lost love, made my own heart clench. "He's waiting for you on the other side of this amulet. Why wouldn't you want to go back to him?"

"I know." Her voice cracked. "Somehow, in my mind, in my heart, I knew the second I saw that stone. I had to have it. I had to take it from you. It's Wyatt's. He's used it to track me before."

"You're suddenly very coherent." I looked toward the others who were still tending to the fallen witches. They hadn't noticed my hushed conversation with Kali. I watched for a second longer, noting that Fiona and Kurt were starting to come to. No devastating damage it seemed. I looked back at Kali, that damn spell still rolling through my head.

"Jet," Amber called. I didn't have to look at her to know what she wanted.

I let the amulet slide away from Kali's chest and then yanked it so the chain snapped. I held the jewel for a few seconds, closed my eyes briefly, *so close*...and then opened my eyes and threw the amulet to Amber. "Do what you need to do."

"Wait!" Kali said, her voice strained. "I can't go back!"

"She's talking now?" Jason came over. He gave Kali a once-over. "She doesn't seem so scary powerful now that she's bound."

Kali flashed her teeth in a snarl. I took that to mean she would rip his nuts off if given the chance.

"The net freezes on contact but it'll loosen up as time passes. She'll be able to move freely soon, but her magic will be bound for a while." I'd seen it in action a few times. Pretty effective stuff that worked consistently. It froze the joints as it hardened but because of how it landed on Kali, her jaw was still working. I kind of wish it wasn't. I'd rather her stay quiet.

"Look at my wrist," Kali said, her eyes darting down.

Jason and I both looked down. Her hand was angled up, her fingers splayed, reminding me just how close I'd come to another blast of her magic. There was a deep scar just above her wrist. A white line.

"Put your finger on it," Kali said.

Neither one of us moved at first. Could we trust her? No. But her magic was a non-issue for the time being so that made her not quite as scary. With a shrug, I touched the line and immediately felt a zap, like an elastic band snapping at a rapid pace. Not painful, necessarily, but unpleasant for sure. I pulled my fingers away.

"It's a boon I owe and it's being called in. Has been for the last ten years. Drives me insane. Literally." She closed her eyes for a moment, taking a deep breath in before letting it out and opening her eyes again. "Your binding spell has dulled it a lot. Gave me my head back. My brain feels so clear right now, it's amazing. So I guess I should thank you." She bared her teeth again. "But it'd be fucking great if you hadn't taken my powers."

"We did what we had to do," I said, feeling that shitty *thump thump* of my conscience flaring to life once again. Nudging me. We'd made her vulnerable. I knew what that felt like. I gave her a once-over. She still looked insane. Dirty, smelly, matted hair, teeth looking a little on the fuzzy side. I nodded to Amber. "Do what you have to do so we can get out of here." Best way to fix all of this was to get the hell off the island.

"You can't take me back." Kali's voice rose, her eyes looking panicked once again. "I can't go back there. Not after what I did. Please." Her voice shook. She cleared her throat. "Leave me here."

"What are you running from, Kali?" Jason's tone held sympathy and compassion that I didn't want to feel.

"We don't have time for this," I hissed. "Those vampires are on their way."

"For sure they are," Kali said, her eyes on me, defiant once again. "Especially now that my wards are down."

I gulped, my gut seizing. If I had to kill Julian I would. If he forced me to. It would happen. But fuck, I just wanted off the island. At home I could think clearly. Develop a plan. Here, everything was wild and unpredictable. I needed some perspective, and I knew I could only get that if we got the hell clear of this place.

Jason looked over at Fiona, who was rubbing the back of her head as she moved closer to us. "I can't echo her powers while she's bound so I can't keep the vamps away either."

"You're a replica?" Kali said with a grimace. "I thought most of you were killed off in the Burning Times."

"My ancestors knew how to blend in and hide. They got so good at it that some of them forgot they were witches. Pathetic really." Fiona's tone was harsh. "You're pretty rare too. A tracker, right?"

"A tracker?" Jason asked.

"She can detect magic signatures and trace them back to the origin. It's why Cassia wants her," Kurt said as he joined us. There was blood dripping from his nose, which he dabbed with his dirty shirt sleeve.

"She wants to drain my blood and take my powers. If she gets my powers then she'll have no trouble locating witches, especially ones with unique power signatures," Kali said.

"And what, she'd just keep collecting the witches until she's all powerful?" I asked. I only knew the very basics of Cassia the Warmonger. She was a witch vampire hybrid who had orchestrated the Dark War with the help of her vampire minions and blindly loyal hybrids. They'd used an environmental anomaly—a giant solar flare along with magic to amplify its devastating effects. In a matter of minutes, they'd knocked out most of North America's electricity grid as well as satellites around the world. The chaos spread pretty quickly, jumping overseas within hours. They'd sent the world into another dark ages and then launched a war against all supernaturals and humans who didn't bow before Cassia. She even had a full-scale hunt on for witch hunters, which at one point, Kali had been.

"She wants me, not just because of my blood or my powers, but because of revenge," Kali said.

Everyone knew that Cassia wanted Kali. The woman didn't hide that fact. There were open contracts for Kali to be captured alive and brought to Cassia. Lucrative contracts that offered immunity and lifelong protection. Under no circumstances was she to be killed though. That, presumably, was for Cassia to do.

"Why, what did you do?" I asked. I'd always wondered. Why did Cassia burn so hard for this particular witch? Sure, she had some unique magic, but there had to be others out there somewhere with Kali's brand of magic. "Is it because of the prophecy?"

Which would make sense, if it were true. Kali was meant to end the war—bad news for Cassia if it actually came to be.

"That prophecy was never what it seemed to be." Kali snorted, then snapped her eyes to me, her expression chilly. "She wants me because I killed her husband, and I started the war. The Dark War, yeah, that was all my fault."

21

WELL, THAT WAS A MIC DROP IF I'D EVER HEARD ONE.

Kali didn't wait for anyone to react. She just nailed me with a hard look and started to spill her guts.

"Wyatt and I made it back home a couple of months after the bombs started dropping. My mom believed I was destined to end the war. And she'd managed to convince all of the Witch's Council too. Even though I was the rebel witch who'd run away from home with a middle finger to the Council years before, they had welcomed me back like I was a prodigal daughter returned."

"You and destiny have a date with a hybrid," Amber croaked. "That's what the prophecy said, right? You were meant to end the war, Kali."

Kali snapped her glare Amber's way. "That's what everyone seemed to believe, yes. And for a while, they convinced me too." She snorted bitterly. "But I didn't know how I could end the war when I didn't even know how to find the woman who started it. Cassia was hiding behind walls of supernatural fighters. The only appearance she'd made was in our heads when she'd used a spell to send a message, but that had been months before. The only things we heard about her whereabouts came from scouts and rumors. She only ever ventured out when there was a reason to—namely the capture of a powerful witch she wanted to drain of power."

She turned her gaze back to me. "My mother told me I had to go back in time and stop Cassia before she became a hybrid, before she started taking blood from other witches, before she went insane."

Fiona snorted. "That's fucked up."

"That's forbidden!" Amber gasped.

"Yeah, it is. Dark magic, dangerous shit." Kali nodded. "But it was the only way to get her, and I was the only witch who could do it."

"Because you're a tracker," I said, piecing the story together. "You'd be able to find her by her signature before it became all muddled up with other magic signatures."

Kali nodded. "The Council sanctioned it. They wanted Cassia dead more than they cared about me messing around with a forbidden spell. I had no experience with time travel. I knew the spell, I could understand the principles, but the actual experience of shifting through time was foreign to me." She swallowed, her eyes moving to the left as she swept the group. "Cassia was pure evil. She'd altered the world in a way that might never be repaired. She'd murdered and destroyed. She'd hunted innocents and pulled witches into her traitorous games, asking for sacrifices that were just too great. She'd cost me loved ones and friends since the war began and yes, she deserved to die for that alone. If I stopped her before she started then I would be a hero, even though only a few people would actually know what I'd done. The alternation of history would erase everyone's memories but the witches involved with the spell. I didn't need the accolades though. It would be enough to know that I'd prevented this from happening at all. I had a death spell with her name on it. I was ready."

"So what the fuck happened then because as far as I can tell, the war didn't end." I crossed my arms as Kali's gaze swept back to me.

"I had to go back fifteen years from that date, the day we did it, to a vampire stronghold in Chicago. Before Cassia became a vampire herself. It was rumored that Cassia had fallen in love with a Strix vampire Master."

"A witch and a vampire? Yeah, right." Kurt shook his head. "Never heard of such a thing."

Because interspecies mingling was taboo. Something the Dhampirs felt strongly about—so strongly that there were cultural laws in place to discourage it.

"As the story goes," Kali continued, ignoring Kurt completely. "Cassia had been captured as a child by the vampire's predecessor and had been used for years as a witch slave. She and her vampire had fallen into forbidden romance, and as usually happens with lust and love, they'd hatched a plan to overthrow the Master of the gang. Together, they rose to lead one of the most powerful Strix gangs in the United States with her first as a witch, and then later as a hybrid. Her lover, the new vampire Master, was killed sometime during her rise, but that didn't slow her down. She maintained control over that gang until she became what she was. A warmonger. A witch hunter. A tyrant. A self-proclaimed queen. Some rumors held that she had been the one to murder her lover, having grown tired of being ruled by a man. But Drake, a soothsayer I knew, had hinted that she was the victim in this whole story. That the war was a result of her broken heart and seeking revenge. It was hard to know exactly what the truth was.

"I was going back far enough to catch her when she was still a young witch. It was possible to bind her powers at that stage but there was no guarantee that she would stay bound. Better to kill her and permanently prevent the uprising. We'd gone through all of the options. This one was the only viable one that ensured no dark war would come to pass."

"Sounds complicated," Jason said. "A million ways that could go wrong."

"It was a sound plan, and the only one that would be worth the effort." Kali sighed. "Witches are all about the complicated plans. Following Cassia's signature would take me directly to her, or at least get me in close enough proximity that I could find her easily. As soon as she was dead, I would tug on the time travelling tether that was bound to Wyatt and he would pull me back through."

"So what happened?" Amber asked. "You did it, right?"

"What went wrong? Something had to go wrong," Fiona added.

Kali lowered her gaze, her whole body shuddered. "I found Cassia, found her signature and was moving down the length of her thread when something snagged my attention. Entwined with hers all of a sudden was another signature...one that I hadn't felt in a very long time." Kali's voice cracked. She sucked in a few deep breaths before continuing. "I felt my sister. Destiny. Her signature was entwined with Cassia's."

"Wasn't your sister brutally murdered by vampires?" Amber asked, then cringed when I shot her a hard look. "I mean, that's what I'd heard."

Kali wasn't listening, she kept talking, her voice raw. "I couldn't stop myself. Even though I felt Wyatt's tug, willing me back on course, I couldn't not go to Destiny. When I landed in a time and space, when I felt the full impact of my sister's signature, I finally understood what my mother's prediction had truly meant. You have a date with Destiny, she'd said. And now, I had to wonder if my mother knew that she was sending me back to witness my sisters' deaths."

Amber gasped and lifted her hand to cover her mouth.

"Cassia was there. Younger, sure, but not the innocent girl I'd been aiming for. My detour had taken me out of the travelling spell too early. But that didn't matter. Not when I could see two of the most important people in my life, still living and breathing.

"I was in the shadows. Unseen. There were vampires, at least twenty deep, standing around Cassia and another male. My fingers moved to my blades. My sisters, Destiny and Leila were there, facing off with the vampires, and I felt like my heart was about to shred to pieces. I had no idea how long it was until Destiny and Leila would be attacked, but I had no doubt that this was the night of their deaths." Kali's words were tumbling out so fast it was almost hard to make sense of it all. "Cassia was a hybrid. Her signature was muddled somewhat, but still strong. My sisters were negotiating. I couldn't hear their words but things seemed to be amping up. It felt wrong. Maybe because I knew what was going to happen next. That's when I realized that I could change it. I could alter my sisters' destinies."

"You deviated from the plan," I said, realizing the gravity of it all. Kali was supposed to kill Cassia at a different time, when she was weaker, less prepared.

"It wasn't like I could step back into the spell and continue forward, not when my sisters were right there, about to die. You have to understand," Kali croaked. "I had a chance to keep my sisters alive. I could take out Cassia at the same time. This was what my mother meant. It had to be. But my sisters, they didn't know that Cassia was a hybrid. Such a thing would be too taboo to even consider. My sisters wouldn't have fathomed that a witch could be a vampire and retain her powers. For all they knew, as most of us had believed at the time, when a witch turned vampire, she gave up her powers. They had no idea how much danger they were in. I felt Cassia's magic rise as she called it to her, her signature pinging me. The vampires, they closed their circle. My sisters prepared for battle. They were outnumbered, no way to survive." A sob punctuated Kali's words. "I screamed at Destiny to run. I tried to kill Cassia. I watched the blade as it turned, end over end. I watched as it embedded deeply into the Master's chest. I watched as Cassia realized what I'd done. I'd murdered her mate. The fury on Cassia's face transformed her instantly, and I knew what a horrible mistake I'd made. She glared at my sisters and uttered the words that I could not undo." More sobs shuddered through her. "I killed Cassia's mate. I started the war. I murdered my sisters."

22

WELL, FUUUUUCK! DIDN'T SEE THAT ONE COMING.

Kali had fallen to the ground, the binding net having finally released her enough so she could move. She didn't seem to notice that she'd crumbled as her story had ended. She was sobbing quietly. A heart-wrenching sound that reminded me of my own losses. Life was a brutal bitch sometimes.

"Wyatt wants you back," I blurted, my voice husky with pent up emotions. "He told me to tell you that things didn't end like you thought they did and that he knows you fear the worst but that history did change."

Kali didn't seem to hear me. I looked over at Jason. He shrugged.

"Kali, listen to me." Suddenly Wyatt's message made so much more sense to me as I recalled the conversation we'd had. *When you find her, tell her that she didn't fail. Tell her that Destiny is alive.* "He told me to tell you that your sister isn't dead." At the time I had been so caught up in myself and the promise of a huge bounty that I hadn't listened properly. I'd just taken his message and shoved it aside, knowing that Kali would be coming home, to him maybe, if the price was right. "Destiny is alive."

That caught her attention finally. That caught everyone's attention. Amber, Fiona, Kurt, they all were looking at me.

Kali glared up, her face tear-streaked, her lips twisted. "You lie!"

"I'm not lying. He told me to find you and tell you those things. I didn't realize that Destiny was the name of your sister."

Kali gulped. She wiped her face with the back of her hand and then seemed to realize that she could move again. She jumped to her feet, eyes blazing, darting around like she was going to bolt. The wolves were there all of a sudden though, crowding her back in place, with the rest of the group closing ranks. She stopped moving, a wry smile on her face as she raised her hands up in defeat. "No magic still."

I shook my head, motioning for the group to move back a bit. Give her some room so that the panicked look of flight left her face.

I raised my hands as I took a step closer. "You need to go home so you can see for yourself."

Kali had gone back in time. She'd altered the future, perhaps causing the war, true, and that was shitty, but no one was perfect and everyone deserved a second chance. Even a crazy witch. I tried not to glance at Jason—there were just too many reasons to avoid his eye.

Everyone deserved a second chance. He'd said that hadn't he?

"My sister isn't dead?" The fire in her voice was slipping. "Are you sure he said that?"

"It appears that your tampering with history may have changed things for you. Big things."

Jason looked stunned by all of the information. The idea of time travel and altering history was mind-bending for sure. I knew the witches could do it—I just hadn't thought they ever would. The amount of power at their disposal was terrifying.

"I don't understand." She looked lost, her hand to her head

like she could force her brain to make sense of things. "How can that be?"

"Obviously, something you did when you went back in time altered things somehow," Jason said, sympathy in his voice.

"It doesn't make sense." Kali's voice quivered. "I saw their bodies. I burned them on a pyre." She rubbed her eyes. "At least I think I did."

"Wyatt said your sister is alive. He said that things as you remember them are flawed now." He'd been talking so fast, and I'd been so distracted. But he'd grabbed my arm at one point, insisting that I convey the one key message. *Destiny is not dead.* "So, you want to go home and see for yourself now or what?" I asked, nodding to Amber.

She had the amulet in her hands. I didn't know how she would perform the spell or what she needed to do to shatter the gem, but I figured now was a good time to get started.

A shiver of awareness was racing up and down my spine, had been for the last fifteen minutes or so. The vampires were closing in. Julian was on his way. We were running out of time.

Amber moved to a nearby rock and picked up a stone, holding it up, posed and ready to pound the gem. Okay, very basic. With her other hand she started pooling a blue glow of magic.

"Wait, what are you doing?" Kali tapped her head, squeezing her eyes shut as she took a step toward Amber. "My brain is so fuzzy. I can't tell what's real and what's not."

"Just relax, Kali. Amber will open a portal that will take us all back," I said, trying to keep the urgency out of my voice. Any second now all hell was going to break loose.

"That won't work," Kali said as she shifted her eyes to Amber. "You break that amulet and it's broken. If you want to get us back, you're going to need to unbind my magic."

"Oh fuck no," Fiona said. "You get your powers back, and you'll go nuts again."

I swayed as a jolt of vampire proximity washed over me. Jason noticed. He raised a questioning eyebrow. We were running out of time. They were too close.

"Do it, Amber, bust that thing and let's go," I said, my voice rising too high.

Everyone noticed.

Kali raised her hand like she wanted to cast. "No!" She grunted in frustration. "She knows what that will do. The blowback from breaking a magical amulet could kill us all."

"No! It won't, I promise," Amber said, her face crunched up with concentration. "I'm sure it will work, and I want to go home!"

"Don't be a fool, witch, it won't work!" Kali was near hysterical. She took another step toward Amber. "Drop that rock before you kill us all!"

I looked at Amber. Who to trust? Was Kali just trying to stall? "Amber, is that true?"

"No," Amber grunted. "This is the only way to get us all back. You have to let me do it."

But her voice quavered as she spoke, an undercurrent of uncertainty.

"Amber," I growled. "Are you sure you know what you're doing?"

"Yes!" Amber's voice rose to a frantic pitch. "I can!" She brought her arm up higher, ready to strike.

"She can't! Stop moving!" Kali yelled back. "You're not powerful enough to use the blowback!"

Jason was frowning, looking from me to Kali to Amber. One of the wolves moved toward Amber, nipping a bit at her ankle so she'd lower her arm.

"Wait, that's true," Fiona said slowly. "Now that I think about it. I've heard that too." She snapped her eyes to Amber. "What are you playing at girl?"

Amber mumbled something, flicking her hand to the side. The wolf skidded, its paws scrambling to find purchase as he tried to get back to the witch. Amber raised the stone higher, a look of mania on her face, the innocent facade crumbling. I didn't know what she was up to. I didn't know who she really was, but I did know that there was no way I was going to let her destroy that amulet. I ran for her and so did Kali, both of us after the same thing. Everything that I thought I knew, it all fell away.

At that moment, when both Kali and I reached for the amulet at the same time, the vampires burst into the clearing. Time slowed down. Chaos descended.

Kurt turned liked a whip, launching one of his bomb spells that shook the forest around us, but he didn't stand a chance—seconds later, he and Fiona were swarmed by vampires, blood spurting in a great arc. The wolves tried to go beast but the vampires were faster and the transformation made them vulnerable. Doug's head was twisted with unnatural force, the cracking sound of it detaching from his body was grotesque and final. Bill went down in a swarm of vampires, fangs ripping through his flesh, sending blood cascading over everything and everyone. I swirled my head just in time to see Jason's chest explode, something spearing him from behind, a look of horror on his face, probably mirroring mine. He reached up as if to stop the spear somehow but whoever was controlling it pulled back, yanking hard and leaving a gaping hole there.

I don't know how Jason was standing, or what was keeping him up, but his mouth was opening and closing and he was looking at me, his hands fluttering at the wound that showed the white of his ribs and the gore of his insides.

In a matter of minutes, everyone else was dead except for me, Kali and Amber.

Survival instinct must have kicked in because somehow I tore my eyes away from Jason and did what I had to do. I pulled a blade, flicked my wrist and nailed Amber in the arm. My fingers touched the amulet first. I snatched it from the rock, and then did the only thing that came into my head.

"Reverted ad me," I shouted as I latched onto Kali's arm, and we were instantly sucked into total darkness.

🜲 23 🜲

HIS COCK PULSED INSIDE OF ME, HIS LIPS SUCKING ON MY NIPPLE, *one hand holding my hip, his other cupping my breast, stroking my flesh and leaving a trail of fire. Each touch wound me up higher, his body pumping and grinding against my clit so I was moaning and writhing.*

"Jason." I grabbed his head with my hands, fingers entwined in his silky hair and pulled him up, crushing my lips to his so our teeth gnashed, our tongues entangled and we were groaning together.

I wrapped my legs around his waist, moving as he moved, arching up each time he ground into me, our bodies rocking with an urgency that I only felt with him. I couldn't seem to get enough, even though the intensity was almost more than I could take.

He crushed me, my tits flat against his chest, his chest hair abrading my nipples. I nipped his bottom lip and smiled when he gave a startled yelp.

His blood dripped into my mouth. And I thought, for a split second, that I wouldn't mind turning for this man. In this moment. I would do the vampire thing just so that I could have more time with him.

But then I remembered.

His chest exploding.

Death on his face.

My orgasm crashed through me, bittersweet waves of pleasure and heartbreaking pain. He roared along with me, coming into my body with hot jets that I could feel deep, deep inside.

As he stilled, he looked down at me, my hands on his cheeks, my eyes burning. He was satiated, his dick still pulsing, the flush on his face warm.

"I could do this forever," he said, his voice husky, a satisfied smile on his face.

"We don't have forever," I said.

"There's always forever, darlin'." He shook his head free, breaking away from my hold so that he could kiss me. Just a soft, tender kiss that made my heart clench harder.

There wasn't forever for him. I knew this.

But I didn't stop him when he pulled out, then flipped me over, nuzzling my neck as he parted my legs and slipped back inside from behind. The press of his cock against my g-spot made me moan hard. He cupped my tits, holding me hard against him as he grunted into my neck.

I rubbed my clit with one hand and reached behind me with the other, holding him, encouraging him deeper, closer.

Be part of me.

I hadn't known the big cat for long. Only a few nights when it came down to it. Not long enough to really know someone. But he'd gotten in. Past my defenses. He'd stuck with me even when I didn't want him to. He'd had my back. I didn't know him well, but I wanted to. I wanted to know him far longer than I had.

I thought I'd loved before. I'd pined for Julian for a long time. I'd missed him so much that I'd had to close my heart so that I didn't die from the intensity of it breaking over and over again. I'd thought he'd died when he hadn't. He'd been alive that entire time. Denying me relief from my heartbreak. Ignoring the possibility that I was dying, slowly dying from it. He'd done that to me.

But Jason, with him, there'd been the potential that I'd been denied.

I knew he was dead. Gone, taken from me so that I'd never know him more. My heart ached.

"I want more time," I whispered, and then another orgasm crashed, sweeping me away in the waves of pleasure, so I couldn't think. I couldn't think about anything but Jason.

24

My head was pounding. And it was dark. So dark that I thought for a minute I'd travelled back in time and was on the boat again. On my way to Vampire Island. But there were no moans of distress. No shifting of water under me. No impending feeling of doom.

I was alone. In the dark. On a bed?

I spread my arms out, feeling the crispness of clean sheets. A waft of laundry detergent making me think that I was dreaming again.

"We need your help." A voice I recognized, but couldn't place, startled me enough so I sat up. My eyes adjusting to the darkness even more. There were shadows everywhere, too many for a room with no light.

"Who are you? Where am I?" I reached for my knives but found that I was wearing track pants and a tank top. My bodysuit was gone.

"If I turn the light on will it hurt you?" another voice asked, this one female, coming from my right.

I shifted toward the sound. My movements were slow, like I

was under water. My reaction time a fraction of what it should be. "What did you give me?" I couldn't detect a foreign presence in my blood stream. No drug running through my veins. But I didn't feel right somehow.

A light turned on, stinging my eyes enough that I squinted, lifting a hand to shield my face. "Too bright!"

The light muted dramatically. "Sorry," the female voice said.

My eyes adjusted once again. I lowered my hand. Now I knew why I recognized the first voice. "Wyatt."

Wyatt was sitting in a chair on the other side of the room, close to a door. I shifted my gaze to the side where a dark haired woman stood—tall, armed, not a witch. Not completely anyway.

"You're a hybrid."

The woman stepped forward, her arms crossed. "My name is Destiny. I'm Kali's—"

"Sister." I nodded. My thoughts were fuzzy but my memory was intact. The pounding ache of my head didn't erase the fact that my heart felt broken Jason... Fuck, there was no way he'd survived that vampire attack. My thoughts drifted to my dreams. My brain so loved to torture me. "So that's how you survived."

"Kali altered history when she came back. I didn't know that until recently, of course, once I escaped."

"Escaped?"

"Kali thought I was dead. Everyone thought I was dead. And for a while I was. Or at least I wished I was," Destiny said. "When the vampires attacked, they killed Leila outright but not me." Destiny's voice cracked a little. "They kept me underfed, never let me take from a witch so I'd get my powers back."

"Obviously you have powers now." I could practically feel the buzz wafting off of the two of them. It made goosebumps rise on my skin.

"I do." Destiny nodded.

"Where's Kali? Did she survive the portal?" I shifted, my body so lethargic that all I wanted to do was lay back down. "Seriously, what the fuck did you do to me?"

"We had to keep you sedated, witch style, for a while so we could figure out what was going on," Wyatt said, still sitting like a king on his throne. He leaned forward, his uncanny violet eyes locked on me. "It'll wear off soon."

I didn't like that they'd drugged me with their magic, but I knew enough to keep my opinions to myself. I was not in a position of power here—not yet anyway.

"I'm going to need some blood." I could attempt to take it from them, but I figured I'd never get close enough, not with the shape I was in. "Preferably fresh."

A pang of pain clenched my gut—could have been effects of their witch shit but my thoughts were circling around Jason. The last person I'd taken blood from. If I focused, I could still taste him. I'd grown accustomed to his flavor. It was like he'd tainted me. Or marked me. And now I was faced with taking from someone else. Like I was betraying him and that felt like shit on so many levels.

I scoffed to myself, shaking my head at that idea. How I'd changed in the time I'd spent on V Island. Irreversibly changed.

Destiny nodded. "There's a cup next to you."

I hadn't noticed. That's how out of it I was. A steaming mug was on the night table by the light. I reached out, a little surprised by the heat of the mug itself. For a split second I wondered how in the hell that was even happening but then I remembered. Witches.

I took a tentative sip. It wasn't as spicy as Jason's but it didn't taste bad either. Better to wash him out of my system. Right? That's what my head was saying. My heart wanted me to spit that blood out.

I forced myself to drink despite the heartache. The first gulp burned all the way down to my stomach. I winced, blew on the steam, then took another tentative drink. The pain of it almost felt good.

"Kali?" I asked again between sips.

"She's recovering," Destiny said. "We've taken care of the boon that was causing her mental instability but she's still trying to sort out everything that's happened. It'll take some time but she's lucid, at least."

"What do you want from me?" They could have dumped me somewhere. These witches were powerful enough to keep me unconscious, so they were powerful enough to do what they wanted. I was under no delusion that I wasn't outmatched, at least until I got my hands on some weapons. Of all the species of supernatural, witches were the most mysterious. And I had a new policy never to fuck with mystery. Not unless you had a way to kill it.

"We need your help," Wyatt said again.

"We want you to access Cassia through your father's connections," Destiny continued, getting right down to it.

I slowly lowered the mug, my eyes wide. "You're out of your fucking minds."

"Your father has allied with Cassia. He has access to her inner sanctum. We want you to convince him to take you to her."

"No." I put the mug on the table, the blood suddenly tasting bitter, just like their hospitality. Fucking witches and their hidden agendas. "I'm a massive disappointment to my father and the last person he wants to see. I'm not the bargaining chip you need."

"No, not the bargaining chip," Destiny said. "The negotiator."

I snorted. "And what am I negotiating?"

"Your father wants to strengthen his alliance with Cassia," Wyatt said. "He's been reaching out to different factions trying to barter for things Cassia wants."

"He's an opportunist for sure, but above all, he's a calculated business man," I said. "I'm sure he has a grand plan that plays into Cassia's desires."

"What he wants more than anything is to bring her the ultimate prize." Destiny nodded toward the door.

It clicked finally. "Kali." It all made sense and I could see how they believed that they could leverage my father's quest to their advantage. "You want me to negotiate handing Kali over to him." I shook my head. "Seems simpler if I just take the bounty that Cassia is offering and bring Kali in myself, bypassing my father."

"She's had other bounties for other witches she covets," Destiny said. "When the contract comes in, she takes the bounty and turns the bounty hunter into a vampire, whether they want to turn or not. She keeps them captive until they comply with whatever she wants from them. And trust me when I say, she has ways of keeping her people obedient." A shudder went through her, subtle but definitely there. "She'll capture you too. You're too high a prize yourself for her to let you go."

"Yeah, I'd be an asset to her army," I said. I'd earned enough of a reputation that it wouldn't surprise me to find out that Cassia wanted me to join her ranks. "That sounds like something a warmonger would do. But I hate to break it to you, my father wouldn't prevent that from happening. He'd use me if it served him in Cassia's eyes. And then he'd kill me himself when my usefulness was expired."

"No, he won't. He'll keep you for himself," Wyatt said. "Like you said, he's an opportunist. Let him believe that you need his help to connect with Cassia. Let him know that you've heard what she does to hunters who bring her bounties and that you'll split the reward with him. Let him think that you'll follow his lead in this."

They clearly didn't understand the fucked-up nature of my relationship with my father.

"He'll want more than that from me," I said, stifling a shudder of my own. He'd want me on my knees begging for his forgiveness. He'd want me to pledge myself to him. If I did this, took this risk, I'd have to make him believe that I was willing to commit to him, give him not only my allegiance but also my immortality. "You're asking for too big a sacrifice."

What my father always wanted from me was my unbreakable bond. To die, drink his blood and create an everlasting commitment that only Dhampir death could put asunder. Some would liken it to incest and, in a way, it was. He wouldn't expect me to be sexual with him, but the unity would give him control over me in ways that I just wasn't willing to allow. He'd wanted it from the moment my mother had died. A replacement at his side. And he'd want it now. Everlasting servitude and obedience.

"We won't let him have you," Wyatt said. "We just need him to believe he does."

That would take some serious acting on my part. My mind shifted to ways I could do that; manipulating my father had always been an aspiration of mine. It didn't seem possible. My father was the master of manipulation. He knew all the tricks.

"And why should I trust you?" I'd been ready to betray Wyatt from the very beginning. He had to know that about me if he knew so much about my father. Probably why they'd decided to sedate me while they sorted shit out. "Why do me any favors?"

"We'll give you a boon. It's an unbreakable promise. You'll be able to call it in any time you want. If we betray you, you can activate the boon and force us to comply," Destiny said and then shrugged. "We need an in. You take Kali, get her close to Cassia, and we'll do the rest. It's time to put a stop to this war."

The witches were scary powerful. They had ways of doing things that I couldn't really fathom. A boon was a starting point, but it still felt like they were asking too much. And suddenly, I just felt so damn tired.

"So why not just go back in time like you planned before? Kill Cassia before she becomes all powerful and insane."

Wyatt shook his head. "That's not an option."

"Kali won't do it again. It's too risky. And without her, we can't track Cassia," Destiny added.

Made sense. She'd lost a lot the first time she dabbled in time travel. "So if a boon is an unbreakable promise, and Kali had one that was driving her insane, how'd you manage to undo hers? You said you dealt with the situation that was causing her to go mental, so what'd you do?" I needed time to think. Time to really sort out the likelihood that a plan involving the witches would not go against me.

Destiny looked over at Wyatt, something passing between them.

"The witch who called in the boon was under the control of your father," Wyatt said. "Drake, a soothsayer, and he had hundreds of boons on his body, had been collecting them for years before the war. Hundreds of witches at his beck and call. Your father forced him to active them, bringing witches to him in droves. They couldn't stop themselves. The fact that Kali had done so for ten years just speaks to her power. It's amazing her brain isn't mashed to nothing by now."

"So what happened to Drake?" I asked. The guy was doomed anyway if he was under my father's control.

Their silence told me what had happened. I would have done the same thing. Was probably more humane anyway.

I let the silence hang for a few more minutes. *This is nuts.* "My father, he'll kill you all. It's not just him, and his powers—he'll make you think you're attacking one another. That Destiny is a threat and you'll turn on each other, right there in battle. He'll get the better of you, distract you, and if you don't kill each other then he'll send his henchmen to do it for him. They're ruthless. They don't play by any rules. Whatever you're expecting, it won't happen."

Wyatt's smile actually gave me some confidence...as well as a shiver of fear. He raised his hand and flicked his fingers. An image appeared, seemingly straight out of my memory. My father on his knees, arms outstretched, begging me to forgive him. It was startling to see. Also impossible. I frowned, blinked hard, the image wavered. And then I felt something crawling on my arm. I looked down to see cockroaches, hundreds of them crawling out of my mug, over my hand, up my arm. I fucking hated cockroaches.

I scrambled back on the bed, dropping the mug, trying to brush the bugs from my body as their tiny legs crawled all over me, a scream trapped in my throat.

The mug didn't spill though. It stayed suspended, the liquid half in, half out.

And just like that, the bugs disappeared and the mug was back in my hand.

My heart was racing like it was going to bust out of my chest.

"Okay, I'll do it." I tried to keep my voice from shaking. Like I'd said, the witches were scary powerful, more so than my dad. "But I have some conditions."

"You wouldn't be Jet Black if you didn't," Wyatt drawled as he leaned back in his chair, a satisfied smirk on his lips.

I ignored his sarcasm. "I want to be there when the showdown happens, and I want in on all the plans. No surprises for me," I said. "And nobody kills my father." But me. "And you don't do anything like that to me again."

Wyatt gave one quick nod.

"Your father is a dangerous vampire, we realize that. We're not underestimating him," Destiny said. "We know what he can do and what the cost is for you. We know what he has done, to you, to others, and what he must pay for. Whatever revenge you seek, it's yours. We just need to get to Cassia, and we'll need to know how to kill a Dhampir just in case we have to take on his army."

That was likely to happen, and I'd be willing to share the secret to Dhampir death if it got me something more from the witches. "Does this mean an alliance? Am I a partner or a hired contract?"

Wyatt glanced at Destiny, his face full of doubt. He knew that the answer would determine how this was all going to go.

Destiny turned to me. "Allied. One of us. You brought Kali back. We are indebted to you for that alone."

I nodded, lowering my head as I sucked in a deep breath. When I looked up, I made sure I was splitting my attention between the two of them. "I'm going to need another one of those amulets."

Wyatt turned his wary gaze back to me and I smiled wickedly.

25

I HAD TO CHOOSE WHO I WANTED THE BOON FROM. I WOULD have liked to get one from each of them, but they weren't having that. So, I had to pick one of the more powerful witches to give me a boon that I already had earmarked for a future plan.

So which one would I choose? Each had their strengths.

I was sitting on the shaded side of the sunroom, enjoying the warmth, thinking. There were a lot of thoughts to mull over. My father, the plans for deceiving him, the boon, the likelihood that we would succeed in our crazy plan, and, of course, Jason. Jason was in my thoughts a lot. More than anything else. I owed him my life, a few times over. I'd been thinking about reaching out to his family. Finding them, offering alliance once this was all said and done. And perhaps that was something I would do eventually. After I'd tied up some loose ends and put some things to rest. There were some scores to settle first.

"They said I'd find you in here." Kali came through the sunroom door looking like a completely different person. Clean, fresh-faced, and although still very thin, it appeared as though she'd gotten some rest, the dark circles under her eyes nearly gone.

I tried not to act surprised at seeing her. It had only been days since we'd come back from the island, and she looked like she'd never been there at all.

"I like this room. It's bright." I took a sip of my blood-infused coffee. Destiny had everything set up at the witch headquarters to cater to her needs, as well as mine. Fresh blood was on hand at the asking and no one blinked an eye about it when I added it to my food and drink.

"The sun doesn't bother you?" Kali busied herself pouring some non-bloody coffee into a mug and fixing it up the way she liked. "More?" She turned toward me with the carafe.

I shook my head as I downed the last of my coffee. "I've had my fill. And no, the sun doesn't bother me like this. It's so muted by the glass enough that it doesn't strain my system. I'd have to go full vampire to tolerate it completely."

"And that's not something you've ever considered?" Kali said as she moved to take the seat across from me.

"I considered it a long time ago. But for my line of work, my ability to feel the vampires and lure them gives me an advantage. It's an asset more than it's a hindrance. Besides, the vamps I hunt mostly occupy the night—the sun doesn't really factor in too much when you're a night owl," I said with a shrug. "The problem with accepting the change in my culture, for me, boils down to inherent and blatant sexism. If I want to go ahead with it, I have to agree to bond with a male. While I know that that is strictly cultural, I'd be hard-pressed to find a willing female Dhampir vampire who would give me her blood. It's been so brainwashed into us that it's too taboo."

"And if you do the change without another Dhampir?" Kali asked in-between sips of her coffee.

I shrugged. "I would be weak, with no clan affiliation. That bond you get from changing is what makes our species as strong as it is. The unity gives us a collective power that ensures our dominance. I wouldn't be able to tolerate that weakness, not with my pedigree or my lifestyle as it is. As much as I despise my father, I will not shit on the long line of powerful vampires I come from. I owe that, at least, to my mother." I tapped my fingers on the table, thoughts rolling around. "But then again, no one has really tried it any other way so who knows? Maybe being blooded by another species would make me stronger."

"Maybe." Kali lowered her eyes for a few seconds, staring into her coffee. "I want to thank you for bringing me home." She raised her eyes to meet mine. "I was really suffering out there. My mind was not my own." She touched her wrist where the boon mark had been. Her skin was blemish-free now, smooth as if nothing had ever been there. "You could have just killed me outright."

"Nah, I'd never get a full bounty out of a dead body." I winked. "But you're welcome. In all honesty, I wasn't always certain I would take you back to Wyatt. I'm pretty motivated by cash, and I didn't care if this war ended or not. I mean, let's not pretend that Wyatt had me all figured out." I chuckled awkwardly. "He knew enough to sedate me when we came through. Smart guy. I'm glad it worked out the way it did but still, I wasn't always thinking with your best interests at heart."

"So what changed your mind?"

That was a million dollar question. Literally. And I'd pondered it for hours. I could say Jason, as sentimental as that was. I could lay the blame on him. His wishes. But my decision had come before his death.

"Your story. I could hear the loss in your words, your sadness. I know..." My voice cracked. "I know that kind of pain. Thinking that your sisters were dead, that you were responsible for the war." Julian had led me to believe he'd died. I'd felt the brunt of that grief for so long that it had become part of my identity.

"It's weird, ya know? I have memories of that night. Two different ones. Destiny, she tried calling me that night, the message was garbled. I couldn't understand at the time what was going on. She kept saying to go home, go home." Kali rubbed her forehead. "And then their funeral. Leila and Destiny, their bodies being on the pyre—that was my old memory. But we didn't have Destiny's body, so we burned an effigy instead. That's my new memory. I have these fractured stories in my head now. It's enough to drive anyone mad."

Silence fell over us. Was she still insane? Her eyes were clear; nothing suggested she was still that person that I'd seen on the island and yet, could you ever really turn that off completely? I believed she would forever be changed by her experiences on V Island, just as I was.

She cleared her throat. "Destiny was alive this whole time, and I didn't know. I was on that island for ten years, and I had no idea that I'd changed history enough to keep one of my sisters alive." Kali's eyes were bright with unshed tears.

"Lost time, I get it." And I did, but now I felt so differently about it mainly because I had no desire to make up all that lost time with Julian.

Kali cleared her throat. "Anyway, I just wanted to be sure you're on board for this. Truly on board, I mean. It's a huge risk for all of us but you in particular. Turning against family and all."

"I haven't been my father's daughter for a long time," I said. "And I owe him a betrayal or two. He's had it coming for a while." It was stage one of settling the score. Father was one of my top priorities.

Kali nodded, sipping at her coffee. "You decide who you want a boon from yet?"

"You're all scary powerful." I chuckled. "But yeah, I think I know who I want to owe me one."

"Who?"

"Wyatt." There were things I needed from him, and after Kali's story, I knew he'd be the one to get the job done.

Kali snickered. "Oh, he's going to love that." She reached over and patted my arm. "You ready for this?"

I sucked back my laugh and nodded. "Yeah, as ready as I'm gonna be."

"Then I guess it's time to gear up and get going."

It hadn't taken long to get my father's attention. I'd reached out to his lieutenant, Luke, but it was my father who'd called me back. These matters were dealt with by him. No one else had access to Cassia, he'd bragged. I'd spoken with him on the phone briefly. Very professional. Very cold. Everything was arranged within a matter of minutes.

"My father is expecting us at sundown."

He'd insisted right away, that very night, probably because he thought I wouldn't be prepared enough to cause him any trouble.

But as usual, my father underestimated me.

THE WITCHES HAD MILITARY-STYLE HELICOPTERS READY AND available for Council missions. They had magic that cloaked the choppers as well. Their armory was stocked full of all kinds of toys and mostly everything I wished for was delivered in some magical way. I had no regrets so far with my alliance.

Two hours later, there was a team of us dispersed between four choppers. My father's compound was in West Virginia, nestled in the mountains with only one access road leading in. The plan was to land the choppers about five miles away and then trek on foot through the dense forest. There was a passage, I knew intimately, connecting my father's property to what was left of the Clan Cross estate. We'd put the helicopters down in the expansive back garden where Julian's mother had spent a lot of her time entertaining us.

My father had never occupied the Cross property after he'd taken over the clan once Julian was dead. He'd just left it like a tombstone, decaying over the years. And it was decaying... Walls had caved in and the roof was cracked in many areas to let nature invade. All of the former Clan Cross had been absorbed into Clan Black—not as blood members, of course, but to work as minions within the clan. It as an insulting slap given their previous high-standing as privileged Dhampirs. To become enslaved was worse than death. I wondered how they'd react, all those former Cross vampires, if they found out that Julian and his mother were still alive, that they'd been tricked just as I had. Abandoned to their fates by the people who were supposed to keep them protected.

Would they feel betrayed? Angry? Just as I did. Or would they fall all over themselves with relief that maybe, just maybe, they'd be rescued?

My father was expecting us to meet his driver at the train station, one of the only somewhat reliable means of travel left in the United States. Of course there was no way we were going to come on the train. The helicopters were silent and we arrived a full two hours ahead of our scheduled meeting time.

Kali and I would be trekking alone, with the rest of the team ready to move when we moved. We were both carrying a variety of different spells in amulet form and etched on our skin. Wards, protections, markers to keep track of us and for me, a portal amulet for a quick getaway. The choppers landed, we got off, and I found us the old path I used to take when I snuck from my home to Julian's. The forest had reclaimed it for the most part, but it was still passable.

My father had access to Cassia somehow. He said she would come when he called, like she was a dog waiting for his command. I assumed that wasn't exactly how things worked with the Queen of War, but my father's version of every scenario regarding women always put them at his disposal. However the situation actually was, my father would think he had control, and perhaps that's what Cassia wanted him to think. I had no doubt she'd come for Kali if she wanted her badly enough, and I doubted she cared what my father thought of their arrangement. The world knew who was in control of things—for now, anyway.

We caught the guards by surprise when we stepped out of the forest and walked across the expansive lawn leading to my father's estate. Though he owned many, this one was home base—also where I'd spent most of my childhood. I felt nothing. No longing or grief, no desire to go up to my rooms and revisit my former space. This was business, and I had a mission.

"Mistress Bridget." A guard whom I remembered was named Anthony nodded, his gun never lowering from where he cradled it against his chest. "We were expecting you by car."

"Yes, well, I always liked to keep you on your toes." I winked and nodded behind me. "I have the prisoner, and I'd like to see my father now."

Kali was bound by metal cuffs. They looked authentic and if you tugged on them, they wouldn't give. But of course, the witches had charmed them so that Kali could break free with a snap of her wrists. My father was a shrewd and cunning man; he'd be expecting trickery; I just didn't think he understood the extent of the witch's powers. If anything his ego would blind him to his weaknesses.

"He's waiting for you in the library."

My favorite place. Chosen on purpose, to remind me of what I'd walked away from. I'd cherished that library, filled from the top of its twenty-foot ceilings to bottom with books. I'd read most of them too, having been a voracious reader from a young age and also confined to the mansion for most of my childhood. Being the daughter of one of the most renowned and powerful Dhampir Lords had made me a target to many rivals. To capture and blood me to a new clan would have been a tremendous insult to my father and a cunning power play. It was part of the reason why he had been so furious when he'd found out about me and Julian and our secret love affair. Now that I knew Julian's motives had been a confirmation of my father's worst fears, a lot of the fire I'd held toward him had burned down to a low simmer. He was still gonna get it—there were many other reasons to seek vengeance on my father—but that one was less important now.

He was standing by the fire, his back to us as we entered the room. The crackling of the flames, the smell of the books, the feel of the room, tugged at my memories. The thing I missed the most was sitting with my mom in one of the plush chairs—not talking, just sitting. Moments of peace that I'd never seemed to be able to recapture after she'd died.

"Father," I said with a tug on the chain that tethered Kali to me.

He turned, and I was taken by surprise by his appearance. Gaunt where he used to be full, cheeks sharp and defined in a way that suggested he'd been ill. His hair was heavily streaked with white, which was not a result of aging but possibly of extreme stress. Dhampir vampires didn't ail from the typical illnesses suffered by humans, but they did sometimes feel the wrath of anxiety and stress in physical ways. He could bounce back with the right amount of potent blood infusion and rest, but his startling appearance made me wonder what else was going on in his life to make him suffer. His eyes were the same. Piercing blue and homing in on me like a dart. His smile flashed gleaming fangs. He did not approach or attempt to embrace me. Surprisingly, I felt the sting of that rejection.

"Bridget, so good of you to come." His voice was smooth, the tone reserved for formal meetings. There was no warmth there, no smile that he used to have just for me. Those days were long gone.

"I have brought the witch, as promised." I rattled the chain for effect. Kali moaned quietly, like she was terrified.

"This is the infamous Kali Richards?" He walked toward us, the heels of his shoes clicking on the wood floor. "She doesn't seem as fearsome as many have suggested, but I suppose the witches have their tricks. It makes me wonder how you so effortlessly captured and subdued a woman who has been sought after for a decade."

"Father, I am very good at what I do," I said, and then wondered why my voice shook. "I found Kali on a remote island, insane with grief. I used a net to bind her powers. She can do no harm to us in her current state. She didn't come willingly at first, but I was able to convince her that surrender was a better option than death." I pulled on the chain so that Kali was forced down to her knees. "Bow before Lord Black, witch."

Father cocked an eyebrow, his smile never faltering. "Ah, yes, you do have that commanding streak in you." He moved to Kali, his hand under her chin to lift her face. "She's insane with grief, you say?"

"Yes." I steeled my voice, straightening my spine as I did. "Her sisters are dead, her mate has rejected her. She spent ten years isolated on an island just to escape the truth of what she has done."

"The Goddess has been looking for you for a long time, my dear."

The Goddess? I tried to control my expression. So now Cassia had elevated herself to deity? What Kali thought of that I could only guess, but I did feel the chain tremble slightly in my hand.

"You have wronged Goddess Cassia and must suffer the consequences of that." He wouldn't release Kali's face, his fingers pressing into her cheeks enough that I could see the tension in his forearm. Kali was playing the part well though—her eyes were tearing, her face crumpling with apparent anguish.

"So you've made contact with Cassia?" I asked.

"Indeed I have. She will arrive shortly. She doesn't travel by conventional methods." Father shifted Kali's face from side to side before finally releasing her. "This witch doesn't look like much. It's rather a disappointment." He brushed his hand on his pants like he'd sullied them with her skin. "Kali also has been charged with the murder of Cassia's mate. The Goddess will take her revenge tonight, and I will be prized as a valued member of her court."

The crowing made me want to punch something. How proud Father was when he thought he had won.

"And my bounty?"

Father cocked an eyebrow and gave me a once-over like I was garbage beneath his feet but said nothing as he turned and started to walk away.

"Father, it surprises me that you are aligning with a Strix. It isn't like you to lower yourself to grovel at the feet of the inferior race." I followed his movement with my eyes, anticipating a strike at any moment.

Father laughed like I'd just cracked the best joke but otherwise ignored the question. My attempt to rile him was just a distraction, but he wasn't rising to the bait. He thought he was the one in control of the situation. His arrogance would be his downfall.

I knew why he was aligning with Cassia. He'd align with Satan himself if it elevated his position financially or politically. Cassia was the most powerful being on the planet at the moment—you were either on her side or dead. It didn't matter that she was half Strix. Or that she was a woman. In Father's mind, I was sure, he had calculated some way to overthrow her at some point. He knew how to worm his way into most situations, gain trust before striking. Not that I really thought he had any real chance to combat the likes of Cassia, especially not in the state he was in.

He moved to the bar on the other side of the room and motioned to the bottles. "Whiskey? I seem to remember that is your beverage of choice."

"No, thank you. I don't drink while I'm working."

"Wise," Father said as he poured himself a glass. "You look good, fit. Well fed."

"Thank you." I crossed my arms. "As much as I would love to

chat with you, Father, as you know, time is money and I have places to be."

"Do you now?" Father's tone altered enough to tell me that we'd be moving at his pace and that I wasn't amusing him. He turned toward me once again, taking a seat like we had all the time in the world.

"You found her on Vampire Island, I heard," Father drawled as he took a sip of his drink. "Did you have a chance to meet the locals?"

I let the fake smile drop from my face. "You knew Julian was alive."

Father's eyebrows shot up. "You didn't?"

"You let me believe he was dead." I kept my voice steady even though his attempt to rile me was working. *You let me grieve for him. I suffered. I suffered brutally.* But I wouldn't voice those words to him. I would never give him that satisfaction.

"Character building and a good life lesson for you, my stubborn, willful child." Father waved his hand in dismissal. "I knew eventually you'd come back to me." He put down his glass and leaned forward in his seat. "Living unturned, Bridget... It's uncivilized."

"You betrayed me," I said with only a slight quaver in my voice.

"I betrayed you?" He rose slowly from his seat, his eyes flashing malice. "You, my darling girl, disgraced me. You have shamed Clan Black with your career path. Look at you, dressed like a warrior when you should be standing by my side, acting as a proper daughter should. You dishonor your mother's memory by behaving as you have. You should be strengthening our clan, not tarnishing it!" He came at me in a flash of movement.

I braced myself for contact. I couldn't match my father in strength, even in his current state. If he decided to end my life right there and then he could.

I *could* match him in cunning though.

I let Kali's chain drop just as my father gripped my neck, lifting me off my feet, his eyes blasting fury.

"You betrayed me, sweet girl, and tonight you will redeem yourself. Tonight you will take your dutiful role and submit to me." He brought me down, forcing me to my knees, still clenching my throat.

A shimmer flashed in the corner of my eye. Movement that made the air look alive.

My father turned his head, a smile forming on his lips. "Ah, perfect timing. The Goddess arrives. Just in time to see my daughter take her rightful role and submit to her Lord."

I glared up at him, my lips twisted into a sneer. "No, Father. Tonight you will submit to me." I slammed my amulet against his hand. "*Indspectus.*"

And in a flash, we fell into darkness.

❧ 26 ❧

I COULD ONLY HOPE THAT KALI HAD SHIT UNDER CONTROL back at the mansion for phase two of our plan. By now, Wyatt and his team of heavily armed witches would be swarming the property, taking the vampires by surprise.

As we landed on the other side of the portal, I had my blade in hand, moving quickly to jam it into my father's throat, slicing deeply across so that his blood flowed in an arc.

He crumpled to the concrete floor of the warehouse where I'd first been dumped, blade protruding from his flesh. "Father," I hissed as I leaned into the blade, pushing it further so that it touched his spine. "I condemn you to Vampire Island, under the control of Julian Cross. He wants you dead and as far as I'm concerned, he's a ghost as well. I give you to each other. An eternity of battle, alone, on this forsaken patch of Earth. To be forgotten."

My father's eyes went wide, pain, anguish there and gone. Movement caught the corner of my eye, and I glanced up to see the image of my mother, her arms outstretched as if to beckon me to her. She'd been a beautiful woman, taken violently while alone at our country estate. The mystery surrounding her death was one that even my father couldn't unravel. At first, I'd thought he had killed her himself but his grief had been just too apparent and deep to think that for long. My father had always been a hard man, a sexist, self-serving man, but he had loved my mother dearly. It was her death that had sent him down a dark path and had changed him forever.

Using her image now to distract me was both weak and insulting.

"Nice try, old man, but that won't work." I plunged a second knife into his chest, deep into his heart. "You're going to be alone here, Father. Alone and without allies. Kill Julian if you can—or he'll kill you—but I promise you this, neither of you will leave this island alive. The witches are in control now, and they've laid claim to this island. You made the wrong alliance."

I released him, taking a step back and then another. There was blood on my hands. It stuck to me like glue, the stench making me want to gag. I watched as he struggled to his knees. Trying to staunch the flow of his blood, to work the blade out of his chest. His mouth was open, like he was attempting to speak. But there was nothing left to say.

I'd had grand dreams of battling both men. Starting with my father, killing him before taking on Julian. But this plan was more poetically just. They could spend the rest of their lives fighting one another, trapped on this island for an eternity. The witches would make sure they never got off, that these two hateful vampires remained isolated like solitary confinement. I smiled as I stepped back, moving away from the spreading pool of my father's blood. I'd gifted them to one another. Now I was done.

I called the amulet to my hand, pulling it from its magical hiding space—a trick that Destiny had shown me. The amulet was rare and packed a powerful punch but I only had five minutes before its portal spell expired.

I watched him struggle, his grunts and groans giving me a

sense of peace. He lifted his eyes to me, his mouth open. I squeezed the amulet tight in my hand and called myself back home.

Where all hell was breaking loose.

The plan was simple. Kali was going to act as bait. As soon as Cassia made an appearance, the magical trap would be set.

In theory, it sounded fucking awesome. The reality was that Cassia wasn't a stupid woman, nor was she an unskilled witch. She'd stolen a lot of power at the expense of many unique spell casters. She was more powerful than anyone was expecting.

By the time I made it back from my little portal trip, there was a full out war raging in my father's library. Or what was left of my father's library. The back wall was gone; books and shelves, furniture strewn all over the lawn.

I ducked to avoid having my head sliced off.

Kali and the gang were battling on all sides. They'd trapped Cassia in the library with a pretty tricky spell from Kali's super grimoire. Even though I wasn't a witch, I could feel the darkness of the magic at work.

Cassia was held in place by a spell that Kali controlled. A spell that seemed to be taking all of Kali's concentration to maintain. But Cassia was no passive victim, she was battling back, attempting to push Kali's boundaries, the bubble that surrounded Kali flexing and pulsing like it could bust at any moment, sparks and flashes of magic rolling between the two.

My father's vampires, the guards who thought they had stood a chance, were fast becoming less of a problem. Wyatt and his team of witches were making sure they fell and didn't rise again. I'd given them insider information. Shared the Dhampir weaknesses so that they could effectively annihilate the horde. I felt no loyalty to those guards. Men all of them, who'd stood by while I was victimized in so many ways simply because I had been born a girl. Even though I outranked them by blood, I'd still been a toy for their mocking and pleasure over the years. They'd stood by, never coming to my defense when I'd been pinched or grabbed or demeaned. Silent bystanders who were only doing their job, and now their job would get them killed.

The rest of Father's clan, I could only assume, had high-tailed it into the panic rooms in the basement, waiting for direction from my father....which would never come. They were not fighters —not one of them brave enough to pick up a weapon and defend their clan. Father, in his lust for control had hoarded all the power to himself. Keeping the rest of the clan untrained in battle.

Cassia's minions, those guards who had accompanied her to the meeting, were engaging in a fierce battle to protect their queen, surrounding her like they could stop Kali's magic somehow. It was valiant. It was impressive, but it was also pointless. The witches had this.

I pulled two knives from my belt and launched them at the same time, taking out two of Cassia's hybrids with little trouble. They might have the combined power of vampire and witch but ultimately they were Strix, easy to drop, never to rise again. They crumbled to the floor, not quite dead but soon to be. I scoffed at how easy it was.

I pulled another couple of blades and jumped into the fray, not discriminating against witch or vampires. As long as they were on the wrong side of the fight, they met the wrong side of my blades.

I kicked, and punched, using my fists to stab, as I brought my knives into flesh, over and over, blood splattering on my face, getting in my mouth, soaking into my body. It was invigorating to blow through the enemy, taking them as they battled with others, not suspecting that I was coming from behind. This was war and in this war, there was no time for honor, Cassia had set those rules herself.

One of Cassia's horde stepped in front of me with a spark of power racing along her fingers. I ducked, dropping to a crouch so I could punch my way up her torso. My blades sank in deep with each stab, the sucking noise as I pulled them out was satisfying. Her screams as she died, more so.

I met little resistance until I reached the very vampire I'd been looking for. Father's second in command, Luke. To him I owed a special kind of vengeance. He'd been the one to hold me back, his arms like vises over my body, keeping me from putting a stop to Julian's murder. He had to have known it was all a ruse. He'd laughed as I kicked and punched, his hot breath on my neck as he licked my flesh and cooed in my ear about how he'd like to test me out. Telling me that I was a whore who'd sullied herself with the enemy. It was vile in all ways but especially so because I thought my heart was breaking for real. I thought I'd lost the one reason I had to live.

He was my father's most trusted henchman. He'd brutally beaten me to teach me to obey.

I sank my blade into his biceps, then ducked as he turned to face me, striking his fist out like a flash. It would have connected with my head if I'd been standing. He was a brute and a fighter; I'd felt the pain of his meaty fists pounding my flesh time and time again but even so, he wasn't that smart.

I swept my leg around, intent on sending the giant vampire to the ground but he jumped at the last minute, roaring as he tried to grab me. His eyes were fierce with bloodlust, his fangs distended.

"You!" he roared. "Betrayer! You will die tonight!"

"The clan is without a leader, Luke. Whatever will you do?" I jumped away from his hands.

"Where is your father, betrayer?" His spit his words as he stalked toward me, moving us out of the library and away from the melee. "I knew this meeting was a set-up. I warned your father not to trust you. What have you done with him?"

"I've removed him from this place." I smirked. "Taken him where he can do no more harm to me or anyone else."

"Your father only ever did what was good for you," he roared.

"My father only ever did what was good for himself," I countered.

He took another swipe, but as I was ducking, he came barreling toward me like a fucking freight-train on steroids. I dove, rolled, skidding to a halt on his other side. But he was there, surprisingly fast for such a huge guy. He gripped my throat, one large hand encircling my neck completely.

I gasped out my last breath, my muscles straining as he lifted me to my tiptoes.

"You are a disgrace, you vile whore," he spat as he squeezed his fist harder.

My eyes watered, my lungs screamed. He kept me just barely on my toes, his putrid breath washing over my face. I latched onto his arm with my nails, scratching deeply as I lifted my legs, pulling all of the strength I had to my core and wedged my boots, with their steel-tipped blades into his gut.

He screamed, I pushed backward, digging deeply and twisting when he finally let me go.

I landed on the marble floor with a hard thud, my bones jarring painfully. Luke held his stomach like he was trying to keep everything from falling out.

I pushed myself back then launched the two perfectly proportioned pentagram throwing blades the witches had given me. A flick of each wrist and the twins went flying. The magic they contained swiped left and right, and took Luke's head clean off. He didn't even register what had happened. Just stared at me with confusion for half a second and then tumbled to the ground in a heap, his head falling a millisecond after his body.

I moved to his side and saddled his large torso. My throat hurt like hell and I was panting to catch my breath but the job wasn't done, not yet. With a heavy grunt of exertion, I stabbed my blade into his chest, pulling down with all of the strength to open him up. His heart beat frantically as if it knew its end was near. I wiped my forehead with the back of my arm and felt the slickness of blood smear into my hair.

Time to end this. I leaned forward and reached into his chest. His heart was hot in my hand, the beat strong. If I left him like this, he would mend, his head would find a way to reattach—someone would help him eventually. I pulled his heart out with a hard tug, using my blade to slice through the arteries. Even without its blood supply, Luke's heart was still beating and would continue to until I burned it.

"Toss it here, I'll take care of it," Destiny shouted from across the foyer.

I glanced over my shoulder to see her covered in blood and waiting for me. I tossed the heart, in a high arc toward her but before it could descend, she lifted her hand and she blasted it with a blue streak of power. Witch fire turned the heart instantly to ash so by the time it started to fall, all that was left were flakes.

"You okay?" she asked.

I nodded.

She nodded back, then dove right into the battle once again.

I'd done what I needed to do. I could walk out the door and leave the witches to the fight. There was nothing more for me there. I had other people to see, more revenge to dole.

And yet I hesitated.

Something prickled against my skin. A bad feeling that had nothing to do with Kali's dark magic. I turned toward the library, watching as the two groups fought. The vampires were falling. Even Cassia's entourage was dwindling.

But Cassia, held aloft by Kali's spell, was laughing. Laughing her fucking ass off.

Did nobody notice? Was nobody watching her? A current of something shimmered in the air around her hands. Power that was invisible. Well, almost invisible. It rippled like a mirage and it was clear Kali couldn't see it—she was too focused on maintaining her spell. Cassia was back-building her power; it felt like a current vibrating just below the surface of magic, so dark that even I could sense it.

I shuddered. This was so not good.

I could walk away. I could leave them to their doom. After all, if the war raged on, I still got paid. There would always be contracts.

I shifted my gaze to the witches.

Wyatt, Kali, Destiny fought, spell after spell, such power, they were all such noble creatures who wanted to save the world, and they didn't see how close they were to danger.

But I did.

I stood up from beside Luke's body but not before picking up the twin pentagrams, my fingers touching the blood-slicked edges. Still sharp as fuck. I moved closer. Watching as Cassia started to lift her hands, raising her power. It was a lot. I could tell. Too much for Kali. Cassia's head was tilted back, her laughter like a cackle.

I moved closer. Still fingering the blades. Was I good enough to get her? To break through that magic she was welding and put an end to the Queen once and for all?

No.

But I had a weapon she couldn't ignore. I lifted the blades to my throat and swiped left and right, opening my veins to let my blood flow freely.

I was, after all, Dhampir.

The smell of my blood hit Cassia just as she was about to launch her magic, a spell sizzling along her fingertips. She whipped her head around, her eyes wide, full of bloodlust, for me, for my Dhampir nectar. It was enough to crack her focus. Enough to give Kali the advantage.

Kali didn't break her concentration; she didn't look to see what I was doing. Instead, she pushed hard, sparks of bright blue magic flew like lightning from her fingertips. As she bellowed her own rage, Cassia's head exploded into white-hot flames.

How do you kill a witch-vampire hybrid queen? You burn her to ash where she stands.

Cassia died within seconds.

Kali saved us all.

Maybe, with a little bit of help from me, she did fulfill the prophecy.

27

ENFORCER. FOR THE WITCHES. THAT'S WHAT I'D BECOME.

It was an alliance that I didn't hate. Although it did mean that I wasn't getting much killing action in my new line of work.

I wasn't getting much of any action really.

I'd become a kind of refugee. Staying at the witches' head-quarters, getting to know them as people. Kali and Wyatt spent a lot of time alone together, understandably. Destiny and I had become friends of sorts. We went out together, hunting wayward troublemakers, shutting down any bids to claim the role of warmonger now that Cassia was gone. Cassia's death hadn't halted the war completely, but it had slowed things down a lot. The fire was gone. Now things were smoldering.

Destiny came with me to hunt the smuggler who'd betrayed me. The man who I'd paid to send me to Vampire Island. He was surprised to see me alive. With Destiny's help, I sent him for an all inclusive, permanent stay on V Island. See how he liked the hot climate and hordes of pissed off vampires. In his desperation to save himself, he'd admitted that Julian had paid him well to betray my trust. He even showed me where his safe was. And yes,

I took the cash, I'm not an idiot. It made my smile all the brighter after I'd told the fucker that he'd be seeing a lot of Julian where he was going.

Destiny's time sensitive portals were handy trick of magic. I zipped the smuggler over to V Island and was back within minutes.

After that, it was just a matter of settling in with the witches. They'd always been powerful beings but since the Burning Times —where humans had successfully hunted and killed their kind— they'd gone underground as much as possible, honing skills and building defenses. While they hadn't been prepared for the Dark War, it hadn't taken them long to rally and rebuild. Now that Cassia was gone, the witches dominated the leadership race.

The American Witch Council had reached out to the humans again in an attempt to bridge the divide. This time the humans were listening and the witches seemed to be the best spokespeople for the cause. They looked like humans and had been blending and intermingling better than any other species for centuries, and the humans owed them one. Unofficially, the supernaturals interested in peace were backing them as well, although no formal agreements or alliances had been made...yet.

I'd checked in with Clan Black since I'd removed my father from their immediate presence. I knew he wasn't dead. Somehow he was surviving on Vampire Island, and the clan could still feel him buzzing through their awareness. The distance was too great for him to make much of the connection. One of my male cousins had claimed the interim role as leader. It was tenuous at best.

The witches had taken over management of prisons like Vampire Island. The humans had done a poor job maintaining control anyway and there was too much corruption and too much opportunity for exploitation. The witches had done something to reinforce the security, something magical to ensure the inmates remained trapped. Despite the appearance of things on Vampire

Island, all of the prisoners were there for a reason. No more female humans would be sent there as prey. The vampires on the island were stuck with shipments of manufactured blood. Nutritionally sound but bland and without any magical kick. True torture if you asked me.

Destiny had done some research about the witches who'd been on the island with me. All of them had committed horrendous crimes. Crimes against other witches.

Kurt and Fiona were what Destiny called mimickers. They didn't necessarily have powers of their own but could echo the natural magic around them. It took time for them to build their reserves and to absorb enough power to fuel their spells. It explained why they seemed to go dormant with the magic usage here and there. They'd saved it for when they really needed it, because they couldn't generate it on their own. They'd been scavenging vulnerable outposts when they were caught. Stealing, burning, pillaging from humans who had very little defense against their brand of violence. They seemed to like the chaos and had left a trail of destruction, taking advantage of do-gooders. To be honest, that wasn't all that surprising to me. Kurt and Fiona had felt *off*, like they were riding an edge of violence that could turn them at any moment.

Amber had been swept up into a cult that was using ritual sacrifice to attain higher levels of power. Destiny said it was a fucked up way to harness dark energy, though effective and quick. She wasn't a key player in the cult, but had been trying hard to be. She'd already killed five babies by the time she was caught by a hunter, sacrificing them in a quest for more power and recognition. The hunter who'd caught her felt that she needed more a severe form of punishment and had sent her to V Island to die. It was a hard image for me to reconcile. Amber and been meek and soft for most of the time I'd known her. She was a powerful elemental, and she'd gotten caught on a dark path.

It was sad, sure, and I hadn't known her for long, but it was important for me to understand what they'd all been about. The saddest, of course, were the wolves. They hadn't belonged in prison. Destiny had somehow managed to track down their pack so I could tell them what I knew. Doug and Bill had died on the island. Their alpha was actually their grandfather. He was gnarled and wrinkly, his face holding deep scars that spoke of a tough life. He'd taken the news quietly, his fierce expression softening. I'd told him about their sacrifice and how they'd saved my life. I'd told him that if I could have saved them I would have, and I'd meant it.

I thought about Jason a lot. He'd died without purpose. There was nothing to be gained from his passing. He'd saved my life, and I'd watched him die. And that was not something I was okay with.

Working with the witches gave me access to their magic. I saw firsthand what they were capable of achieving, how much power they actually had. I didn't want to live my life without Jason and somehow, maybe because I was living with the most powerful creatures on the planet, I felt positive that I wouldn't have to.

But first I had to make sure I was the strongest possible version of myself.

"You ready to do this?" Destiny was sitting next to me, a sister I never knew I needed. Strong, determined, willing to sacrifice an element of her life for me.

Why? I can't say for sure. Maybe it was because I'd brought her sister home. Maybe it was because she was just a good fucking person, selfless like you hear people can be. Whatever the case, I'd asked for a favor. Not a boon, a big favor. She had no obligation to give it to me. But she'd said yes.

And so, this night I would die. But I would not die alone. I would bleed myself out, using, ironically, the same method that Julian had chosen—a spiked collar, because really, it was the most effective. I would drain my blood and die and I would trust that Destiny would be there with a vein for me to drink. Taking her hybrid blood without knowing exactly what it would do was a risk, sure, but it was a risk I was willing to take. Strix and Dhampir didn't ever mix. As far as I knew, being blooded by a Strix had never, in the history of my species, been done before. But I always liked trying new things. And really, what was the worst that could happen? I'd die for real? Would that be such a loss?

"I'm ready," I croaked against the collar. The feel of my blood dripping was a strange kind of soothing, if only because this time I was in control. "I'll be dead by morning. And I'll need at least two pints from you to kick-start my heart. And then after that, you can give me the bagged stuff. It won't matter as long as I'm being fed."

Destiny was powerful. Her witch powers could enhance my transformation. I had no idea what to expect or how my DNA would interact with what her blood gave me. I was forging new territory, risking my life to see what would happen. Sounded brave, right? For the first time in my life, everything I was doing was not motivated by selfish needs or wants, rather by my desire to save Jason somehow and bring him back to life.

"There's no undoing this, right? You take my blood; if I bring you back, we're bonded, right?"

"I'll be like an honorary witch." I winked, wincing around the pain from the deep gouges in my throat. "I'd owe you my life and I'd be bound to you for eternity. I'll feel you; you'll feel me. You sure you can handle that? I can be a pain in the ass."

Destiny laughed, her smile warm, no doubt in her eyes. "You've got a reputation, Jet, I'll give you that, but if this gives you freedom and independence from the patriarchy of your world, then I do it gladly. Enthusiastically. Whatever you need."

I smiled back, or tried to anyway. Every move I made, however subtle, pulled at the slices in my throat. An unexpected wash of warmth ran through me, despite all the blood that was draining from my body. "Thank you."

I'd changed. Somehow, through this whole ordeal, I'd become a different person. I was ready to embrace that change in a physical way as well. Time to amplify my strength and step into my vampire heritage, just on my own terms.

"We've got this." Destiny took my hand, and settled in to wait with me as I slowly bled to death.

🎐 28 🎐

WYATT WASN'T HAPPY ABOUT MY BOON REQUEST BUT HE HAD to do it because, as soon as he started to protest, I activated it. That sealed the deal.

He hadn't stopped grumbling since. He'd even attempted to ignore the pulse of the boon mark, but that had only lasted two days. Two days of complaining about my request, trying to talk me out of it, demanding that I rephrase so that he wouldn't have to follow through the way I wanted him to. It wasn't just that I wanted him to do something he didn't want to do—I wanted him to do something that was dangerous...for me...and for some reason that bothered him.

On the night of the second day, he found me sitting with Destiny, talking for the hundredth time about how to make it work, with or without Wyatt. He was a strong witch, sure, but we could do it without him. Probably. And Destiny was willing, if it meant giving me what I wanted.

"Don't be foolish. Destiny can't do it alone." Wyatt's eerie violet eyes flashed hot when he was pissed off. He nailed me with a hard look. "Your boon isn't just impacting me."

"I know." I was itching for action. My whirring thoughts

became less and less tolerable each day that slipped by. I had a plan. Wyatt knew my plan. It was doable, according to him. "You remember when you found me and demanded I help you locate Kali?"

Wyatt crossed his arms.

"You said that I had to do it, that if I didn't find her, I'd be condemning you to lifelong pain. At the time I didn't care. Not about you, not about Kali." I softened my expression. "But I didn't understand what it all meant. Now I do. Wyatt, if you don't do this for me, you'll be condemning me in the same way."

"It's too risky. It's a spell for one person. One single person goes in, one person comes out. There's a good chance that you'll go in and not come back out."

"Not the way we have it planned," Destiny said quietly.

Wyatt scowled at her.

I crossed my arms and leaned back in my chair. "You know you have my loyalty and unending servitude. I'll owe you for this, and you've got me for an eternity." Thanks to Destiny. "It'll work. I know it will. I'm asking you to help me."

The transformation to vampire had gone as well as could be expected, with some unplanned bonuses. I'd lost my Dhampiric senses, sure, but I'd gained so much more. Speed, strength, a few tricks from Destiny's hybrid blood that I was still discovering, like the ability to perceive magic boundaries. When a spell was cast or magic was floating around, I could tell how powerful it was, where it started and stopped, where it was weakest. Destiny thought, perhaps with some training, I could even wield some spells of my own without the aid of amulets or etching. Future planning that would have to wait until later.

"The Council won't approve," Wyatt said but his tone didn't hold conviction.

"When has that ever stopped you?" Kali slipped her hand into his as she moved into the room, a smirk on her lips. "I'll help."

That took me by surprise. "You will?"

Kali nodded. "I'm not going in, no way, but I'll help bolster the spell."

"So will I," Destiny offered. "Between the three of us, we can manage. It's a small coven but it'll do."

"You witches have been working this out behind my back, haven't you?" Wyatt growled. "Plotting this little rescue mission like there isn't a fuckload of danger attached. Have you given any thought to the magic load it will demand? Three witches aren't nearly enough."

"Five," a voice said from the door.

We all turned to look.

"Ally," Kali said, not sounding surprised at all.

Wyatt's eyes were wide. "You called her?"

Ally, once upon a time, had been Wyatt's wife. I didn't know the whole story, only that Ally was one of the reasons why Kali had left home in the first place, all those years ago, before the Dark War was even a possibility. After her sisters had died and Wyatt had left her for Ally, Kali had run. She'd run so hard and so far that she'd lost touch with what made her a witch and maybe with what truly made her who she was as well.

Kali nodded, detaching herself so she could go to the other woman who was at least eight months pregnant, by the looks of the bulge of her belly.

"Grant and I are in," Ally said as she wrapped Kali in a warm looking embrace, whispering something that only Kali could hear.

When they pulled away, Kali nodded, her eyes sparkling with tears. "What's this, number four?" She touched Ally's stomach.

Ally beamed and patted her belly, taking Kali's hand and pushing it to one side. "Five actually. And he's a fierce one. Kicking my guts out." She winced at the same time that Kali's eyes grew wide.

"Holy shit, yeah he is!"

The man behind Ally had his hand on her shoulder, looking just as proud. "It's good to see you again, Kali."

In the time that I'd been a part of the witch's world, I'd learned that a marriage bond between two witches was meant to be forever. The magic that united them could not be broken and it was through that bond that witches were able to conceive a child. In the time that Kali had been on Vampire Island, Ally and Wyatt had found some way to break the marriage bond so that she could go on to be with the true love of her life, Grant, leaving Kali and Wyatt to finally have their forever after.

Kali glanced over at Wyatt, whose expression softened. He beamed back at her and I swear my heart melted a little bit more. How funny that I'd developed these feelings for someone I'd been hunting only months earlier. It seemed totally odd that my life had changed so much that my perception had flipped completely.

"You can't risk the baby," Wyatt said as he started to pace again, his tone not as hot as it had been. "This is asking too much." But the look he gave me wasn't as hard as it had been either.

"Wyatt." Kali frowned as she approached, her hands up to halt him. "Jet brought me home. You can't put a price on that. We owe her this and you know we can do it. With all of us working the spell, no one is at risk." She leaned up and kissed him, soothing the beast of his anger.

"Well, I for one want to get this party started." Ally waddled into the room. "Let's do it!"

"Here?" I was expecting some kind of special room—the catacombs or a pentagram at least. "Don't you need some kind of magic conduit or ancient room or something?"

"Yeah, sure, if this was sanctioned, but we want to keep the Council out of this," Destiny said as she touched my arm. "There's so much free floating magic around these days thanks to the war that we can create our own magic circle right here. You can feel it right?"

I nodded, noticing for the first time that there was quite a bit of magic on the air. I'd gotten so used to it that I barely perceived it.

"No worries. We've got this." Destiny slipped an amulet into my hand with a nod.

"As usual I'm the last to know all the plans," Wyatt grumbled but he didn't say no.

"We knew you'd just need a bit of nudging." Kali smiled as she entwined her hand in his and tugged him toward the rest of us. "Wyatt and Ally will anchor the spell—they're the most experienced and will build the foundation." Kali motioned to Grant and herself. "Destiny will get you there and pull you back. Your bond with her will make that easier."

"Less than a minute," Wyatt said. "That's how much time she can have."

Kali winced, expecting an argument no doubt.

"That's all I need," I said. If the plan were going to work, it wouldn't take longer than a few seconds. I'd been practicing the gifts I'd inherited from my father, stretching the limits of my powers. "You know place and time, right?"

Wyatt nodded. "You don't have to worry about that. I'll get you there."

"And I'll get you back," Destiny said with another reassuring hand squeeze.

"Okay, then I'm ready, let's do this." I nodded.

Thanks to my father's DNA, I'd been gifted with the skill of visual manipulation upon turning. I'd need some way to switch the scene around. To make people see what I wanted them to see. Past me had to believe that when Jason's chest exploded, he was as good as dead. Past me had to leave that island with Kali just as I had. Everything that had happened had to be left perfectly intact for my plan to work.

With everything I'd learned from the witches so far, that was the most important lesson of all. History could really fuck with you if you fucked with it.

So I was going back to a key moment in the hopes that I could alter how things had gone down and not impact my current reality. Wyatt's concern was justified... One wrong move...

"You fuck this up, you could fuck us all." Wyatt shifted past me, getting close enough to brush against my arm.

"I know what I'm doing." I held his glare and was surprised to see a flicker of concern there. Concern for me? For everyone involved? Or just the witches? Hard to tell with Wyatt. He was a vault when it came to his feelings on things, except when he disapproved. I wouldn't fuck it up though. I'd practiced and practiced and laid out a plan for every contingency.

The witches were all positioning themselves. Ally and Grant were seated on a small couch and Wyatt, Kali, and Destiny were in a kind of circle, across from them. I didn't need direction. I knew where my place was. I replayed the plan in my head, making sure every action was locked in.

The witches didn't signal me, they just got to work. I felt the magic rise swiftly and powerfully around me as they began their spell-casting. They were drawing on the magic that naturally swirled around, weaving it in a way that made me feel confident in what we were doing. I made eye contact with Destiny, knowing intimately what she was feeling because I was connected to her. She had faith so I had faith. She was excited, so I was excited. This would work—no room for doubt. She smiled, a reassuring expression.

I sucked in a deep breath, let it out and then stepped into the circle.

The magic wrapped me up like a million hands. I felt as if I was falling. For a brief moment of pure panic, I thought something had gone wrong because all I saw was darkness and all I heard was white noise. I opened my mouth to scream for them to stop but then Destiny was with me, a voice in my head, a hand clasped on mine.

"*We're good. This is fine. We've got this, Jetty. Hang tight.*"

So I focused on what I needed to do, my thoughts on my new powers of manipulation. What did I want to show? What did the past me need to see? But I knew the answer. No alteration. The image of Jason's chest exploding was vivid in my mind. I'd have no trouble projecting that.

When I felt the ground beneath my feet grow solid and smelled that forest aroma that had become so familiar to me, I acted without having to think too hard.

I landed behind Jason just as chaos descended and took in the scene. Although I couldn't feel them anymore, I knew the vampires were there, swarming, ready to attack. I saw my past-self diving for the amulet just as Amber was about to obliterate it with her rock. If slow motion was possible, it was happening right then. Kurt and Fiona spun like they were going to run. They didn't get very far.

I had seconds.

Jason didn't see me. I hit the ground behind him. I could have gotten distracted by everything that was going on, the disorientation of seeing myself in action, but I fought to maintain focus. I was there for a reason and I had less than sixty seconds to achieve it.

"Don't move," I whispered in his ear. He froze, intuitively knowing my voice, and my intention somehow.

I wrapped my arms around him, placing the amulet against his skin, pressing flesh to flesh and as the magic took hold and Destiny tugged me back, I cast out the image that was vividly burned in my memory. Jason's chest exploded, death in his eyes. That's what my past self would see. That's what I would think had happened to him. It's what would drive me to this very moment.

"Hang tight, Jason," I whispered. *"Reverted ad me."*

Destiny pulled hard, harder than I was expecting, a kind of desperate twinge radiated through our bond. It felt wrong.

Something lashed at me, a tendril of darkness, a whip of pain slapped at my side. Jason bellowed, his body shuddering. I smelled blood. His blood. I couldn't see what was happening, couldn't tell where the danger was.

"*Reverted ad me*." My voice was frantic, panic landing hard on my nerves. "Destiny, help!" I reached out to Destiny through our connection, stretching into the darkness while still clinging to Jason, his blood coating my arms.

I told him I'd get him off the island and that's what I was going to do.

"Destiny, *reverted ad me*," I screamed for the third and final time.

JASON WAS HURT. REALLY, REALLY HURT.

We landed in the middle of the witch circle, and I was screaming, trying to hold Jason's guts inside his body while blood gushed between my fingers.

His muscles were tense, rigidly hard, and his eyes rolled back in his head, his body shook with a violent force and blood foamed on his lips.

"He's having a seizure." Destiny's hands were on my hands, helping me to keep his insides inside.

"Wyatt, do something," Kali's eyes were wide, panicked.

"That's unfixable." Wyatt didn't move. "He's meant to die."

I growled at up him, teeth bared.

Wyatt lifted his hands like he could do nothing. "I warned you that something could happen and now it has. Fate has intervened."

"What the fuck are you talking about?" I screamed. Jason's body was vibrating but not as hard as before. "My boon request was to get Jason back safely. You haven't fulfilled your obligation to me! You're a fucking healer, so heal him!"

Wyatt's calm demeanor crumbled, he cursed, then slid off his chair then laid his hands on Jason. "This probably won't help," he said before closing his eyes and pumping his healing magic into Jason's body.

Hours passed. Hours of us watching as Wyatt's magic sealed Jason's gaping wound, hours of Wyatt working to knit back together what was broken in Jason's insides. I felt his powers at work, the edge of them hot, rolling through Jason's body like jolts of electricity. Kali was helping too, doing something that kept Jason calm and eased his moans of pain.

"Why isn't he waking up?" I asked, my hands shaking and coated in blood. Destiny had finally pulled me away, giving me a cup of tea infused with blood. I was exhausted, emotionally, physically. My whole body hurt, muscles aching, along with my heart. "Why aren't Wyatt's healing powers working?"

Destiny rubbed my back, watching as I watched. Jason was cycling through seizures, his whole body shuddering.

"I don't understand how this happened. Was it a vampire that managed to strike just as I was pulling him away? Some kind of spell from Amber? Something else? I don't understand. How did he get hurt?" I asked.

"The only thing that can penetrate a witch's portal is fate," Kali said, worry all over her face. She was sitting back on her heels, her hands no longer on Jason. "I mean, if you believe in that kind of thing."

"Fate?" I frowned. What were we talking about here?

"Capital F Fate," Wyatt said with a sigh. He pulled away from Jason too, his shoulders slumped, exhaustion clear on his face. "I've done what I can. The rest is up to her."

"Who?" I could not be more confused, scared, or upset. "Will someone explain what's going on?"

"Fate. Some people believe her to be a supernatural of some sort," Kali said. "It's possible that Fate stepped in while you were pulling Jason through the portal. Perhaps she didn't like that you were altering history."

"Why me though? I mean, Kali altered history and nothing like this happened." It made no sense. Things like that were myths—like the idea of karma being a person or the four horsemen actually existing. They were stories meant to teach lessons.

"Didn't it?" Destiny snorted. "I lived in captivity for years. My life was hellish. Kali lived on thinking she'd killed me, going mad on an isolated island. We both paid for her actions."

She hadn't said it in a harsh way but all the same, Kali flinched.

"Any time you use a time travel spell, there seems to be some kind of backlash," Wyatt said, motioning for Kali to come with him as he stood.

"Why didn't you warn me?"

"I did." Wyatt tried to glare but his hard expression slipped quickly. Kali moved into his embrace and he kissed the top of her head.

"You didn't warn me that Fate would have an issue with what I was doing." I leaned my head down.

"Would it have stopped you?" Wyatt countered.

No, it wouldn't have. I looked back at him.

"There's no proof that Fate exists," Kali said. "It's just something some witches believe." She rolled her eyes pointedly up to Wyatt. "Just like some witches follow the three-fold law. Whatever we put out will come back to us three-fold. I've never had that happen though and there's no consistency with the Fate idea either. Could just be coincidence."

But she didn't sound confident. Something had attacked Jason in the portal. Something had split him open and had done catastrophic damage to his insides.

"Some of us have seen it work too many times not to believe," Wyatt said.

Kali shifted so she could look up at him, some quiet communication passing between them.

"Will he survive?" I felt defeated. I moved to Jason and kneeled at his side, tracing my fingers over his cheek, his neck. His skin was clammy, a bit too cool to the touch.

"Like I said, it's in Fate's hands now." Wyatt ran his hand over his face. "I've done what I can. He's not bleeding, his bones are mended. Now we wait."

Destiny came to my side and took my empty cup. "We'll get him cleaned up and into a bed upstairs, okay?" She held a hand out for me to take. "You need to clean up as well and get some rest."

I nodded, feeling on the brink of tears. I'd done all this to keep him safe, to bring him back, but instead I'd made things worse.

What have I done?

♊

MY DAYS BLENDED INTO ONE, TWO, THREE, WITH NO beginning or end. I'd wake up next to Jason, touch his face, and put my hand on his chest to make sure he was still breathing. I'd whisper in his ear to wake him up. I'd sigh with disappointment when he didn't.

Three days. That's what it took to get him back.

"So I guess we're even now, right?"

I froze, standing in front of the mirror in the bathroom, the door only slightly ajar. I was detangling my hair with my fingers, water droplets dripping to the floor. I had a towel wrapped around me. I turned slowly, pushing the door open wider as I did.

"What, you're not talking to me now?" Jason was sitting upright, hair a haphazard mess, wry smile on his lips.

"You're awake!" Relief flooded through me.

"I am." His eyes sparkled like I remembered, his lips curled into a bigger grin. "You look happy to see me."

I rushed toward the bed then stopped. "I thought...I mean...

you almost died." I glanced down at my open hands, remembering how I'd held his intestines there.

Everything was too intimate. Too real.

"So you saved my life?"

"Something like that." I let out a long breath.

"You going to tell me where we are?" He pushed himself up higher, wincing a little as he did. "And what the fuck is going on?"

"You're safe. I got you off the island."

"Oh really? I thought this plush bed and expensively decorated room was part of the cavern." His eyes were filled with laugher. "You know that's not going to cut it, right?" He patted the bed next to him. "I'm going to need the full story version."

I slid next to him, wanting to reach up and touch his face like I had every morning.

"And a kiss."

"Huh?"

He chuckled softly, then leaned toward me, his hand on my back, pushing me down so he could capture my lips with his. Something tender, quick, and then he was pulling away again.

"There's something different about you." He was studying my eyes, his fingers trailing down my spine, then along my hip.

I flashed my fangs, which were longer now that I was a full vampire.

His eyes went wide. "You've bonded with someone?"

"In a way, yes." When his expression crashed I leaned in and kissed him. "Not like that."

He pulled me onto his lap, wrapped his arms around me tightly, and kissed my forehead. "You'd better start talking."

And so I did. I told him everything that had happened. I didn't hold anything back. The plan to set my father up, Cassia's death, my transformation thanks to Destiny, and then the trip back in time to save him.

"Wyatt believes in Fate?" Jason widened his eyes. "The way you described him, doesn't seem like the type."

"I know, seems strange. He's such a level headed guy."

"Oh well, yeah, sure, but Fate does exist." Jason squeezed me. "I've met her."

"Um...what?" I pulled away a little. "Are you serious?"

"For sure, she's a fickle woman, I'd say more like a goddess, actually. And she deals fairly. Seems to favor the shifters, though, if you ask me. Wolves more so than cats."

"Wait a minute, you're telling me that there's a supernatural being who goes around making sure that people's destiny plays out as it should?"

"She tries to keep things in balance. It's a hard job and sometimes she gets it wrong." He ran a hand through his hair. "She's super powerful though. Probably more than any supernatural we've ever met."

"So how'd you meet her?"

"That's not a story you want to hear." He chuckled.

I pushed back from him so I could look him in the eyes. "Oh really?"

He chuckled again, leaning in to nuzzle my throat. "Yeah, don't want to get you all jealous. Not after you went to so much trouble to keep me around."

I smacked his chest lightly, then trailed my lips along the side of his throat. The heat of his pulse teasing me, my fangs aching to sink in.

"I missed you," I whispered. "The taste of you. The feel of you."

With his hands on my ass, he urged me to straddle him, the sheet and towel between us quickly discarded.

He slipped inside of my soaking wet pussy, heat rushing up my core as his cock filled me up and stretched me out. He bent to suck on my nipple, flicking, biting, soothing with his tongue.

I rocked into him, using my momentum to slip and slide, my head back, reveling in the feel of him all over me.

"Jet," he moaned. "Take a bite out of me."

I looked down then, a smile on my lips. "You'll get addicted."

"I'm already addicted." His expression was wicked. "And now I owe you my life so you're stuck with me. Might as well make it more permanent."

He wanted me to blood him. I'd feed from him then he'd feed from me. Dependent on one another. It was serious business. It would put his life in my hands. I slowed my movement, rocking only slightly as I contemplated him.

"You almost died." My voice cracked. "I mean, maybe this is something we should wait to do...once you're completely healed."

"Jet, I feel good." He nudged upward, pressing his dick deeper into me. "Really fucking good."

"You don't owe me anything. You rescued me and I rescued you. We're even."

He flipped us over so he was looming on top of me, his cock still pulsing inside of me. "We don't know each other very well, Jet. I get that. But I want to get to know you. I want to be a part of your life in this new world. You're fierce and loyal, and fucking hot as all hell."

I grinned up at him.

"And you came back for me." His smile shifted to something more sentimental and tender. "You didn't leave me behind. You challenged Fate for me."

Which I hadn't known I was actually doing. Had no idea I was stepping on the toes of an actual being. I'm sure that meant that Fate had a bone to pick with me, but I'd do it again in a heartbeat.

"I promised I'd get you off that island." My voice was husky with emotion. "I couldn't stand to leave you there, to let you die." I gulped down the lump in my throat. "I want to get to know you better too. I want you in my life."

"So bite me, baby." He was grinning again. "Give me your blood. Let's do this right."

He kissed me, his soft lips on mine, his tongue delving inside, stoking me up. My body burned for him.

I pulled away from his kiss, lifting his head with my hands on his cheeks so I could look in his eyes. "I'll always have your back, Kitty."

His eyes flashed, "You too, Fangs."

I kissed him again, then trailed my lips down his throat to the pulse point there. It beat against my lips, demanding I break through his flesh. Saliva pooled in my mouth, desire flooding through me. I broke his skin with a moan, his blood hitting the back of my throat in a gush. His taste was the same as I remembered. Hot, spicy, masculine. I drank and he pumped into me, his cock so hard, his moans so deep that they burned through me.

He lifted my wrist to his lips and dug in there, biting me back, taking my blood as I took his. We would be tied together as long as we exchanged blood. He would have a part of me inside and I would have a part of him. A strong union that only made me melt more for the man.

My orgasm rose swiftly, pushing me to the upper limits of pleasure. He rubbed his cock along my clit, his thrusting became more urgent and forceful. He pulled away from my wrist to cry out, loudly as he spurted his cum and I tipped over the edge into my climax.

He was breathing heavily, chest heaving, arms wrapped around my hips. "That blood of yours will help with the stamina won't it?" He waggled his eyebrows.

I smiled back, trailing my fingers over the twin holes now healing at his throat. "It will." I rolled my hips when his cock pulsed and hardened once again. "Round two?"

"We've got some catching up to do." He kissed me again, tender, soft. "And an eternity to do it."

EPILOGUE

JASON CLEANED UP REALLY GOOD...LIKE REALLY, REALLY GOOD.
If we weren't about to board a helicopter I'd be pulling him back
to our room for a marathon sex-plosion.

He was off to the side talking with Wyatt, the men in deep
conversation about something undoubtedly super important. He'd
trimmed his hair and his beard; I wouldn't let him shave it
completely. I loved the scratch of it against my skin. He was
wearing a pair of beat-up looking jeans and a black sweater. He'd
put some weight on in the last few weeks as well, which looked
fucking fantastic and only accentuated his bulk and build. I could
stand there drooling over him all damn day.

But, as it was, we were already running late for our takeoff,
and our pilot was giving us dirty looks as we wrapped up our
goodbyes with the witches.

"Don't forget, if you two get yourselves into a sticky situation,
you can always use the summoning stone." Destiny gave me
another big bear-hug.

"We're not leaving the country, I think we'll be okay," I said as
I squeezed her back. I didn't love the idea of leaving without her,
but Destiny's place was with her family. Although we were bonded

with blood, I didn't need her to sustain me—that was now Jason's job.

"Wyatt will be transporting the witches that were being protected up north over the next month or so back here," Kali said as she took her turn to hug me. "Jason's cat colony is not too far from that stronghold. If you run into trouble—"

"I appreciate the concern, really," I laughed. "But I am Jet Black, remember? I think I can handle things."

"We know you can." Kali let me go and smiled. "But it's still pretty hostile out there, even with Cassia gone."

"We just want to make sure you stay in one piece."

"You two witches worried that the cats will take a bite out of her?" Jason came up next to me and slid his arm around my waist. "Because really, it's just my sister who—"

"Hey, I thought you said she'd love me?" I shoved him with my elbow.

"No, I said you reminded me of her...which I'm pretty sure is going to make her go all big sister on you." He squeezed me closer when I tried to shove him away, then leaned in and kissed my neck.

We were going home to Jason's clan with provisions, mostly food and some witch-infused medical supplies. Jason's grandmother was ill, and Wyatt had provided a few broadband tonics that he hoped would help her get well. We had a few amulets for transportation if we needed to bring her back to Salem for treatment. Jason had said she wouldn't want to leave the clan though so it was last case scenario.

"You know I can feel every time you two fool around, right?" Destiny looked disgusted. "I mean, the bond between us is super fresh still."

Jason sucked on my neck and I melted just a little bit more, feeling the zing of desire as I usually did when he touched me.

Destiny reached up and rubbed her neck, looking thoroughly grossed out. "Seriously, guys, quit it!"

"You should be happy we're leaving then." I laughed. "Because there's no way I'm quitting it with this guy around."

"I think you'd better get going." Kali motioned behind us. "The pilot looks ready to take off without you."

There was one last round of hugs, and then Jason and I hopped onto the helicopter and put the headphones and seatbelts on.

I waved down at the witches as we started to lift, feeling a tug of sorrow that was new to me. It had been a long time since I'd cared enough about people to be affected by their absence. Even though the plan was to come back to witch headquarters in six months to reconnect, I still felt pretty sad to be going. The witches, all of them, had become my family.

Jason didn't know what the state of things would be back home. The witches had offered refuge to the cats, but that was a decision that his sister would have to make as leader. If she wanted to stay put, then so would he...which meant so would I. While the bond to Destiny would weaken somewhat with distance, I would forever feel a connection to her, and I could live with that. Being without Jason though, yeah, totally not going to happen. I loved the guy, okay? Full on heart-pounding in love.

Jason took my hand. "You okay?"

I tore my gaze away from Destiny and Kali and smiled at him. "I will be."

"You know I was just joking about Natalie. She'll most likely love you." He nudged me, a wide smile on his face.

"Most likely." I snorted. "That's comforting."

He wrapped his arm around me and pulled me closer. "Wyatt said that there's a coven not too far from where my family is. He said he'd send word to the high priestess there to offer sanctuary if we need it. I don't think that will be necessary but all the same, he said they'd come and help if there were repairs that needed to get done to our structures."

"Do you think we'll need it?"

He shrugged, his eyes going dark. "I haven't been home in over a year. I left to make some money and to scavenge some medicine for grandmother. Once I was captured, that supply chain stopped. I don't know what we'll find when I go home. Things weren't great when I left, but Nat was holding it together as best as she could. The clan is young—most of the girls are under twenty and more interested in play-fighting than in keeping the homestead in working order. The few men are all over sixty and even less inclined to get work done. We aren't the strongest of lynx clans or the most industrious, despite my sister's best efforts to rally everyone. I just hope nothing bad has happened while I've been gone."

I squeezed his hand and leaned closer. We both knew being in a war meant that something bad most likely had happened to some degree. "We'll handle it. We'll take care of things."

"Yeah, I know, big bad Jet Black to the rescue." He lifted my chin so he could kiss me tenderly before I could protest.

I'd never get tired of those kisses.

Salem to northern Maine was about a five-hour trip and by the time we landed, it was late in the afternoon and I was pretty wired. Which was good because we had another hour of hard trekking to get us to Jason's family's place. The pilot had set us down as close as he could get without being too close to the nearest town, or what was left of it, High Landing. We didn't want to run the risk of meeting up with the locals before we'd had a chance to suss out the situation fully. So, loaded up like pack mules, we set off into the dense forest and kept ourselves on high alert the entire way. You never knew what kind of hostilities lurked in the shadows. A place like this, so far out of the way, it was likely word hadn't even gotten around that Cassia was dead. As far as these folks were concerned, the war was still on.

Even with my vampire strength, the hike was difficult. The forest was overgrown; there were no tracks to follow. Jason had some kind of uncanny homing ability, knowing just where to head so that we encountered less resistance from the wilderness.

Just when I thought my arms were about to fall off and my legs would quit working, Jason held his hand up for me to stop.

He craned his neck and scanned the perimeter. That's when I noticed that the birds had stopped chirping and the bugs had stopped buzzing.

"We're being stalked." Jason slowly lowered his pack and crouched low, motioning for me to do the same.

I slumped down with little ceremony. "By what?"

Jason jumped up and, in a flash, had transformed into his kitty self. Instantly on alert, I pulled my arms out from my pack and pushed myself into a defensive crouch, my blades already in both hands.

Jason gave a low, grumbling growl and then darted off into the bush, leaving me turning in circles, hunting for the source of concern.

Something rustled to my left. A branch broke to my right. I twirled just in time to lift my blades against an attack from a furry predator. It jumped over my head, maneuvering sideways as I twisted my knives so that I wouldn't gut the thing. The jump had been meant to scare me, not hurt me. A warning. No way was I going to stab first—not when we were in lynx country. It landed on the other side of me, fangs bared, spit flying, looking like it was pissed and ready to take a bite out of me.

"Nat, it's good to see you." Jason came out of the tree line behind me, arms crossed, looking equally as pissed. "You didn't have to put on a show."

The cat growled one more time before swirling into the weird transformative magic the lynx seemed to have—into a tall, athletic-looking, gorgeous blonde. "Where the hell have you been?" She barked. "And who the hell is this?"

Before he could answer though, Natalie stomped to him,

threw her arms around his shoulders and practically picked him up in a tight embrace.

"Whoa, big sis, you're killing me here." He laughed and squirmed his way out of her arms.

"I'm so glad you're home. Jay, I thought you were dead." Tears glistened in her eyes. "Why were you gone so long?"

"It's a long story," he started, then shook his head and looked over at me. He smiled and I walked to his side, letting him wrap me in a one-arm embrace. "Natalie, this is Jet—the woman who saved my life."

Natalie gave me a hard once-over, so hard that I thought she was about to go all wildcat on me again. "You're a vampire."

I nodded.

"And you saved my brother's life?"

"I wouldn't be here without her." Jason squeezed my side. "I got caught up in a raid, ended up on Vampire Island."

Natalie's eyes went wide and she nodded slowly. "Well then, Jet, welcome to the family." She bypassed Jason, pulled me into her arms and whispered. "Vampire or not, you hurt him and I'm gonna stake that cold, dead heart of yours."

I laughed and whispered back. "I'm not going to hurt him, but if I did, I'd let you."

She chuckled as she pulled away, her eyes sparkling. "I like her, Jason. She's funny." She wrapped one arm around Jason and kept one arm around me. "Now, let's get you two back to home base before grandma comes out here looking for me." She shook her head. "She is going to piss herself when she sees you've brought a vampire girlfriend home."

I glanced over at Jason. He winked, his smile so bright that I knew, no matter what came next, I'd do anything to keep him smiling like that. Jason was home, and now so was I.

AFTERWORD

Thank you for taking the time to read *Fortune's Fool*. If you enjoyed it, please consider telling your friends or posting a short review. Word of mouth is an author's best friend and much appreciated.

Thank you again,

Angie

My newsletter is a spam-free zone. If you're interested in hearing about my next releases and upcoming events, contests and other fun stuff, please sign up.

ACKNOWLEDGMENTS

Every time I go through the editing process I think, thank fuck for Holly because without her this story would suck! Holly Atkinson, my beloved editor is first on my list of invaluable people to thank. I seriously don't know what I'd do without her.

Also a big thank you to my cheerleaders of unending support, who come out to book signings in the middle of nowhere and always say nice things about my characters (in no particular order, you're all my favorites) Dianne Waye, Tammy Crosby, Anna Sotiropoulos, Kate Riddell, Bev Woodfine and Linda Farnes-Copan. I wouldn't survive without D.B. Reynolds who is not only a forever-friend, but also a trusted source of common sense. I'm not thanking Michelle von Enckevort here because I dedicated this book to her. I basically wrote it for her too, she's just that important to me.

I also want to give a special shout-out to Diana K. who spoils me with surprise packages in the mail.

Thank you to my husband and kids who put up with a messy house and don't whine too much about proper meals when I'm in the writing zone.

I also want to thank my parents who believe in me no matter what I set out to do.

A CONVERSATION WITH ANGELA ADDAMS

This book didn't go in the direction that a lot of people were expecting. You want to walk us through why?

I love the world of *The Dark War,* and I know this follow-up book has been a long time coming. When my old publisher, Samhain, closed a couple of years ago, I was just about to start writing this book...and then my writing world got majorly derailed. It was a setback that I hadn't seen coming...although I probably should have. By the time things settled, too much time had passed since the release of *The Dark War,* and I knew I would have to write a different kind of book two. Not a sequel per se, but a continuation of the world itself. I'd wanted to write about Jet Black for years—I just didn't realize she would fit so well in this world. When the time came to get this book written, I knew it was her voice I needed to tell the story. I also knew that ultimately Kali needed to fulfill her destiny and that her path to becoming the hero she was meant to be would not be an easy one.

Let's just get this question out of the way now: Is this the end of The Dark War books?

No! I have another book in my head, and if the timing of all other things works, I should start writing it in the summer of 2019. These books are definitely darker than my *Witch Hospital Series* but if you're looking for something else to read, you could check out that world for a bit. If werewolves are your thing, you may like my *Order of the Wolf* series. There are witches in those books as well—just a different version of them.

Okay, so what comes next in this series? Is the Dark War really over? Like, did Kali truly end things?

When I first started writing this series it was actually not with *The Dark War* but with three other books (which will likely never see the light of day). All three of these books were written AFTER the Dark War begins—many years after, in fact—in a world that is trying to heal from the ravages of this war. Those three books never actually went anywhere (they were my first attempts at writing novels). Even though they helped me get my first agent, they really weren't fit for publication. But the ideas from those books spawned *The Dark War* world. It was my good friend, Michelle von Enckevort, who really wanted to see how the war started and because I did too, that's the book I wrote. So *Fortune's Fool* actually puts me time-wise exactly where I want to be. The catalyst of the war may be dead and the primary battles over, but that doesn't mean things are all calm and peace. There are treaties to write and alliances to form, a world to rebuild, and an open society of supernaturals who are not going back into their various closets. *The Dark War* might be over, but the story has just begun. Characters I introduced in those first three unpublished novels I wrote years ago will likely start making appearances in upcoming books, just better written and with solid stories this time. *You have a lot of vivid detail in your worlds from the creatures you create to the hospital itself. Where do you get these ideas?*

Everywhere! I am always pushing my imagination to come up with things that I would find interesting if I was reading my books for the first time. I love writing about magic and witches and I want to give my readers a vivid experience as they're going through my stories. While my first drafts are usually very lean, I add a lot of description with each editing pass so that I do my best to paint a picture for readers and hopefully create a world that they would want to revisit.

What comes next in your publishing schedule?

Next up is likely going to be a contemporary erotic romance (genre-hopping, I know!) that I have contracted through my publisher (Entangled). It's very different from all of my other books. For one, there's no paranormal creature in sight and for two it's a fun, relatively light, read about a struggling newly graduated young woman who needs to produce the perfect boyfriend for her mother.

The problem is, she doesn't have a boyfriend...but there is a regular customer who comes into her work who sure as hell looks like the guy she described to her mom. She ends up asking the guy she serves coffee every day to be her date to the family reunion. Unbeknownst to her he's an ex-con, luckily with a heart of gold, and he agrees to play along. They are from completely different worlds, and that makes for some crazy adventures. So they get into all kinds of shenanigans and a ton of hot and heavy and it's definitely happily ever after. If that sounds like something you'd be interested in, then keep your eyes out for release date info on my blog and social media...or sign up for my newsletter where I'll keep you posted.

I'm also almost finished writing book three in my Witch Hospital Series, so that's another possibility for the next book to release. If I can manage it, I'd like to get it out before the summer but we'll see. I'll definitely keep you all posted but no matter what, you haven't heard the last of me. Muwahahahahahaha!

That's it for me! Catch ya on the witch side!

BONUS CHAPTER

Dear Readers:

When I started thinking about writing the sequel to *The Dark War*, my previous publisher was still in business and so it made perfect sense to continue writing from Kali's perspective. Unfortunately, Samhain closed its doors, leaving me in a bit of a limbo for several years while I sorted things out with my new publisher. When I sat down to continue The Dark War story, I realized that I would have to appeal to new readers as well as satisfy existing ones...so I came up with a plan to set the story ten years later with new characters to fall in love with. It was hard for me to leave Kali behind though, so I had this scene awkwardly dangling in the middle of the novel where it had no business being. I had to cut it for the sake of story flow and now it's here. You'll see some crossover phrases and sentences between *Fortune's Fool* and the scene where Kali tells the others what caused her to fail her mission. I tried to keep the heart of Kali's story without changing point of view in the novel. For those of you who have read *The Dark War*, this deleted scene should be the perfect bridge between the two books and give you Kali's perspective on what went wrong. I hope you enjoy reading it!

꜠

10 Years ago
American Council of Witches Headquarters, Salem Massachusetts.

I carried the grimoire everywhere with me. Couldn't be parted from it. Wyatt kept telling me that I was too dependent, but with the war waging, I needed to learn as much as I could. And besides, the damn thing had saved our asses a few times on the road.

We'd made it back to Headquarters a couple of months after the bombs started dropping. Rick's apocalypse shelter had served us well and gotten us through the nukes without too much damage. But when the humans stopped with the explosions, we needed to get a move on.

The grimoire had provided some nifty tricks, like proximity detectors for any hostiles coming our way. And a few handy flash strikes that not only blasted bright, eye-piercing light, but also packed a pretty big acoustic punch. But the ultimate had been on the night we'd been surrounded by vampires, outnumbered and about to be swarmed when I remembered the portal spell. It was dark magic, to be sure, but a little rip in the time stream and I was able to close the distance between us and safety in a matter of seconds. Bye, bye vamps. I'd been bitten before—it wasn't pleasant or something I wanted to repeat. It was dangerous on all sides, but no one had lost an eye so the dark magic proved, once again, to be worth the trouble.

Even though I was the rebel witch who'd run away from home with a middle finger to the Council years before, they had welcomed me back like I was a prodigal daughter returned.

Everything had been put to rights immediately. Some of the most powerful witches in the country resided at Council head-quarters. They had lifted the curse that had made me invisible; one I'd cast on myself and my hunter friend Billy in an attempt to save our asses from hunters that Cassia had sent. And the Council had restored Wyatt's powers, lifting his lifetime ban on magic because they desperately needed his powers for battle. In serious times, you didn't hobble your best fighters. It seemed like all was forgiven. No questions asked. Blank slate.

We were back to our normal selves, and I had a huge fucking destiny hanging over my head.

"It's chaos out there." Wyatt was animatedly describing how dangerous our journey had been.

And it *had* been dangerous. War, especially between supernat-urals, was not something to be taken lightly. I'd seen things that I never wish to see again. Wyatt had to dose me some nights with his healing powers just so I could sleep and keep the nightmares away. The way he was describing things though, it sounded like a lot more fun and adventure than it had been. His audience was a group of scholars who were following his story with rapt atten-tion. Scholars who would never step foot outside of Council head-quarters. They lived for wild tales from the world, and Wyatt was playing it up for them.

I'd heard it before. Wyatt sure did love telling a good story, especially when there was a captive audience.

With a sigh, I flipped through some of the pages of my grimoire. It had been a gift from a special friend. My heart clenched at the thought of him. Billy was a dependable witch hunter; I'd worked with him for many years at the Witch Hunter's Union before leaving to start my own company as a bounty hunter. He'd remained a committed member of the union, and a die-hard witch hunter. When all hell had broken loose, he'd been by my side, helping me fight against the witches who had been sent to kill us. We'd watched our friends die. Sharing that heartbreak in the moment that their lives were brutally taken. I'd cast the invisibility spell to save our own asses and then when it was all over, I couldn't walk away with him and continue the fight at his side. I knew I'd never see him again. I made a choice to come home with Wyatt.

Billy was a good friend. But he was only a friend. Wyatt was my forever, despite the fact that Wyatt was married. It was a marriage of obligation only, to another witch. We had yet to see Ally upon our return. I could call her my nemesis, but she honestly hadn't done anything wrong—not willfully anyway. Certainly not maliciously. Her only crime was in loving Wyatt and trying to help him help me. She'd had her powers bound as well, a punishment for breaking a sacred witch law. Time travel was forbidden—too many things could go wrong. A slight alteration of history could transform the future. But Wyatt had been determined to get revenge for me and my sisters and he'd needed Ally's powers to help him do it. Of course she'd gone along with his plan, which had gotten both of them magically bound in punishment. I had to assumed the Council had reversed Ally's binding also—she was just too powerful of a witch to let sit on the sidelines while a war raged.

"Sweetheart." My mother's voice was something I would never get tired of hearing.

I turned to watch her slowly make her way down the grand staircase that would take her to the main floor. Wyatt was still chatting away with a few of the scholars who had caught him as they were coming out of the library on the second floor. I was somewhere in the middle. Walking in circles, lost in thought as I usually was when I had the grimoire in my hands. I closed the book and slipped it into my satchel.

"Mom." I kissed her cheek, wrapping her in a hug. I inhaled her scent—also something I would never grow tired of. Jasmine and honey, with a hint of something spicy. Fuck, I'd missed her. "I was going to come up for a visit just as soon as Wyatt and I check out the armory."

Things had been such a whirlwind since we'd arrived back home. It had only been a few days, but already it felt like we'd been back for an eternity. Part of me was itching to climb into bed with my mom, snuggle up with her and sleep for days, but another part could feel the tension riding just beyond the Headquarter grounds, and I wanted to load up with weapons and get out there. Help as many witches as I could. The war would claim them. Cassia, the War Queen as she was being called now, was out to gather all of the uniquely powerful witches so she could drain them dry and take their powers. She wanted me too, but I had other plans for her.

"I wanted to speak with you." My mom leaned closer so only I could hear. "Without anyone hovering."

She meant my dad. His interference in the past had cost me my sisters. I wanted some time with Mom alone so I could make sense of this prophecy she claimed she had. I patted her hand, slipping her arm around mine, and guided her down the hall toward a little sitting room I knew would not be occupied. It was too small for war talk and strategizing and too pink for the men to tolerate for longer than a few minutes. Sounds silly, sure, but it was a fact. The Rose Room was the epitome of stereotypical girl-vomit decorating.

Mom was moving gingerly, her body so frail, hardly there at all. Having been out of commission for so long meant her muscles were very sore and tired. Her trip out of bed would cost her. She'd probably have to sleep for a full day to regain her strength. That's why I knew whatever she wanted to discuss with me was super fucking important.

"Here, sit. I'll make some tea." I maneuvered her over to the most comfortable chair in the room, a plush white lounger where she could elevate her feet.

Once she was settled, I moved to the tea service and got to work.

"My darling girl, I don't think I will ever tire of seeing you back home." My mother's voice was strong, unlike her body at the moment. Her words, while tender, came out like a punch. Or at least, that's how I felt it.

I should never have stayed away for as long as I had. Even though she had been in a catatonic state for all those years, she would have known if I were around. I swallowed down the lump in my throat and dropped in two bags of tea to steep once the water was ready.

"Come, sit by me while we wait. I want to hold your hand."

I clenched my fingers on the wood of the table, fighting back the tears that burned my eyes, gulping down those emotions that threatened to turn me into a sobbing, inconsolable mess. I was a strong woman, but even the strongest can't combat the Mom guilt-trip, whether she intended it that way or not.

I forced a smile then turned to face her, taking her in as I walked to her side. She was so thin, bones sticking out from her skin, making her flesh seem like tissue-paper. Her cheeks were sallow and skin so pale I could see her veins. Her eyes were green, vibrant and sparkling with a mischievous glint that was always there. Her white hair was tied into a ponytail with a blue ribbon to keep it in place. She didn't look old—not to me, anyway—and she wasn't, not really. She was just recovering. Wyatt had been helping, giving her a dose of his healing gift each morning and night since we'd been back. He'd brought color to her cheeks when he dosed her, and she had started to regain her appetite.

"Oh dear, you can't pull off that smile so stop trying." She winked as she patted the arm of the chair, which was big enough to accommodate my ass.

I let the smile slide from my aching cheeks and nodded, doing as I was told.

She entwined her fingers with mine, then used the nails of her other hand to glide along my arm, barely touching the skin and giving me a shiver. "You traded a boon." Her nails touched Drake's boon mark, giving me a whole other kind of shiver.

"I did."

"Was it worth it?"

"Yes. I got information I needed to hunt down a hybrid."

"Was it so hard out there?" she whispered, her voice cracking as she resumed tracing my arm. "When you were alone in the world all that time I was in my head? Was it too hard to bear?"

"No." I cleared my own throat, fighting to keep my emotions in control. "I liked it, and I needed it. Being alone helped me gain some perspective."

"We were all so heartbroken," Mother said, and I knew she wasn't talking about me. She was talking about the loss of my sisters, Destiny and Leila. Killed by the fangs of a Strix gang. Murdered while on a mission for the Council. A mission my father had sanctioned. "We all needed time."

I looked at her then, our eyes meeting with a sudden shared understanding. She had withdrawn into herself after Destiny and Leila died, and I had walked away from everything and everyone I knew. Choosing to isolate myself away from witches. Choosing to hunt them instead. My work had had meaning back then. Keep the bad witches in line. Make sure they weren't exposing us to the humans. Keep them from risking all of our lives that way. We'd lived in fairy-tales and myths. As long as the humans thought we weren't real, we were safe. Now it all seemed meaningless. Humans weren't the big bad we'd all feared for centuries. There were bigger monsters out there in the world.

"I missed you," I said, squeezing her hand, letting my eyes well.

She had tears too. "We did what we needed to do." She had a firm grip on my forearm, turning my arm and bringing my palm up so she could trace the lines there. Destiny. Life. Love.

"The prophecy is real," she said, her tone fierce and filled with power. "You have a date with destiny. You must end the war, Kali. That is what you were born to do."

"I don't know how." I was lost when it came to the hero stuff. How could I end the war when I didn't even know how to find the woman who had started it? Cassia was hiding behind walls of supernatural fighters. The only appearance she'd made was in our heads when she'd used a spell to send a message, but that had been months ago. Now the only things I heard about her whereabouts came from scouts and rumors. She only ever ventured out when there was a reason to—namely the capture of a powerful witch she wanted to drain of power.

"You have the answers in your grimoire." She nodded at the bag I still wore on my hip. The heavy weight of it was something I barely noticed anymore. It was just there, a part of me, bolstering my powers with the information it contained. For the first time in my life, I took spell casting seriously. Memorizing spells, both light and dark, working to master the language and nuances of the words to get the correct rhythm so that the spells would work as they were meant to work.

"But how will I know what to do?" I patted the grimoire through the canvas of my bag, feeling the outline of its hard leather cover.

"Kali, sweetheart, you'll always know what to do. You always have. You always will. It's your destiny."

"So how do I find her? Cassia isn't exactly waiting in plain sight."

"Darling, you're a tracker. You've tasted her signature. It's in your senses. Locked in there."

"You mean when she pulled us into that summoning spell?" It had nearly killed me, that damn summoning spell of hers, but Mother was right. It had also given me a taste of Cassia's signature.

My mother nodded, her fingers still tracing my palm. Her eyes riveted there. "Yes, that's right. You have her natural signature.

The one she used when she was a pure witch, not a hybrid. You'll use that to track her."

"But her signature is mixed now with the blood of all of the witches she's stolen from." As a hybrid witch vampire, Cassia needed the blood from other witches to retain her powers—otherwise she'd just be like any other Strix vampire, vulnerable to sunlight and to a stake.

"No, honey, I mean, find her before she became a hybrid, when her magic was untainted."

I frowned, my thoughts jarring to a halt. "You mean you want me to go back in time?" Like I said, time travel was a forbidden spell. A dangerous use of dark magic. The Council would never agree to it, and I hardly believed I was powerful enough to wield it.

My mother looked up at me, her eyes still sparking with that look that spoke of devious things. "Yes, darling, you're going to go back in time. You're going to find Cassia before she becomes a hybrid, and you're going to kill her."

It was honestly a brilliant plan. Crazy as all hell but brilliant. Even so, I was not on board. And neither was Wyatt. At least, that's what I thought.

"She insists that the prophecy is directed at me and that the only way to end the war is to stop it before it starts." For the first time in days, Wyatt and I had some alone time where we weren't so exhausted all we wanted to do was sleep. We'd made use of it, a few times. It felt good to be loved again, to share my life with someone and to have that sense of home.

He had his head in my lap, his fingers trailing designs on my bare legs. I loved it when he did that.

"Do you think you could do it?"

That was not the response I expected from him.

"Huh?" I shifted so he'd have to raise his head.

He looked at me like I'd just disturbed him unnecessarily, running his hand through his hair as he sat up. "You've been studying that grimoire every chance you get. There's a time travel spell in there. I've seen it."

I cocked an eyebrow, wondering just when he'd had a chance to snoop. I literally had the thing with me every moment of the day.

"You do sleep, you know," he said with a wry smirk. "And I'm not saying you should do it—I'm asking if you think you can."

I glanced over to where the book was now, a lump in my bag that I'd tossed on the floor when we'd stumbled into our bedroom, ripping our clothes off in a hasty attempt to reconnect. Sex had been quick and dirty the first round. We'd taken a little more time the second and third. My body was craving more, always more from Wyatt.

But there was urgent business to attend to. My mother's time travel solution for one, and also Wyatt's reunion with his estranged wife, Ally. She'd been holed up at his family's home since he'd left years before to hunt me down. He'd honored their marriage agreement to protect her despite the fact that neither one of them loved each other that way. Or so he claimed. I'd see for myself when Ally arrived...in about twenty minutes.

I sighed as I shifted from the bed, searching for my clothes. "Yes, I think I can do it. Not alone, but sure, I could get where I needed to go and do what I needed to do." Kill Cassia. "But I don't think I should do it." And not because of some moral objection to killing.

"Even if it means stopping the war?"

I ducked down to grab my jeans and panties, untangling them from Wyatt's clothes. "Murdering Cassia doesn't guarantee the war will not come to be. You know how prophecies go. Usually it's when you try to change something that they come to pass exactly as they say they will."

"I think it's a pretty good shot in this case. You're not trying to avoid the prophecy; you'd be doing exactly what it was predicting you to do. And you know your mother's ability to decipher prophecies is solid...or at least better than your father's."

Good ol' dad was a self-made prognosticator. He'd never been very good at it though. Nothing beat my mother's natural talent. And Wyatt was right—she was normally very good at figuring out what the, often cryptic, messages meant. You and destiny have a date with a hybrid, that's what my mother had originally said.

Wyatt moved to the edge of the bed and grabbed my hips, pulling me closer so that he could lay the side of his face against my belly. "I want to grow babies in there."

His words stilled me.

"What?" I literally froze in place, my hands raised with a pair of pink panties clenched in my fingers.

He looked up at me, his violet eyes blasting with such tenderness I wanted to crumble. "You're ovulating. I can feel it." He traced his fingers along my thigh, the warmth of his healer's touch enough to give me a tingle of pleasure. Now that his powers were fully back, even his healing magic was supercharged—his touch rejuvenated me and revved me up. "I want to live in a world that's safe for our children."

Our children. Two words I never thought I'd ever hear come out of Wyatt's mouth. "Ally..."

He closed his eyes briefly, then sighed. After kissing my belly first, he pushed away from me. I mourned the loss of that tender touch.

"You're right. Let's get dressed. We need to go downstairs and speak with her."

"We?" That had so not been a part of my plan for the night. Sure, I'd imagined a quick hello but then an equally quick goodbye as I moved off to somewhere I actually wanted to be, alone or with my mother maybe. Certainly not hanging out with Ally while she and Wyatt caught up on things.

He shot me a hard look. "You in this with me or not?"

I winced. "Of course. But don't you think Ally will want to speak with you alone? Especially when you tell her that you and I..."

"I spoke with her already." He lifted his hand before I could respond. "Earlier. She wanted to make sure you would be comfortable with her coming here to see me. She wants to see you, actually. So that you can hear her give her blessing."

I frowned. Also not what I was expecting to hear. Wyatt had been my first love and if I was going to be honest, my only true love. Ally had swooped him away from me when we were younger. But I didn't blame her for that—not much. Wyatt was captivating. He was also an ass. He'd used her to hurt me back then. Stupid, foolish games that were meant to create jealousy. Which was exactly what had happened. Too much jealousy for me to see clearly. I believed that he'd fallen in love with her and out of love with me. And then my sisters had died, and I just couldn't take any more emotional trauma. So I'd left. And when I'd left, I'd created a hole that needed to be filled. Wyatt had married her, out of obligation, he said, but I knew part of it was because I'd ripped his sorry-ass heart out when I'd turned my back on him once and for all.

"She's found love too," Wyatt said.

I thought my eyes would bug right out of my head. "Um...what?"

"One of my cousins. Grant. He's been watching over her for years now, and I kind of hoped something would develop. They are really perfect for each other."

Somehow I got my tongue working again. "So what does that mean for your marriage vow?" A witch's marriage vow was for life. Breaking that bond could mean death for either witch, depending on how much power had gone into the spell in the first place. With Wyatt and Ally, that was a debatable variable, but it was still risky enough.

"You got anything in that book of yours that reverses a pact?" Wyatt chuckled. "Honestly, I don't know. We're kind of stuck with the vow for now."

"Which means you can't bond with me and she can't bond with Grant." I felt a heavy weight in my chest. "Which means there won't be any babies for us as long as that pact exists." Because witch bodies were loyal to the vows even if the witches themselves weren't. Without that pact between Wyatt and me, we'd never carry a pregnancy to term.

Wyatt stood from the bed and pulled me close, kissing the top of my head as he did. "Sweetie, as much as I know we'd have a lot of fun trying, I promise you, I will find a way to break this vow so that we can have babies together. Pacts can be dismantled and reversed. I just have to find the right witch to do it."

And there were witches out there who could. But those were witches that Cassia would be looking for as well. Rare and priceless witches with huge bounties on their heads. So they'd be hiding or hidden and no way they'd come out at our beck and call —at least, not while the war raged.

Wyatt pulled back enough so I'd look up at him. "You end this war and they won't be hiding," he said, as if reading my mind. "You're a tracker, babe. Once this war is over, we'll go find ourselves a pact-breaking witch."

He smiled. I smiled. Okay, so maybe my mother's idea wasn't so crazy after all. And then I pushed myself up and kissed him good and hard so that he knew exactly what we'd be doing once we got this meeting over with.

"Wyatt."

Ally was demure where I was not. She was petite and soft-spoken. She had beautiful long, red hair and green eyes and was just gorgeous, put-together and polished.

I could never, in a million years, compete. Old feelings of jealousy spiked as she moved to give Wyatt a hug, her pink, manicured nails and stunning jewelry made her look like a priceless doll.

"Kali?" A tall dark-haired hulk of a man had his hand extended to me. "Grant, the other man."

I cracked a smile and tore my eyes away from Wyatt and Ally as they hugged like long-lost friends. "I guess that makes me the other woman."

"Or the original woman. Wyatt was a fool for letting you go the first time." Grant's smile was wide and his eyes sparkled like he was ready to burst into laughter at any moment. He clasped my hand in both of his and gave me a warm shake before pulling me into a giant bear-hug.

"Once a fool, always a fool." Wyatt was there when we parted; ready to take his turn hugging his cousin in a hearty, back-slapping way. "I told you this would all work out."

"No, you didn't. You told me that your luck was shit and that you were an asshole and she'd never take you back." Grant winked at me. "Which he is, but you took him back anyway."

"Boys," Ally said sweetly as she waved her hands for the men to part, her eyes lighting on me with such warmth that I couldn't possibly do anything but smile back. "Kali, I'm so happy to see you again."

I wanted to balk at that. I wanted to say something snide and mean. Instead, I swallowed it all and stepped into Ally's embrace. She smelled like flowers. She felt like silky petals. I wanted to hate her, but that was fleeting because how could I hate someone who gave such warmth?

"Why don't we have some wine?" Ally suggested as she pulled from our embrace. Still smiling, still comfortable. Not an ounce of weirdness that we'd all committed adultery and were all seemingly okay with it. It felt surreal.

Wyatt grasped my hand and gave it a squeeze before

motioning for me to follow Ally to the seating area. Grant moved off to the bar and started to uncork a bottle of red. "There's white here too, if you'd prefer that."

I raised my hand and shook my head. "I'm more of a whiskey girl."

Wyatt was already on it though. He moved behind the bar to pour us both something harder.

"Wyatt told us about your mother's prediction," Ally said as she leaned back in her chair. "And about the plan."

I glanced over at Wyatt, wondering just how much time he'd spent talking to Ally on the phone earlier. A soft touch on my leg had me shifting my eyes back to Ally.

She was leaning closer to me, her gaze intense, her smile gone. "You have my support. I'll build the time travel spell with you." She flicked her eyes to Wyatt as he approached with my drink. "I've done it before."

Ah yes, the infamous attempt to help save my sisters. Wyatt and Ally had worked a spell that sent him back in time in an attempt to prevent my sisters' deaths. He'd gotten there too late. But later, once he was back and his punishment for performing a dark spell was in full effect, he'd hunted down every single one of those vampires and killed them all. Revenge for my sisters. Revenge for me. He'd made a huge sacrifice in doing that spell the first time. The Council had punished him severely.

Wyatt gave me a short glass with ice tinkling inside. The smell of whiskey was a comfort. I downed it in one gulp.

"The Council will forbid it." I coughed. "I mean, they bound your magic for doing it that time."

Ally leaned back, accepting the wine glass from Grant. "The Council is all for it. In fact, they have agreed to bolster the spell so nothing goes wrong."

"You're kidding!" I blurted, my eyes wide.

Ally was already shaking her head, but it was Grant who spoke next. "Not kidding. As soon as Ally heard the idea, she petitioned the Council. They have been in a meeting with your mother since then to iron out the details. All we need is for you to agree."

"Why does it have to be me?" But I knew why. I had to go back because I was the only one who could find Cassia for sure. They could send me to the right time and the right general area, but they needed my tracking ability to accurately locate Cassia.

Nobody answered. Nobody had to. Wyatt put his hand on my shoulder. "I'd go with you if I could, but the spell works better when it's carrying one person. We don't want to take any chances by making the spell-load too heavy."

And I wouldn't ask him for that either. I didn't want to risk his life while I was hunting another's.

It took a tremendous amount of power to wield a spell like that. The fact that just Ally and Wyatt had been able to do it, and years before, was a testament to their natural talent and sheer will. They could do it again; I knew it.

I lifted my glass to Wyatt. "I'm going to need another drink." Then I sighed with total resignation. "Okay, I'm in. Let's do this. Mom says I have a date with destiny. I guess it's time to figure out what that means."

❧

There was no time to waste, according to the Council anyway. I was feeling the sudden urgency as well. End the war; get on with life. And suddenly life, with Wyatt, with my mom, and, I suppose my dad as well, it all seemed brighter. It held more promise. Time to reconcile differences and maybe, if we were lucky, find a way to undo the marriage pact so that we'd all be happy.

The hour-long meeting between my mother and the Council had tired her out, so I'd only had a few hasty moments with her before going to the spell chamber. She'd patted my hand, reassured me that I'd know what to do once I got there, and then had fallen asleep. No *I love you*, no wish of luck. But even that didn't sway my hopeful feelings about what we were going to do. It was dangerous, sure, but with the witch power I had backing me, I didn't foresee any major hiccups.

The Spell Chamber was in the basement of the Council headquarters, or rather in the sub-basement because it was below even the lowest floor. Dug deep into the bedrock, it was a sacred chamber that remained largely a mystery—even to witches. Not many of us had had the honor of venturing down there. Whether because of the centuries of spells performed there or just some natural phenomena, anything magical that happened in the Spell Chamber was amplified to ridiculous degrees. You could feel it on your skin—a strange tingling that made your hair rise along with goosebumps. For the unpracticed witch, the Spell Chamber could mean death. Uncontrolled spells would backfire and cause a lot of damage. Only the most powerfully trained witches got the opportunity to descend the roughly cut stone stairs and enter into the vault itself.

There were thirteen Council members standing sentry—a suitable coven number—lining the roughly hewn hallway. They wouldn't enter the chamber to bolster the spell, they would do it from a safe distance. The kind of power that Wyatt and Ally were going to wield could kill anyone in the vicinity, especially with the chamber's supercharging effects. I didn't blame the coven for wanting to keep safe; I wasn't totally keen on the idea of being blown to bits while trying to do good by the world either.

They wore hoods that covered the faces and I only knew, by the brief touch of a hand on my arm, which one was my father. He'd be there of course. A powerful witch in his own right. I hadn't spoken with him much in the time that I'd been back, and suddenly I felt some regret for that. I'd held such hate for him for so many years for the role he'd played in sending my sisters to their deaths. It was hard to set that aside in a matter of days. It would take time, but with my new vision of the future, perhaps we could come to some kind of truce and work on rebuilding our relationship going forward.

Wyatt was holding my hand as we stood in the center of the room. A pentagram had been etched in black on the floor centuries ago, but it still looked recent. The black was stark against the muted grey stone. I toed the circle with my boot and felt a surge of power race up my leg. It made me shiver. Wyatt squeezed my hand tighter.

"Grant will anchor you," Ally was saying with a nod to her boyfriend. "And Wyatt will be your tether. But you will have to home in on Cassia's signature quickly if we're going to make the best use of this spell."

"How long do I have?" I had no experience with time travel. The actual spell was now part of my repertoire, but I had yet to experiment with it. I couldn't imagine that it was going to be pleasant. Playing with dark magic always started with a sickening surge in my stomach. It passed as the power took hold, but at the beginning, it always felt wrong, dirty, almost painful, and definitely something I wanted to expel from my body.

"I'm not sure. Not long. It doesn't flow linearly when you're in there, so it's hard to say. What passes as many minutes for you are only seconds for us." Ally worried her bottom lip like she was trying to calculate time for me in a way that I could understand. "You'll need to be focused and quick. Your mother thinks it's best that you kill Cassia rather than bind her powers. Are you okay with that?"

The way she asked it though suggested that she knew I was. It was no secret what kind of life I was living as a witch hunter. I'd killed my kind before. That wasn't my preference but I didn't have many qualms about it either. Sometimes a witch was so evil that it just had to happen.

The beauty of the time travel spell was that everyone involved would retain the memory of what had been. We'd all know, from the thirteen Council members in the hall, to me, Wyatt, Grant and Ally, what had been avoided. If I succeeded and came back to the Spell Chamber having killed Cassia, the world would be different but we would all be the same, knowledge intact. We were altering history, a calculated risk with threads of unforeseen outcomes, but none of them likely as bad as what Cassia was doing right now. At least in theory anyway.

"I'll do what needs to be done." I let Wyatt's hand go and checked that my weapons were in place. Knives on my belt for throwing, as well as for close combat if required, although I didn't plan on getting that close to Cassia—a death spell would do what I needed it to. Silent, painless, removal of life. More dark magic, true, but I had Wyatt tethering me, so I knew I wouldn't get lost to it. I traced my fingers over the other side of my belt. A couple of steel stakes for the vampires. Anything pointy could kill them, but these had some really neat finger grips that would allow me to slip them on and then punch my way through flesh to heart.

After a lifetime spent being the bad kid, refusing to memorize even the simplest of spells, I was now probably the most knowledgeable in the room and that was strange feeling for me. While Ally and Wyatt were building the foundation of the time travel spell, I'd be shaping it with a sensor in place to target Cassia's signature in the time stream—complicated weaving that I would have never been able to do before the grimoire. It was a spell that would ensure it was taking me where it needed to take me, directly to my target.

"You know where you're headed?" Ally asked as she moved into the pentagram, flexing her fingers, her own powers sparking a little along her palms.

"Fifteen years ago, to this date, Chicago. Cassia will be in the vampire den."

There was no way of knowing the layout of the vampire den other than that it was in an industrial building so it would be huge. I'd have to use my tracking abilities to find Cassia in the building as well. With the internet down, and no means of researching using that method, I'd had to go on the archives that the scholars had found me. Mapping the layouts of notorious vampire gang strongholds had been an ongoing occupation of theirs for centuries. It was always best to know thy enemy. The scholars had enough intel—even though it was probably outdated —for me to get by. The warehouse had two underground floors located at the south end. Following Cassia's signature would take me directly to her, and Wyatt's tether would pull me back.

"Let's get started," Wyatt said. He glanced at me, his hand snaking out to touch mine briefly, fingers curling.

We'd said our goodbyes upstairs. We'd kissed. Made love. Shared promises. Tonight was a necessary parting, after which we would be together, with nothing pulling us apart ever again. I wouldn't allow it. Wyatt and I had wasted too many years away from one another. After tonight, there would be no more barriers, and my goal was to be so together that we got sick of each other. I smiled at that thought. He smiled back. Then he let my hand go and settled himself on the floor, his legs crossed like he was about to start a yoga meditation. Shoulders squared, arms resting so that his hands were on his knees, palms down. Ally was doing the same across from him. Both of them closed their eyes, and I felt the power rise immediately. With a deep breath, I stepped into their circle of magic.

It took hold of me, no time to waste. Gripping me around the waist and flinging me up, or so it seemed. The sensation of flying was disorienting, unsettling. It took me a few seconds to establish that I would not get my bearings, not while I was moving. Instead, I pulled my own power to my core, giving me a base to weigh me down and keep myself from flying off in the wrong direction. Wyatt's tether was there, a comforting hold that pulsed with his magic. I concentrated on my destination, on the time period and the place. Muttering my own spell to home in on Cassia, I plucked at the signatures that were whipping past me to find hers. It was chaos, madness. My head pounded with the pulses of so much power. Exhilarating in a way that I knew dark magic to be. Dangerously addictive. I could see the magical threads of so many witches. Pulsing ropes of light, the intensity giving me an idea of just how much power was out there. In the wrong hands, my tracking abilities really were quite dangerous. Tugging on any one of those pulsing threads could take me directly to the witch attached to it.

The whiff of Cassia's signature came to me, tingling my senses and I homed in on it. I rubbed my fingers along the colorful wisp of red, a tendril reaching out as I beckoned it closer so that I could latch on. And as soon as I did, I was moving faster, zooming toward my goal. Her power was so strong, as I had expected it to be now that she'd been feeding on powerful witch blood as a hybrid. What I needed was to trace her power back to its purest form, before she'd been tainted by so much violence.

But as I was moving down the length of her signature, something snagged my attention. Something that gave my heart a hard thump and my stomach a kick. Entwined with her signature all of a sudden was another one...one that I hadn't felt in a very long time.

Tears sprung to my eyes. Destiny. My sister. My dead sister's signature was entwined with Cassias.

Why? Ah fuck, why?

I couldn't stop myself. Even though I felt Wyatt's tug, willing me back on course, I couldn't not go to Destiny. When I landed in a time and space and I felt the full impact of my sister's signature, I finally understood what my mother's prediction had truly meant. You have a date with Destiny, she'd said. And now, I had to wonder if my mother knew that she was sending me back to witness my sisters' deaths.

Cassia was there. Younger, sure, but not the innocent girl I'd been aiming for. My detour had taken me out of the travelling spell too early. But that didn't matter. Not when I could see two of the most important people in my life, still living and breathing.

I was in the shadows. Unseen. There were vampires, at least twenty deep, standing around Cassia and another male. They made a stunning pair. Cassia with her long blonde hair and angelic face and her mate, tall, muscular, dark hair and piercing eyes. My fingers moved to my blades. My sisters, Destiny and Leila were there, facing off with the vampires and I felt like my heart was about to break into pieces. There was tension. I could feel it prickling on my skin. I had no idea how long it was until Destiny and Leila would be attacked, but I had no doubt that this was the night of their deaths.

Cassia was a hybrid. Her signature was muddled somewhat, but still strong. My sisters were negotiating. I couldn't hear their words but things seemed to be amping up. It felt wrong. Maybe because I knew what was going to happen next.

I could change this. I could alter my sisters' destinies.

I pulled a blade and a spike, sliding it onto my finger as I slowly, stealthily moved closer to the group.

I had a chance to keep my sisters alive. I could take out Cassia at the same time. This was what my mother meant. It had to be.

"We aren't here to battle with you over territory. As a witch you're bound to the same rule of law as the rest of us, no matter who you affiliate with," Leila said, her voice stern. "The Council—"

"The Council has no governance here," the vampire said, his eyes flashing dangerously. "And Cassia is no longer a witch."

A flicker of doubt flashed on Leila's face. She didn't understand. She had no way of knowing that Cassia was a hybrid. Such a thing would be too taboo to even consider. My sisters wouldn't have fathomed that a witch could be a vampire and retain her powers. For all they knew, as we all believed when a witch turned vampire, she gave up her powers. They had no idea how much danger they were in.

"Cassia may be a slave to your gang but—"

"I am no slave, witch," Cassia said, her words filled with bitterness and hate. "And I reject your offers and your threats."

Destiny's fingers twitched, a subtle tell that she was preparing her magic.

I felt Cassia's magic rise as she called it to her, her signature alerting me.

The vampires closed their circle. My sisters prepared for battle. They were outnumbered, no way to survive.

"Destiny, run!" I screamed as I launched myself forward. Kill Cassia, take her out and save my sisters.

Destiny turned her head toward me, eyes wide, questioning and in shock that I was even there. I could only imagine how I'd cost her concentration but it was too late to pull back.

The vampire Master moved, ready to take down my sister in her distraction, and I reacted. I cast and threw, my blade whirling through the air at a sonic speed, faster than any vampire could move. Time really did slow down when something critical was happening.

I watched the blade as it turned, end over end. I watched as it embedded deeply into the Master's chest. The look of shock. Pain. And finally death that came over his beautiful features all happening in seconds.

I watched as Cassia realized what I'd done. Murdering her mate so that he died as he fell into her arms and they both fell to the concrete floor. The fury on Cassia's face transformed her instantly, and I knew what a horrible mistake I'd made. She glared at my sisters and uttered the words that I could not undo.

"Kill them," she roared, pointing at Destiny and Leila.

I started to move again, wanting to intervene, add to my sister's power even if it was useless. They were marked for death.

I took a step toward them and then I felt Wyatt's tug on me. Grasping me round the waist once again and yanking me hard and fast until I fell on the cold hard floor of the Spell Chamber, unable to move.

I let out a sob, my body crumbled on the ground, tears tracking down my face.

I'd killed Cassia's mate.

I'd started the war.

I'd murdered my sisters.

Read Kali and Wyatt's Story

Even destiny can't get in the way of what is meant to be.

Hazel Knight is a Promised One—a witch born with unique magic abilities. As a result, her future is laid out for her. She is to join the Circle and spend the rest of her life meditating, chanting and devoting her healing magic to bolster her fellow witches. It's a commitment Hazel is proud to make, and she's just one internship away from fulfilling her destiny.

But just because Hazel's committed to her destiny doesn't mean she can't have some fun before she takes the final step. For the past year, she's enjoyed many clandestine nights with a man who has given her a lifetime of memories to take with her. A mysterious lover whose name she's never asked, whose face she's never fully seen.

Yet when her internship begins, she has no trouble recognizing Healer Duke Hart, the exquisitely sexy witch whom her mother has handpicked to serve as her mentor.

Hazel only meant to have a little fun before she devoted herself to a life of servitude, but Duke is bound and determined to prove that nothing, not even destiny, is written in stone.

CHAPTER ONE

"So you're slumming it tonight? For real, Haz? You're going to ditch me?"

Hazel snorted lightly as she held up yet another wispy gown. "It's not slumming, Mahdyia, and yes, I'm definitely going. Wouldn't miss it. You should come." But she knew before her cousin barked her disdain that that would never happen.

"Hang out with the humans?" She made a gagging noise. "Not on your life." Her voice echoed, the phone on speaker suddenly amplifying in an obnoxious way. "It's our last night of freedom! How can you do this to me?"

Last night of freedom. The night of the Spring Moon Festival she'd attended every year since she'd been old enough to get into trouble.

"What would your mother say?"

Mahdyia would never say a word to Hazel's prudish mother and they both knew it. All the same, the threat was enough to make Hazel gasp.

"*Mother* won't find out. She never finds out. She has no interest in human rituals. Besides, I've been going for years and I'm not missing this one. It's fun, Mady. Seriously. A night of drinking, dancing—"

"And fucking. Yeah I get it."

"Making love, under the stars," Hazel corrected. "You're acting like I'm some angsty teenager. I'm a grown woman, about to embark on the next phase of my predetermined life. I'm allowed to have a little fun." She sighed. "I know you had big plans for our last night of freedom but I have to go."

"To see him."

Hazel's heart squeezed. *Him*. He'd texted her to tell her he'd be there. In town for work, he'd said. "It'll be the last time. Forever. And then you'll have me by your side, training, working, for the next year of our witchly lives."

A silence hung between them. One year was all they had left together.

"It's dangerous to play with humans. They could mess with your destiny." Mahdyia's tone was mocking, but not in a biting way.

Hazel knew Mady felt the same about Hazel's destiny, forged in stone on the night she'd been born, as Hazel herself did at that moment. Shit luck that she had been born into the Knight clan and to one of the most powerful white witches of all time.

"But it's such fun," Hazel tried to keep her voice light. Every moment she got to spend with him was delicious torture because she knew it was fleeting. "I have to say goodbye to him. I can't leave him wondering forever."

"Oh Haz." Madhya scoffed. "Such a romantic. Fine, go, spend time with your human. See if I care. I'm going to have the time of my life tonight anyway. Don't be late tomorrow. We have to make a good impression." She gave a little harsh laugh. "Or at least, I do."

"Reputation is everything, darling," Hazel chirped, mimicking her mother's tone.

"Easy for you to say." Mahdyia made a kissing noise that sounded more like a squawk. "Love ya. Don't do anything I wouldn't do."

"Love ya too. And I plan on doing all the things you wouldn't do." She waved her finger and disconnected the call.

Hazel went back into her closet and pulled down the dress she'd been avoiding. It was stunning with its sheen of gold and slips of gauzy material. It dipped low on her chest, almost showing her nipples, and cinched at the waist, leaving her back exposed as the rest of it cascaded to her toes. And if it caught the right light, like when the ritual fires flickered against the dark night sky, yeah, it was damn near see through.

Was she bold enough to pull it off?

It was hardly practical, the chill she'd feel when she danced away from the flames would be unpleasant, especially if the wind was whipping like usual. She'd get it tangled on the low hanging branches and brush as she ran through the woods, chased as a part of their fun and games. He liked hunting her. She liked being hunted. Her dress would snag for sure. But what did it really matter? Before the night was through, he'd have her in his arms and they'd both be naked on the grass, her dress forgotten somewhere along the way. And she wouldn't need it after tonight.

She had a year to prepare her body, mind, and skill for her inevitable journey to her destiny. There would be no time, no room, for romantic fantasy, especially not under her mother's watchful eyes.

With a sigh, she held the dress up to her frame once again and examined herself in the mirror, a small smile creeping on her lips. Yes, for him, it was worth the snags and chills. One last time.

The city was off in the distance, blazing with the light of typical modernization. Much of its inhabitants still clung hard to the old ways, with over eight hundred practicing witches among them. Human witches. The city was nestled in woods so thick you wouldn't even know it was there if it weren't for the massive highway connecting it to the rest of the world and the big billboards advertising its existence. A tourist attraction that boasted all sorts of enticing and accessible forms of magic: love spells, fortune telling, crystal healing and perhaps a few curses here and there. They catered to the curious of their kind—humans who wanted to learn about witchcraft and all things Salem. Including the notorious witch trials that had almost ended Hazel's kind.

The humans, even the non-witch ones, paid tribute and honored the fallen. The human witches were harmless dabblers in natural magics, making fistfuls of cash on the tragedy. She didn't fault them for that. Everyone and *everything* had a price.

Hazel felt a chill from her vantage point on the grassy hill, looking down at the twinkling lights of the city. It was the only appealing thing about Salem—the city and its believers, the pulse she got from their worship made her almost giddy. Her mother didn't value it—the humans were hardly worth her notice, even though they did provide a boost to the Healer's magic. Her mother felt their power was minor and insignificant, but she'd never ventured outside of the walls of White Willow Hospital, other than to come home and instruct Hazel in all the ways to be a proper white witch. She was a strict woman with high standards, expecting much, maybe too much, from her only daughter.

Hazel turned, scanning the horizon for White Willow itself. There, off in the distance, it stood, muted lights hazy in the darkness. Only witches of the non-human variety could locate it. A haven for those in need of magical healing, and soon to be her place of residence for the next year. There she'd train before ascending to her role as a Promised One, designate for her mother who was far too important, far too powerful, to ever give up her role as the Great Mother of all Healers.

Music wafted toward Hazel, floating on the breeze, pulling her from her dark thoughts. Away from the city and from White Willow was a small ceremonial valley where a cluster of cottages stood. She called it The Village—it was where the human witches assembled to celebrate their faith. Only the elders of their kind actually lived there but it was mecca to the city witches and to Hazel as well. The bonfires were already burning in the center of the village. She could see the wisps of flame calling to her.

Her dress billowed behind her, the wind tickling her thighs. He was waiting for her. Somewhere down there where the fires were warm and the music was loud, where the wine flowed and the food was laid out. He was there, she knew it by the flutter of her heart. She lowered her mask, covering most of her face, as was the custom for the festival. With a jolt of excitement, she picked up her dress, freed her legs, and ran down the dirt path, her feet barely touching ground.

❧

"You are the most beautiful woman I have ever seen." His breath on the back of her neck made her shiver in a delicious way.

She swayed backward, feeling the warmth of his body just behind her. "You've never actually *seen* me," she teased.

He chuckled softly as he lowered his lips to her neck, sending another sweep of pleasure over her. Goosebumps rose all over her body. Somehow, even though he was barely touching her, he noticed. "Are you cold, sweetheart?"

On a sigh, Hazel turned, closing the small distance between them as she wrapped her arms around his waist and pressed her face to his chest, inhaling his scent. Sandalwood, mint, maybe a bit of vanilla. "No, not anymore."

His long dark hair was tied into a ponytail, the tips swishing against her forearms. "Mmm." She could feel his heart hammering as he wrapped his arms around her, encircling her with strength and warmth. "Your dress is very impractical for this weather."

She pulled away just enough to look up at him, his face shielded by his own mask. He had a wry smirk on his lips.

"Would it be better if I was covered in dowdy cotton?"

He licked his lips. "It would be better if you were covered in me."

She could have giggled with giddiness. His mask only revealed full lips, a strong chin and dark sparkling eyes, glinting with wicked intentions. "So you missed me then?" she teased again. He made her feel so alive. So cherished.

"I think about you every day. All day." He leaned into her, his lips brushing hers so tenderly. "Yes, I missed you."

And then he really kissed her. His tongue lunging deep, stroking her, loving her, making her want to gasp and moan. He gripped her ass, urging her to lift her legs to wrap around his waist as he hoisted her up. Her breasts pressed hard against his chest, nipples aching, heart pounding.

This was how it always was. A flame that never seemed to diminish, no matter how many days passed between their visits.

How she would go without him for the rest of her life, she didn't know.

He moved them away, to their secret spot shielded in the woods, and worshiped her body. Licking her every inch as he slowly dismantled her dress, slipping parts away to expose her flesh to his roving lips and tongue. Every spot he touched tingled with pleasure. When he sucked hard on her nipples, laving them then nipping, cupping her breasts with his palm before flicking with his fingers, she was on fire. He slipped the dress down her body, then nestled between her thighs to lick and stroke there too, sucking so hard on her clit that she exploded with a loud cry of pleasure.

And she did the same to him. Wound him up, rung him out. His cock was long and thick. Her lips were barely able to wrap around the width and no way was she taking his shaft all the way down. He was a big man in general—six foot four at least, with a broad muscled chest, like he worked out, or worked hard. His skin was olive, sun-kissed with no tan lines. Dark hair curled lightly around his nipples, trailing down in a line to that fine cock. She liked to take him down to the back of her throat, not all the way down, he was much too big for that, but as far as she dared while cupping his balls. She loved to make him moan and writhe beneath her. Especially when she replaced her mouth with her pussy, riding him hard and fast under the blanket of stars.

They made love for hours, her orgasms shattering her each

and every time, making her forget, if only for a bit, that she was meant for greater things. Things beyond human understanding. Heartbreaking things that demanded sacrifice, great sacrifice. For those blissful moments, she couldn't think what could possibly be greater than this.

She lay panting in his arms, her body feeling light, a sheen of sweat making her shiver. "It's always so amazing with you. You make me feel really good." She knew she shouldn't gush, that it made her sound young and inexperienced. Which she was, really, since the encounters she'd had with him were the only ones she'd ever had—the only ones she *would* ever have. He had this way with her, making her feel cherished and exotic, beautiful and loved, just with his body. With his penetrating eyes and his tender lips.

He sighed deeply, running his fingers up and down her arm. "I feel the same way. I wish we could stay like this forever."

Her heart clenched. They didn't have forever. What a stark reminder. She opened her mouth to speak, then closed it again quickly. What would she say? What could she tell him? Despite the fact that he was a practicing Pagan, and wore a forearm tattoo that branded him so, it was forbidden for her to tell any human about her witchy status. It could put White Willow at risk. Humans had turned on them once before. Even though she believed he never would, she couldn't confide in him about being the Promised One. Not that. Not ever.

"I'm in town for a while. The coven is preparing for a solstice celebration." He gripped her tight and pulled her almost on top of him, his cock growing hard at the slight touch. "You could just stay here until then."

Summer Solstice was in a matter of days. Despite the fact that she would be so close, hidden away at White Willow, she wouldn't be able to get away, not even for a few hours. Disappointment crushed her. He'd never stayed longer than one night at a time usually. "I'm sorry. I won't be able to get away again for a while." It felt like her heart was shattering.

His fingers stilled, he released his grip and her body slid back down to his side. "Sweetheart, I know that something is wrong, I can feel it. Be honest with me. Is there someone else?"

Yes. My mother. "No." She raised her head and turned, propping herself on her elbow so she could look down at him. "I have..." She searched for the right words. "A family obligation."

"Your mother again?"

She'd told him only a little about her mother's controlling ways, trying to paint herself as a normal human girl. It was often her mother who prevented her from attending various ceremonies anyway. She could only sneak out unnoticed at certain times, when her mother was consumed with other very important things. Otherwise she kept her life very secret, like her identity. She and her lover didn't even know each other's names, texting only when they could sneak away to see one another.

"You should tell that woman to shove her obligation up her—"

"Let's not talk about her." Hazel leaned down and gave him a soft kiss.

"She's controlling, manipulative, from what you've told me—"

She opened her mouth over his, licking him, stroking him, silencing him. He moaned. She reached down to stroke his growing erection, his tip slick with a mixture of her cream and his.

As she pulled away from the kiss she felt a tug on her mask. "Let me see your face."

She gasped, flung up her hand to stop him. "No!" And then she said more quietly, "You always say the mystery is what keeps you coming back."

"That's not what keeps me coming back." He smiled wickedly. "For once, I'd like to make love to you without any barriers."

He started to lift his own mask. Hazel caught a glimpse of high cheekbones. "No!" She stopped him once again. "Not this time. Please. I'll find a way to come to the solstice. We'll reveal ourselves then." How she would do that she didn't know, but she'd have to find a way. There had to be a way. She needed to see him one last time.

He sighed, lowering his mask. "As you wish, sweetheart." There was such disappointment in his voice.

"I think we can make better use of this time." She slid herself on top of him, slipping him inside, enjoying the feel of him filling her, consuming her, making her feel something more than obligation, duty, and the overwhelming press of her destiny.

ABOUT THE AUTHOR

Every day is Halloween for author Angela Addams. Enthralled by the paranormal at an early age, Angela spends most of her time thinking up new story ideas that involve supernatural creatures in everyday situations. She believes that the written word is an amazing tool for crafting the most erotic of scenarios and has recently started down a dark path to disturbing thrillers and erotic horror.

Her Order of the Wolf series, featuring kick ass Amazon warriors and their mates, and her Dark War series, set in a world of witchcraft and war, are available from Entangled Publishing.

She is an avid tattoo collector, a total book hoarder, and loves anything covered in chocolate...except for bugs.

She lives in Ontario, Canada in an old, creaky house, with her husband, children, four cats, and a couple of weird guinea pigs.

Visit her website or sign up for her newsletter for more information!

ALSO BY ANGELA ADDAMS

Witch Hospital Romance
The Witches of White Willow
Feral Heart

The Dark War Series
The Dark War
Fortune's Fool

The Order of the Wolf
Cursed
Wolves' Bane
Spell-Weaver
Valiant Heart
Beast Rising

Single Titles
Burning Kiss
The Temptress
Assassin
Ghost Bride